The Prince and the Whitechapel Murders

Saul David

HODDER &
STOUGHTON

First published in Great Britain in 2018 by Hodder & Stoughton
An Hachette UK company

1

Copyright © Saul David 2018

Map drawn by Louise David

A CIP catalogue record for this title is available from the British Library

Hardback ISBN 978 0 340 95368 6
eBook ISBN 978 1 444 70836 3

Typeset in Sabon MT by Hewer Text UK Ltd, Edinburgh
Printed and bound in Great Britain by Clays Ltd, St Ives plc

Hodder & Stoughton policy is to use papers that are natural, renewable
and recyclable products and made from wood grown in sustainable
forests. The logging and manufacturing processes are expected to
conform to the environmental regulations of the country of origin.

Hodder & Stoughton Ltd
Carmelite House
50 Victoria Embankment
London EC4Y 0DZ

www.hodder.co.uk

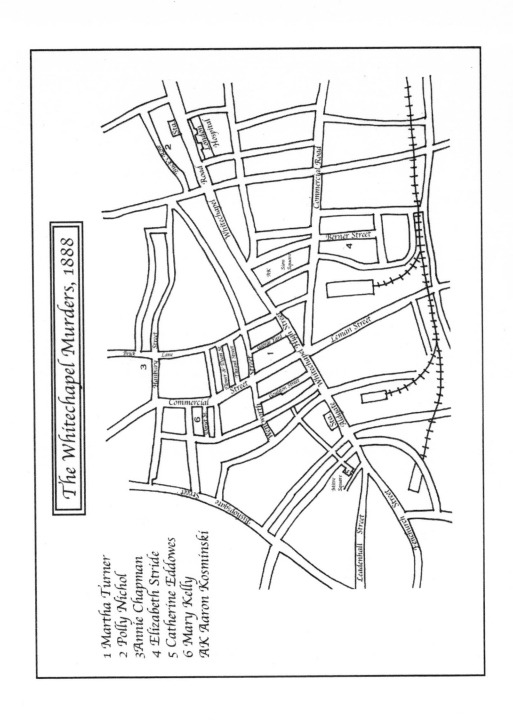

The Whitechapel Murders, 1888

1 Martha Turner
2 Polly Nichol
3 Annie Chapman
4 Elizabeth Stride
5 Catherine Eddowes
6 Mary Kelly
AK Aaron Kosminski

For Pete

I

SS Britannia, The Solent, off southern England, summer 1888

George leant on the guardrail and watched the familiar shoreline of the Isle of Wight slide by the port side of the comfortable P & O steamship he had boarded two days earlier in Gibraltar. He had not set foot in England since departing on a covert mission to Afghanistan nine years earlier, and was both nervous and excited at the prospect of meeting the man he strongly suspected of being his long-lost father: Field Marshal HRH the Duke of Cambridge, cousin of the Queen and Commander-in-Chief of the British Army.

The duke had never acknowledged his fatherhood, but there were enough clues: George's actress mother telling him, on his eighteenth birthday, that his father was a man of *considerable influence*, already married but with a penchant for thespians, who had given George financial incentives to do well as a soldier because his other sons in the military had *disappointed him* (the duke's acknowledged sons had done just this); an undercover officer who, shortly after saving George's life in British India, admitted that he had been sent to keep an eye on him by the duke; and, finally, one of the duke's sons telling George that his father had had an affair with a young actress in 1859, the year that George was born.

It was not as though George wanted this possible royal connection publicly acknowledged. That would turn his life upside down, and he had no desire to be known as the royal bastard whose career was dependent upon his father's patronage. Moreover, he still resented the fact that his father had chosen not to be a part of his and his mother's life, yet at the same time had tried to bribe him to make a success of his career by offering large cash incentives to win a Victoria Cross, reach the rank of lieutenant colonel and marry respectably by his twenty-eighth birthday. Now at that age, he had only fulfilled one of his father's conditions, and it still irked him that a man who had played no part in his upbringing had felt the right to interfere. But George still wanted to know the answer to the question that any fatherless child was bound to ask: who am I and where do I come from? It was simply a matter of identity, of belonging, and he hoped the duke could bring himself to admit privately they were related – if indeed they were.

There was also the perennial issue of money. In short, his suspected father had plenty and he had none. He had long ago spent the VC bonus of £10,000, partly on his mother's IOUs, but also because he and Lucy had run up debts of their own. She was a profligate spender; he was addicted to gambling, particularly card games like baccarat and chemin de fer. Bored by garrison life in Gibraltar, he had spent even more time at the tables than usual, and his debts were now a crippling £1,500, give or take a few pounds. Hitherto he had regarded active service – with its generous pay and opportunity for booty – as his only hope of avoiding bankruptcy. But it was just possible that this summons from the duke might offer an alternative. Only time would tell.

With the Isle of Wight now behind it, the steamship entered the narrow channel that led to Southampton Docks, a gaggle of seagulls following close behind. Eager to be on land, George put on his spiked helmet and smoothed the creases in his bottle-green patrol jacket. As he turned from the rail he almost collided with a colonel from the Devonshire Regiment. 'I'm sorry, sir,' said George, saluting.

'Not your fault, Major,' said the colonel. 'I didn't look where I was going.'

He glanced down at George's chest and spotted, alongside the campaign ribbons for South Africa, Afghanistan, the Transvaal, Egypt and the Sudan, the distinctive crimson flash of the Victoria Cross. 'Heavens!' uttered the colonel, 'it is I who should be saluting you, not the other way around. Forgive me. You've certainly seen a bit of action. Your name?'

'Hart, sir. Major George Hart.'

'Rings a bell. Of course! You were at the defence of Rorke's Drift and won the VC at Kabul, didn't you?'

'I did, sir.'

'Well, it's a pleasure to meet you. I'm sure your family must be very proud.'

'They are, sir. Or at least some of them are. I'm not sure about the others.'

The colonel raised his eyebrows, but chose not to inquire further. 'I see you're a rifleman. Are you stationed in Gibraltar?'

'Yes, sir. We moved from Egypt in eighty-seven.'

'A good posting if you want a quiet life. But a fire-eater like you must be bored to distraction.'

'I am, sir, but my wife likes it.'

'I bet she does: plenty of sun and no danger. Is she with you?'

'No, she's still in Gib with our son. I've been summoned back by the commander-in-chief.'

The colonel looked impressed. 'Have you, indeed? Sounds very conspiratorial. Well, if the duke himself has asked for you, it must be important. Any clues as to what it might be?'

'Not a thing, sir. I know there's trouble at Sikkim in north-east India, and that sooner or later there'll be a reckoning with the killers of General Gordon in the Sudan. But I doubt either is the reason for my recall.'

'Well let's hope so, for your wife's sake if not your own.'

*

The anteroom at Schomberg House, the handsome red-brick building in Pall Mall that had served as the headquarters of the British Army since 1871, was much as George remembered: packed with officers from most branches of the service, all hoping for a private audience with the duke that might further their career. As before, George had barely arrived before his name was announced and he was escorted up to the commander-in-chief's office on the third floor.

George could feel his heart racing with nerves as he mounted the stairs. He knew the duke would greet him like any other officer, as he had at their previous meeting. Yet, for George, this time was different, because he now had good reason to think the duke was his father.

The aide knocked on the door, giving George a brief moment to compose himself. 'Enter!' came a voice from within.

George found the duke writing at his beautiful oval walnut desk, once the possession of the great Duke of Wellington.

He was informally dressed in a dark blue patrol jacket, but with four orders of knighthood sparkling on his left breast and, a little higher, his Crimea medal with clasps for the battles of 'Alma', 'Sebastopol' and 'Inkerman' that resembled the metal labels on a port decanter. He was a little thicker of waist than George remembered, but with the same bald pate, white moustache and mutton-chop whiskers. He looked up and smiled. 'Thank you for coming at such short notice, Major Hart. Do take a seat.'

George sat down.

'It's very good to see you again,' said the duke.

'It's . . . uh . . . good to be back, Your Royal Highness,' said George, slightly taken aback by the duke's familiarity.

'How long *has* it been?'

'Nine years, sir, since you introduced me to Lords Beaconsfield and Salisbury in your house in Mayfair.'

'Ah yes, I remember. That dreadful Afghan business. You did well, very well, under the circumstances. The VC was the least you deserved. I'd like to have pinned it on you myself.'

'Thank you, sir.'

'And now you're a major and . . .?'

'And married, sir.'

'Do I know her people?'

'I doubt it, sir. Her father is a farrier.'

'A *farrier*?' The blood drained from the duke's face. 'Am I hearing you right? Are you telling me your father-in-law is a carer of horses' hooves?'

'Yes, sir. From Devonshire.'

'My god, a bloody farrier,' said the duke, shaking his head. 'You do realize, Major Hart, that the choice of a wife can make or break an officer's career? The daughter of a farrier is hardly a suitable companion for an officer and a gentleman.'

George frowned. 'Forgive me, sir, but I don't agree. Farrier's daughter or no, my wife is worth two of any of her finely bred contemporaries. She's a remarkable woman: intelligent, brave and, well, we've been through a lot together.'

The duke looked unconvinced. 'I'm sure you have, but that still doesn't . . .' He paused for a moment. 'How old are you, Major Hart?'

'Twenty-eight, sir.'

'That all? I just don't understand men of your generation. There doesn't seem to be quite the same sense of duty, of doing the right thing. If you want something, you take it and damn the consequences.'

Aware as he was of the duke's unorthodox domestic life – married to an actress and with two, possibly three, children born out of wedlock – George could detect more than a whiff of hypocrisy. But he also knew that the duke had been driven to distraction by the profligate ways of his errant acknowledged sons, and so understood what he was getting at: he didn't want George to go the same way, but feared that he might. His choice of a wife was obviously not a good sign.

The duke seemed to be waiting for a response. When he didn't get one, he said: 'Well, let's hope you don't regret it. Anyway, down to business. The reason I've called you back from Gibraltar is that I have an extremely unusual and delicate task that I think you might be perfect for. You served, for a short time, did you not, with my young cousin Prince Albert Victor of Wales when he was posted to your battalion in Gibraltar last year?'

'I did.'

'What did you make of him?'

'He seemed a very nice, down-to-earth young officer, Your Royal Highness. I found him kind, modest and unassuming.'

'Yes, yes, Major Hart. I know the prince is an engaging fellow with great personal charm. But is he a good officer?'

George hesitated.

'Speak your mind, Hart. This will go no further.'

'Well, sir, he was not always punctual and occasionally neglected his duties. Once, when duty officer, he overslept after a night carousing.'

'Yes, that sounds like Eddy,' said the duke, using the royal family's pet name for the prince. After a pause, he continued, 'What I'm about to tell you is highly confidential and must not be repeated outside these walls. Is that clear?'

'Of course, sir.'

'Good. The prince is a charming and likeable fellow, as you know, but he's never shown much interest in his studies. Nor at a young age did his father, the Prince of Wales, it's true, but Eddy's difficulties seem more profound. He finds it hard to concentrate and has struggled academically. Imagine my horror,' said the duke, throwing his hands in the air, 'when I spoke to him at Sandringham of the Crimean War. He knew nothing about it! Nothing about the Battle of Alma! It is past all conceiving!'

After a pause the duke continued: 'Even now, as an officer, his knowledge of his profession is not what it should be. On a recent inspection of his cavalry regiment, I wanted Eddy to demonstrate an elementary piece of drill. But his commanding officer begged me to desist, as Eddy had no *idea* how to do it! Of course, not wanting to expose him, I let it alone. Yet I was determined to see an improvement, and under

Major Miles's instruction, he has made great strides. I know that he is not unteachable, and that much of his ignorance is down to the inadequacies of his former tutors, Dalton and Stephen. He has his father's dislike for a book, and never looks into one, but learns all from conversation, and retains what he has learnt.'

The duke rose from his seat and, hands behind his back, stared out of the bay window behind his desk towards St James's Park. 'I've always loved this view. But as dusk falls, the park fills up with some very disagreeable characters.'

'I'm sorry, sir, I don't get your meaning.'

Turning, the duke said: 'I'll explain. It's not just Eddy's indolence that is troubling his father and the Queen. It's also the fact that he forms close and potentially compromising relationships with young men of questionable morals. At Cambridge, for example, he spent all his time with his tutor Jim Stephen and a small circle of students who were members of a secret society known as the Apostles. It extols the virtues of the philosophy known as "Greek love", claiming that one man's affection for another is the highest form of love, pure and disinterested, and unsullied by sex. In truth the practice is rarely innocent, any more than love between men in Ancient Greece was. What is worrying is that these same young men – all now barristers – are Eddy's closest friends.'

'Are you suggesting, sir, that the prince might be homosexual?'

'I don't know. What I *do* know is that he's young and impressionable, and eminently capable of being led astray. Now I fully appreciate that young men can be infatuated with each other. I myself experienced something similar as a junior officer. But an infatuation is one thing, sodomy quite another.'

George was only half convinced by the duke's reasoning. His own love for his best friend Jake had been both intense and innocent. Yet he was prepared to concede that other young men of his acquaintance – particularly at Harrow – had experimented sexually. Did that make them homosexual? Probably not, and the prince might be similar: able to form strong attachments to young men, possibly even to have sex with them, but also to marry and have children.

'I can see from your expression,' said the duke, 'that you're wondering why any of this matters. Why can't Eddy have his youthful flings before reverting to heterosexual type? I'll tell you why. He's not some minor royal, but the eldest son of the Prince of Wales and destined one day to be king; and since the recent change of law, it isn't just sodomy but all types of homosexual practice that are illegal. So even a minor indiscretion – say kissing another man – would put Eddy at the mercy of criminal or even political blackmailers. We can't allow that to happen, which is why I need a resourceful fellow like you – one used to undercover work – to "shadow" Eddy and make sure that he stays out of trouble, at least until we can marry him off to a suitable German princess. Of course you'll need to exchange into the prince's regiment, the Tenth Hussars. That way you can get to know him socially and pick up any hints about his sexual proclivities. You've been a cavalryman so you know the ropes.'

After a pause, the duke continued: 'Now, I appreciate that the role of prince's nursemaid may not fill a hero like you with enthusiasm. But there is another far more dangerous element to this assignment that should be more suitable for a man of your martial abilities. I'll let the man outside explain.'

9

The duke rang a bell on his desk and an aide appeared. 'Show him in, would you, Reynolds?'

Moments later the door reopened and in stepped a tall, impressive-looking man with a thick moustache and dark thinning hair swept back from a side parting. He was wearing a dark blue double-breasted jacket and white shirt with a wing collar, and an expression of quiet confidence. 'Do take a seat,' said the duke, 'and explain to Major Hart what you do and why you're here.'

'Certainly, Your Royal Highness.' He turned to George. 'My name is Detective Inspector John Littlechild. I'm the head of the Metropolitan Police's Special Irish Branch that was formed a few years ago to deal with the terrorist threat from the Irish Republican Brotherhood, or Fenians, as they're more popularly known. Their most infamous outrage was the murder of Lord Frederick Cavendish, the chief secretary to Ireland, in Phoenix Park in eighty-two. You have heard of the Fenians?'

'Yes of course. I was born and brought up in Dublin. Their aim is an independent Ireland, and they're prepared to use any and every means to achieve that.'

'Exactly so, and these methods include the detonation of dynamite in public places. They even targeted our headquarters in Old Scotland Yard, blowing off a corner of the building and destroying my office. Fortunately I had tickets for the opera that night or I wouldn't be talking to you now. In recent years, thanks to the use of surveillance and informers, we've managed to arrest most of their bomb-makers. That still leaves, however, the threat of assassination, and we have reason to believe – from intelligence supplied to us by an American informer – that His Royal Highness Prince Albert Victor is on their list of targets. We've offered to provide the prince with personal protection but he refuses to take the threat seriously and has declined—'

'Which,' interjected the duke, 'is where you come in, Major Hart. If the prince won't agree to a Special Irish Branch bodyguard, we need to have someone near him that we can trust to keep an eye on him. You're a few years older than him, and senior in rank, but there's no reason why, once you're in the same regiment, you can't become friends. Just encourage him to like and trust you. It shouldn't be difficult: he knows you slightly from Gibraltar and he's already demonstrated with his Cambridge tutor a willingness to be mentored. What do you say? Will you act as the prince's unofficial bodyguard?'

'I . . . I'm flattered, of course, Your Royal Highness,' said George. 'But I'm a soldier, not a bodyguard, and feel my talents are better suited to active service.'

The duke scowled. 'This *is* active service. The threat to the prince is serious and we need a bodyguard in place as soon as possible. But I can promise you this: if you agree to take this on, and carry out your duties successfully, you'll receive another step in rank and a posting of your choice.'

'Anywhere I choose?'

'Anywhere.'

'And how long will this assignment take, sir? You didn't say.'

The duke turned to Littlechild. 'What do you think, Inspector? Would a year be enough?'

'That would more than suffice, Your Royal Highness, as we'd hope to have the Fenian threat neutralized long before then.'

'A year it is, then,' said the duke. 'After that, Major, you'll be free to resume your former career. Will you do it?'

George leant back in his seat to mull over the duke's proposal. He'd been hoping to see more action, possibly back in southern Africa where Zululand was still unsettled and there was unfinished business with the Boers. But as a war with either seemed unlikely in the near future, he could think of worse jobs than protecting a royal prince for the next twelve months, and it would make a welcome change from the monotony of garrison life in Gibraltar. Then there was his family. Lucy would be delighted at the thought of returning with little Jake to Britain. She hadn't been back since their hurried departure in '78, after George had killed in self-defence a private detective who was trying to stop her from leaving. The detective was acting for her former employer, and George's former CO and nemesis, Sir Jocelyn Harris. Harris was long gone – killed at the Battle of Majuba in 1881 – and, though there was no longer any reason for Lucy to stay away, she had preferred to follow George from one posting to another. Her one regret was that her parents had never seen their grandson Jake; this would give them the opportunity. There was also the prospect of promotion and more war service. He knew he'd be a fool to turn the offer down.

But still he hesitated because none of these benefits would solve his most pressing concern: an acute lack of cash. It was time, he decided, to test the duke's determination for him to take the job. 'I don't mean to sound *too* mercenary,' said George at last, 'but is there any extra pay on offer? I only ask because I'm a bit strapped for cash at the moment. That, if I'm honest, is why I was hoping for a foreign posting: the pay is better and the cost of living cheaper.'

'I thought you'd get around to money,' said the duke, frowning. 'You youngsters can never have enough, can you?

What happened to old-fashioned notions like duty to your sovereign? Does it exist any more?'

George shifted uneasily in his seat and tried to avoid eye contact.

'Obviously not. But to answer your question: yes, there is an incentive. You'll receive a lieutenant colonel's pay, a signing on bounty of three hundred pounds and a final lump sum of a thousand pounds, if you keep the prince safe and out of trouble for a year. Is that enough to tempt you?'

George nodded imperceptibly. Not only was the extra money almost enough to cover his debts, it bore an uncanny resemblance to the financial incentives his father had offered him in a letter when he was eighteen years old. Was the duke trying to tell him something? He couldn't decide. But either way the potential cash had removed his last reason for refusing the duke's offer. 'Yes, sir,' he said at last. 'More than enough. To whom will I report?'

'To the detective inspector.'

'Your cover will be as a cavalry officer,' said Littlechild, 'but you'll actually be working for the Special Irish Branch with the right to carry a firearm at all times and make arrests. I'll see you're issued with a Derringer pistol. It's small enough to fit in a pocket or hidden holster. You may need it.'

After Littlechild had been shown out, the duke poured two glasses of brandy and handed one to George. 'Your good health,' he said, clinking glasses.

George took a gulp and nodded appreciatively as the smooth, fiery liquid warmed the back of his throat.

'I wanted to thank you,' said the duke, 'for not mentioning the other matter we discussed. I trust Littlechild, of course, but the fewer people that know about Eddy's foibles the better. Best to keep it in the family, so to speak.'

George glanced at the duke. Had he confessed at last to being his father? he wondered. Or was that simply a figure of speech? He couldn't be sure.

The duke raised his eyebrows. 'Anything the matter, Major Hart?'

'No, Your Royal Highness,' said George, draining his glass. 'Far from it.'

2

Knightsbridge Barracks, Central London

'I would like to introduce you all to Major George Hart VC,' said Colonel Anson, gesturing to the officer beside him, 'your new squadron commander.'

George gazed at the 160 officers and men standing to attention on the parade ground before him. All were wearing, like him, the undress uniform of the 10th (Prince of Wales's Own) Hussars: a peakless gold and blue cap, dark blue stable jacket, blue trousers edged with two gold stripes, and shiny black riding boots with spurs. The main distinction for officers was a chained-pattern pouch belt that they wore over their left shoulder.

Anson continued: 'Major Hart has considerable combat experience and we are lucky to have him. His most recent service was as a rifleman, but he started out with the First King's Dragoon Guards and later joined the Natal Carbineers, so he knows one end of a horse from another. I'll leave you in his capable hands.'

Having spoken to the men, George called a meeting of the officers in the squadron office. The last of the seven to shake his hand was Captain HRH Prince Albert Victor of Wales, the commander of E Troop. A couple of inches shorter than

George, the prince had inherited the good looks of his mother, Princess Alexandra, and was strikingly handsome: a thin oval face, light complexion, full lips, aquiline nose and widely spaced piercing blue eyes. He was also immaculately turned out, with dark, side-parted hair, a waxed moustache turned up at the ends and a closely fitting tailored uniform. His one physical flaw, George remembered, was a long neck that was cleverly hidden by an oversized collar.

'I'm very glad to make your acquaintance again, Your Royal Highness,' said George. 'How're you enjoying your time in the cavalry?'

'Very much, sir,' said the prince, smiling. 'I get to play polo twice a week, but I find the incessant drill a bit of a bore.'

'A necessary bore, I'm afraid, and vital training for war. I hope you'll give it your full attention.' George turned to the other officers. 'That goes for all of you. I have high stand-ards and I trust you do too. Carry out your duties diligently and efficiently, and you'll find me an easy officer to work under. Neglect them and there'll be hell to pay. Do we under-stand each other?'

'Yes, sir,' they said in unison.

Once the meeting was over, George asked the prince to stay behind. 'Whisky?' he offered, pulling a flask and two glasses from a drawer. 'I don't usually at this time. But as it's my first day . . .'

They clinked glasses. 'Your good health,' said George. 'And congratulations on your recent promotion to captain.'

'Thank you, sir. I'm not sure that it's deserved.'

'Well, any praise from me will be.'

The prince took a gulp. 'Do you mind if I ask you a ques-tion, sir?'

'Not at all.'

'How did you end up in the army?'

'The usual route: Harrow and Sandhurst. But you don't mean that, do you? What you're really asking is how did someone as dark-skinned as me,' said George, tapping his tawny cheek, 'become an officer in the British Army? Well, it's complicated. I was born and raised in Dublin by my mother who is – or was – a celebrated actress of Irish and African parentage. She always told me my father died when I was young. In fact he's very much alive, but chooses to remain anonymous because he was married before his affair with my mother. It seems he's both wealthy and high born: how high I can only speculate. He used his influence to get me my first commission in the KDG – not that that did me much good – and tried to bribe me to do well in my career.'

'Well that seems to have worked, sir. I already knew a bit about your service, of course, from my time in Gibraltar, but not the details. So when I heard you were joining us I looked you up in the Army List. You've seen more action than most colonels twice your age. Zululand, Afghanistan, the Transvaal, Egypt, the Sudan. And you're what, twenty-nine?'

'Twenty-eight.'

'That's incredible! And a VC winner as well. Do you mind telling me, sir, how you won the Cross?'

'Not much to tell, really. We were defending the cantonment at Sherpur, near Kabul, when fanatical Ghazi warriors broke into a trench held by the Guides. I knew that if the defences were breached, the fort would fall and we'd all be killed. So I led a counter-attack and we retook the trench. That's it. I really had no option. Anyone would have done the same.'

17

'I'm sure there's much more to it than that,' said the prince, 'but like all heroes you're far too modest. Tell me, is your father British, do you know?'

'Yes, and a soldier apparently. He served in the Crimea. It's my mother who has foreign blood. Her grandfather was a Zulu chief.'

The prince's eyes widened. 'Zulu? How exotic.'

'You think so? My schoolfellows at Harrow were not so kind. Which is why I had to stand up for myself. I've been doing it ever since.'

'It seems, sir,' said the prince, 'that we have more in common than you might think. My father, as you know, is colonel of the Tenth. He wants desperately for me to shine as a soldier; probably because he did not. But I can't help feeling I'm a disappointment to him. Mama, on the other hand, just wants me to be happy. She's Danish and hates court formality. She never imposed much discipline when we were children. We used to run wild at Sandringham. Grandmama did not approve.'

George chuckled inwardly at the prince's casual reference to his grandmother the Queen. 'So you're close to your mother?'

'Very close, sir. She always takes my side when—'

'When what?'

'When Father accuses me of not trying. I *do* try, but not always successfully.'

'All that anyone can ask of you, Your Royal Highness,' said George, draining his glass, 'is that you do your best.'

*

George stopped in front of number 69, a pretty whitewashed mews cottage set back from the main road, and murmured, 'A good choice, but not cheap.'

He had taken the underground train from Knightsbridge to Hammersmith, and then walked the short distance to his rented house in Alnwick Grove. He turned the key in the lock, pushed the door open and called out, 'Lucy?'

His wife appeared at the top of the stairs, her finger to her mouth. 'Sssh!' she said softly. 'He's just gone to sleep.'

She was simply dressed in a white blouse and long dark skirt, her curly chestnut hair piled high on her head, with just a couple of errant strands framing her lovely pale oval face. 'Was he as you remembered?' she asked, coming down the stairs.

'The prince? Yes he was. No airs and graces. I like him. We have a lot in common.'

'Do you? Well that's good,' she said, her voice still retaining a faint trace of Devonshire burr. She leant forward from the first step and kissed George. 'After all, you'll be spending a lot of time together.'

Yes, thought George, but not in quite the way you think. At the duke's request, he had not told Lucy the real reason for their return to Britain. The less she knew the better, apparently, which is why he simply explained that he had been posted to a new regiment, the 10th Hussars, among whose officers was Prince Albert Victor, the heir apparent. Lucy was delighted: not only would her husband be rubbing shoulders with royalty, but he would also be, for the first time in years, out of harm's way. Or so she thought.

'Shall we toast to the future?'

'That would be nice.'

They went through to the simply furnished front parlour: two easy chairs and a sofa grouped round a small fireplace. George poured two whiskies and handed one to Lucy who, by now, had kicked off her shoes and was lying full length on the sofa. 'Tired?'

'Exhausted. You try chasing a seven-year-old round the Natural History Museum. But he loved it, particularly the birds and the dinosaurs.'

'I thought he would. When do you plan to visit your parents?'

'I wrote today, suggesting two weeks from now. I can't wait to see them. It's been almost ten years.'

'I know,' said George, sinking into an armchair. 'I haven't seen Mother for almost as long.' He thought back to their hurried departure from Plymouth by boat in 1878, George having just shot and killed the private detective who was trying to stop Lucy from leaving. 'It's hard to believe it turned out like that.'

'What do you mean?'

'The last ten years. Who would have thought we'd get involved with Barney Barnato, the "Diamond King" of Cape Colony, for goodness' sake! Heavens, that really was a low point when I got your letter in Karachi saying you were engaged to Barney. It was only then, when I was about to lose you, that I realized that I'd loved you all along. What a self-absorbed fool I was!'

'Yes,' said Lucy, her smile fading at the memory. 'Don't remind me. Colonel Harris was threatening to expose me as a murderer if I didn't return with him to London. So my only hope was to marry Barney. But I didn't love him and the only reason I needed his protection is because *you* kept rejecting me.'

'I know,' said George, reddening at the memory.

'Oh well, the main thing is that you came back for me – eventually. It's in the past, but I haven't forgotten. That's all I wanted to say.'

'I understand,' said George. 'And I'm sorry.'

'And now, thank Heavens,' said Lucy, her face brightening, 'we're cosily ensconced here with Jake and I no longer . . .'

'Yes?'

'. . . have to lie awake at night and wonder if you'll come home in one piece.'

'Ah, that. Well even London has its dangers.'

'Such as?'

'Such as the Irish Fenians,' said George, without thinking.

'The Fenians? Were they behind the recent bombings?'

George nodded.

'Why would you be in danger from them? You're a soldier not a policeman.'

'Yes, but everyone in uniform is a target.'

'Well, better the Fenians than the Mahdi's followers. Didn't you once tell me you agreed with their cause?'

'The Mahdists?'

'No, silly. The Fenians.'

'Agree with indiscriminate murderers? No, not at all. But I accept that life is tough for Irish Catholics and something has to be done. The answer, I think, is Home Rule. It will give Catholics a stake in government, and break the Protestant stranglehold over politics and property.'

'I'm confused. I thought the leader of Irish Home Rule was a Protestant.'

'Parnell? Yes he is. But he's also an Irish patriot who knows that the political system has to change if the country is to prosper. He hopes that by relinquishing some of their power, Protestants can share in the future government of a semi-independent Ireland that retains the Queen as a monarch and remains a part of the British Empire. That's a long way

from Fenian demands for a complete break and the establishment of a republic.'

'I can see that. So you support Parnell?'

'Not as such. As an army officer I have stay out of politics.
But privately I applaud what he's trying to do. Meanwhile
the Fenians will continue their campaign of indiscriminate
murder, which is why we soldiers have to be on our toes.'

3

Chiswick Mall, west London

So far, so good, thought George as he strolled in evening dress – black dinner jacket, wing collar and white bow-tie – up Chiswick Mall to The Osiers, a pretty stone cottage overlooking the Thames that was owned by Harry Wilson, a close friend of the prince's from Cambridge. Wilson held regular dinner parties for the prince and his inner circle, and it was testament to George's ability to charm the heir apparent that, despite their fairly recent acquaintance, he had been invited to join them.

It was, in fact, quid pro quo for George's offer, the day before, to tutor the prince in equitation and, in particular, the basic cavalry manoeuvres – such as moving a troop from closed column, four riders abreast, to the two-rank-deep line formation used in a charge – that any cavalry officer was expected to be able to perform with his eyes shut. Sadly the prince could not, a fact that had become painfully clear to George during the weekly squadron drills in the riding school at Knightsbridge Barracks. 'It's very good of you to help me,' the prince had responded. 'And in return you must join me and a few particular friends for dinner.'

Those friends – George discovered on arrival – were three in number, making the party five in all. They consisted of the host Harry Wilson, Jim Stephen, the prince's tutor at Cambridge, and an ex-Oxford man by the name of Montague Druitt. All three were talented sportsmen and noted scholars at university who had since been called to the Bar. They were also strikingly handsome and, if the Duke of Cambridge was to be believed, almost certainly homosexual or bisexual.

Of the three, Stephen was the most physically imposing: tall and broad-shouldered with a wide face, prominent nose, dark moustache and wavy hair. Slightly older than the others, he was clearly the dominant personality, eyeing George with his wide-set green eyes like a cat observing its prey. Wilson, by contrast, was much shorter and more softly spoken, with white-blond hair and blue eyes. He was clean-shaven. Druitt was the best looking of the three, with a classically hand-some symmetrical face – aquiline nose, full lips and brown eyes – that was framed by dark, slicked-down hair and a dark moustache. Though not as tall as Stephen, he seemed to George to possess the wiry frame and strong wrists that are typical of talented cricketers.

They had barely sat down to dinner in Wilson's small but beautiful oak-panelled dining room when Jim Stephen began quizzing George on his connection to the prince. 'Forgive the inquisition,' said Stephen, pushing back an unruly lock of hair. 'It's just that Eddy hasn't mentioned you before.'

'Leave him be, Jim,' said the prince, who was sitting directly across from George. 'It's quite simple. We're brother officers. George has just joined the Tenth as my squadron commander. He also happens to be a bona-fide war hero who will, I hope, have a positive effect on my soldiering. If I can't go to war, being exposed to someone who has excelled in combat is probably the next best thing. I'm certain that's what my cousin the duke had in mind when he made the appointment.'

'I'm sure he did,' said Stephen. 'But I must confess I've never taken the business of soldiering seriously. Oh, it's fine to play at soldiers, like you do Eddy. But war means killing to order and often indiscriminately. That's not something I could ever do.'

The prince frowned. 'Come now, Jim. There's a little more to it than that.'

'Actually, he's got a point,' said George. 'I haven't yet fought in a war that I felt was entirely justified, particularly not the first against the Zulus. But that might say more about me than the average soldier.'

'In what way?' asked Stephen. 'You don't look like a typical British officer, if you don't mind me saying. So why did you join the army if it makes you feel so uncomfortable?'

'Why indeed? I've often asked myself that very question. I don't think I really had a choice. My father arranged my commission and then offered me financial incentives to do well.'

'He bribed you?'

'Yes, something like that.'

'Why didn't you tell him to go to hell?' interjected Wilson.

'I should have. But I needed the money and, moreover, I didn't know my father's real name. He was already married before I was born, and didn't want his first wife to know. So he paid my mother an allowance in return for his anonymity. I still don't know who he is – though I have my suspicions.'

'He sounds like a charming fellow,' said Stephen. 'But what's to stop you from chucking it all in now? You've proved you can do it. You've won medals. Why not resign your commission and do something useful?'

'Like law, you mean?' said George. 'Truth is, I enjoy soldiering. I'm good at it. I don't mean the killing. Only a man with no empathy enjoys that. What *I* love is the camaraderie, the shared sense of purpose, the willingness to lay down your life for others. It's hard to explain to the uninitiated.'

'It's even harder to understand,' said Stephen.

'Well I do,' said the prince. 'I haven't been to war, but I have felt the bonds of friendship and mutual trust that bind together any group of soldiers. It's like a large family.'

Stephen snorted. 'What rot! That doesn't sound like any family I know. Certainly, not yours Eddy. Your father is one of the most selfish men I know and, when it comes to personal morality, is clearly a match for George's pater.'

Shocked by Stephen's display of *lèse-majesté* George looked to the prince for a reaction. But the younger man just sighed. 'Please don't bring my father into this. I know very well he's no angel. One day, however, he will be king, and the institution, if not the man, is deserving of respect.'

'Fair enough,' conceded Stephen. 'I'll say no more.'

After a brief pause, Druitt turned to George. 'You mentioned earlier that you didn't think any of the wars you'd fought in were justified, particularly the fight against the Zulus. Why do you say that?'

'Because it's true. The Zulu war was deliberately engineered by Sir Bartle Frere, the governor of the Cape, so that he could confederate South Africa and win himself a peerage. Other senior figures were motivated by military glory and financial gain. Almost no one on our side comes well out of the sordid tale, bar the odd mid-ranking officer

– Redvers Buller and Evelyn Wood come to mind – and the ordinary soldiers, of course. They fought like lions, particularly the defenders of the hospital at Rorke's Drift. They wouldn't leave without the wounded, and it could easily have cost them their lives.'

'What about the Zulus?' asked Druitt. 'You're not suggesting they deserve our sympathy?'

'No. They're a brutal and ruthless tribe. But don't imagine we're any better.'

'I don't for a minute,' said Stephen. 'That's my point about soldiering: you think it brings out the best in men; I think it brings out the worst. But enough of war. Let's talk about love. Are you married, George?'

'Yes I am.'

'Happily?'

'I doubt any marriage is like that all the time,' answered George. 'Mine has its moments.' It was a less than truthful response, but one he thought necessary given the company.

'That's probably the best you can hope for,' said Stephen, nodding sagely. 'I, for one, have no intention of pleasing the guv'nor by settling down with a suitable spouse.'

'Me neither,' said Druitt.

George turned to Druitt. 'Why the certainty? You'll never know if marriage suits until you try it.'

Druitt smiled. 'I *know*. You'll have to take my word for it.'

After dinner, as they sipped coffee and port in Wilson's drawing room, Stephen gave a reading of his poetry. The first verse was entitled 'Malines' and was inspired, Stephen explained, by a train journey in Belgium and an unfortunate encounter with a clumsy-footed native. 'Belgian,' he began, in his deep baritone voice, 'with cumbrous tread and iron boots,

Who in the murky middle of the night,
Designing to renew the foul pursuits
In which thy life is passed, ill-favoured wight,
And wishing on the platform to alight
Where thou couldst mingle with thy fellow brutes,
Didst walk the carriage floor (a leprous sight),
As o'er the sky some baleful meteor shoots:
Upon my slippered foot thou didst descend,
Didst rouse me from my slumbers mad with pain,
And laughedst loud for several minutes' space.
Oh may'st thou suffer tortures without end:
May fiends with glowing pincers rend thy brain,
And beetles batten on thy blackened face!

George joined the others in their enthusiastic applause, though he had been made to feel a little uneasy by Stephen's theme of righteous vengeance for a minor, almost certainly accidental, injury.

'Thank you, thank you,' responded Stephen, with a little bow. 'I will never know if the brute got his come-uppance; only that he richly deserved it. And now, for your delectation, a slightly longer poem that will, I hope, put the demerits of both sexes into proper perspective. It's called "A Thought".'

If all the harm that women have done
Were put in a bundle and rolled into one,
Earth would not hold it,
The sky could not enfold it,
It could not be lighted nor warmed by the sun.
Such masses of evil
Would puzzle the devil
And keep him in fuel while Time's wheels run.

But if all the harm that's been done by men
Were doubled and doubled and doubled again,
And melted and fused into vapour and then
Were squared and raised to the power of ten,
There wouldn't be nearly enough, not near,
To keep a small girl for the tenth of the year.

The misogyny implicit in these lines was unmistakable, and George's applause was half-hearted at best. He was hoping that Stephen's next poem, 'Men and Women', would adopt a more generous tone towards women. The first two lines dashed his hopes. 'As I was strolling lonely in the Backs,' read Stephen, 'I met a woman whom I did not like.'

The poem went on to describe a 'loose-hipped, big-boned, disjointed, angular' woman with an unappealing face, clothes 'devoid of taste or shape or character' and boots 'rather old, and rather large'. Stephen continued:

She was not clever, I am very sure,
Nor witty nor amusing: well informed
She may have been, and kind, perhaps, of heart;
But gossip was writ plain upon her face.
And so she stalked her dull unthinking way;

Stephen seemed to be referring to a particular type of blue-stocking he had encountered at Cambridge, and his antipathy, based chiefly on her looks and manner, was shocking to George. But nothing could have prepared him for the casual violence in the poem's final verse.

I do not want to see that girl again:
I did not like her; and I should not mind

If she were done away with, killed, or ploughed.
She did not seem to serve a useful end:
And certainly she was not beautiful.

'Bravo!' shouted Druitt, as he and Wilson clapped enthusias-
tically. George stared open-mouthed, too shocked to applaud
poetry that he regarded as both distasteful and of poor quality. Only the prince voiced his doubts. 'I admire your poetry,
Jim, you know that. But I really wish you'd lighten the tone
and go a little easier on the fairer sex. I have nothing but love
and admiration for my mother. She is, as you know, a much
greater force for good in the world than Papa.'

'Yes, yes,' said Stephen. 'We're well aware of your deep
regard for your mother. Let's just say she's an exception and
leave it at that. Now, who's for a nightcap at Hammond's
Club?'

'Where is that?' asked George. 'I've never heard of it.'

'It's a private members' club in Cleveland Street, Fitzrovia,'
replied Stephen. 'Eddy loves it. I'm sure you will too.'

George opened his pocket watch and saw that it had gone
eleven. 'I think it's a little late,' he said. 'His Royal Highness
and I have to be on duty at nine o'clock tomorrow
morning.'

'True enough,' said the prince, 'but I don't need much
sleep to function and Hammond's is only a little out of my
way.'

'We won't stay long,' pronounced Stephen. 'I promise.
Harry? Monty? You both coming?'

They nodded.

'George?'

He hesitated. The hour was late, his earlier good humour
had been rather soured by the misogynistic tone of Stephen's

poetry, and Fitzrovia was certainly out of *his* way. Yet it sounded as if the prince was keen, and he knew his duty was to keep an eye on him. 'All right,' he said at last. 'I'll come. But just for a drink or two.'

*

They were met in the entrance hall of number 19 Cleveland Street, a modest four-storey Georgian townhouse in Fitzrovia, by the proprietor Charles Hammond, a rotund swell, with thinning dark hair and a magnificent waxed moustache, whose eyes lit up when he spotted the prince.

'Welcome back, Your Royal Highness, gentlemen,' said Hammond, obsequiously. 'Thomas will take your overcoats. Would you like a drink first or get straight down to business?'

'Softly, softly, Hammond. We have a new boy with us,' said Stephen as he removed his coat, 'and he doesn't know the ropes yet. A table in the long drawing room if you please.'

'As you wish, Mr Stephen.'

Hammond led the way upstairs to the opulent drawing room: all gilt mirrors, plush sofas and potted plants. The twenty or so occupants were a mixture of well-dressed gentlemen like themselves and attractive youths, some barely into their teens. A few were even dolled up like women, complete with wigs, floor-length gowns and lipstick. George had never seen anything like it.

Once champagne had been brought, Stephen offered a toast: 'Good times!'

'Good times!' chimed the others, clinking glasses.

Already George was regretting his decision to come to what was clearly a male brothel. He consoled himself with the thought that the prince would probably have come anyway, and that it was better that he was here to keep an eye on him. But what would he do if the prince took a fancy to one of the male prostitutes? It was a question that became more acute a few minutes later when they were approached by a dark-haired lad, no more than sixteen, who was wearing the tight-fitting blue uniform of the General Post Office. 'Mind if I join you gen'lemen?'

'Please do,' said the prince.

The boy squeezed onto the sofa between George and the prince. 'Name's Charlie Thickbroom. Pleased to meet ya.'

'And we you,' said the prince.

'Did you say Thickbroom?' asked Stephen from an easy chair opposite.

'I did, sir.'

'How wonderfully apt. I trust it's a name you can live up to?'

'I don't get your drift, sir.'

'Never mind.'

'How did you hear about the club, Thickbroom?' asked the prince.

'I was told 'bout it by 'Enry Newlove.'

'Newlove!' said Stephen. 'How droll.'

'Quiet Jim,' admonished the prince. 'Pray continue, Thickbroom. Who's this Newlove?'

''E's a telegraph boy, like me. We're based at the GPO in the City. Anyways, one day Newlove persuades me to go with 'im into a cubicle in the basement lavatory. After we'd done some fings, 'e tells me I can earn four shillings a time by letting the gentlemen at Mister 'Ammonds 'ave a go between my legs. 'E said he did it regular, and enjoyed it. So I thought, why not? I earns the same in one night as the GPO pays in a month.'

'And Hammond,' asked George. 'How much does he pocket?'

'Enough,' said Druitt. 'It's a sovereign a go.'

'Well gentlemen,' said Thickbroom, 'is any of you in need of my services?'

'Not tonight,' responded Stephen. 'But thank you.'

'Then I'll bid you good evening.'

The plan to come for just a drink or two was quickly forgotten as the drink flowed and George began to enjoy himself. He had imagined a male brothel to be a cheap and sordid place where unwilling prostitutes were routinely exploited. Hammond's Club was the complete opposite. The young prostitutes seemed to be there by choice and the atmosphere was relaxed and jolly. Now and again, one of the gentleman clients would leave the room with a youth, presumably to retire to a bedroom. But most were content, like the prince's party, to enjoy the fine wines, music and ribald conversation. It was a place, George reflected, without convention and rules, where you could be yourself. No wonder it was so popular with people like the prince who, for so much of their lives, had had to live within a strict social code. As practising homosexuals, they were all – by definition – outsiders, which was why, George reasoned, he felt so relaxed in their company. He was an outsider too – just not for the same reason.

One of the patrons looked familiar to George – a large, ample-girthed man with magnificent ginger whiskers – but he could not place him. Eventually the man strolled over and said to the prince, 'Good evening, sir.'

'Good evening, Podge.'

'I know all of your guests but one,' he said, nodding at George. 'Would you introduce me?'

'We don't use surnames here, Podge, as you know. His Christian name is George.'

'Pleased to meet you, George.'

George nodded.

'Are you military by any chance?'

'Yes.'

'Sudan.'

'That's right.'

'I thought so. Well, enjoy your evening.'

As the man walked away, George suddenly remembered his name: Major Lord Arthur Somerset of the Royal Horse Guards. They had met briefly in the Sudan when George was on the Staff and Somerset had been part of General Stewart's Heavy Camel Corps. Lord Arthur had covered himself in glory at the Battle of Abu Klea by helping to drive the Mahdists out of the British square before recovering the body of his dead commander, Colonel Fred Burnaby. A younger son of the Duke of Beaufort, Somerset was generally regarded as the beau idéal of a British cavalryman and highly attractive to the opposite sex. What then, George wondered, was he doing in a male brothel?

Stephen had similar thoughts. 'I dread to think of your father's reaction, Eddy, if he knew his intimate friend and equerry, the superintendent of the Royal Stables, was a regular here.'

'Not half as volcanic as his temper would be,' responded the prince, 'if he ever learned that I come here too, and that Podge first proposed me for membership. Let's just hope, for all our sakes, that he never finds out.'

George looked at his pocket watch. 'Good heavens, it's one in the morning. I must go.'

'Must you?' said Druitt. 'I've a mind to head for Whitechapel for a bit of fun.'

'At this time?'

'Yes. What of it? This is *the* time to go. The streets are quiet and dark, and the pleasure discreet and suitably earthy. You should try it.'

'Not tonight. I have to be up early, as does the prince.'

'George is right,' said the prince, 'and more importantly he's my superior officer. I'd better call it a night too.'

'Will anyone come with me?' implored Druitt.

'I will, Monty,' said Wilson.

'So will I,' added Stephen.

George and the prince left first, and headed south to the junction with Goodge Street. As they were waiting for cabs, the prince asked George if he had enjoyed the evening.

'Very much so. The dinner was excellent and I enjoyed the company of your friends. I wish I could say the same for Jim Stephen's poetry.'

The prince chuckled. 'Yes, it's not to everyone's taste. Jim can be a little choleric, but he's a brilliant man and destined for great things. I'm certain of it.'

'Maybe so. But I thought that, at times, he was a little disrespectful towards you. Was I imagining that?'

'No. He sometimes forgets he's no longer my tutor. Though he has, I think, my best interests at heart. So what did you think of the club?'

'I enjoyed it. It's not the sort of place I'm familiar with, but I liked the fact that everyone could relax and be themselves without fear of censure. I've always felt outside mainstream society, for obvious reasons, and I suppose many people of "that" persuasion are in a similar position.'

'It's not quite as simple as that, George. You talk about "that" persuasion, as if it's one or the other: homosexual or heterosexual. In fact many people are a mixture of both. I know I will have to marry one day. My future role as monarch requires it. But until then I want to enjoy myself with like-minded people and no strings attached. Is there anything wrong with that?'

'Not if you're discreet. But never forget that all homosexual acts are now illegal. You would risk much less by taking female lovers like your father.'

'Would I?' barked the prince, his anger evident. 'The sort of women my father consorts with are no better than high-class whores. They all hope to supplant my poor mother and to feather their nests. They're nothing but scheming harpies, and he's a fool to be taken in by them. My male partners expect very little in return.'

'Yet they still present a very real danger. What if you're caught in the act? What if the press discover that you visit clubs like Hammond's? Can you imagine the damage that would do to you, the regiment and, more importantly, the royal family?'

'I won't be exposed. Most of my lovers have no idea who I am. Those that do would never betray me. There's nothing for you or anyone else to worry about.'

'I hope you're right. Here's your ride home,' said George, hailing a passing hansom cab.

The driver reined his horse in and leant down from his perch behind the small two-wheeled carriage. 'Where to, sir?'

George turned to the prince. 'It's Marlborough House on the Mall, isn't it?'

'Yes it is, but I really must insist you take this one. After all, you're my commanding officer. I'll get the next one.'

'Are you sure? I'm happy to wait.'

'Yes I'm sure. It's my fault we've finished so late, and you have further to go.'

'All right then,' said George, turning back to the cabbie. 'The address is Sixty-Nine Alnwick Grove, Hammersmith.'

'Very good, sir.'

George shook the prince's hand. 'Goodnight, then.'

'Goodnight.'

As the cab took him home, George ruminated on the events of the evening and the fact that, in many ways, the duke's very worst fears had been confirmed: the prince was indeed 'young and impressionable' and 'eminently capable of being led astray' by his Cambridge friends. Their visit to the male brothel, and the conversation they had just had on the street, was proof that the prince was having sex with men and, as a result, was a potential target for criminal or political blackmail. George's job was to protect the prince from both sexual misadventure and Irish terrorists. He'd assumed the first task would be the easiest to accomplish. Now he wasn't so sure.

4

Kilburn, northwest London

George got off the train at Kilburn and Brondesbury Station, and walked south down Kilburn High Road. Dressed in the working man's uniform of shapeless jacket, collarless shirt and flat cap, he knew he would not look out of place in a community dominated by poor Irish immigrants who had flocked to the mainland in recent years to work as low-paid labourers. Yet the sight of so many shoeless children and dilapidated houses was still a shock. 'Spare a penny for me, mister?' asked one grubby tyke more in hope than expectation.

'Get out of here,' said George with a sweep of his hand. He felt bad, but knew that his cover demanded such a reaction.

Reaching the junction of Burton Road, he could see directly opposite The Kingdom public house. It was, according to Inspector Littlechild, a notorious pro-Fenian watering hole and an obvious place to begin his undercover work for the Special Irish Branch, the SIB. His task was to infiltrate the local Fenian network and, if possible, disrupt their plan to assassinate Prince Albert Victor. He would do this by masquerading as Tom Quinn, a Dublin-born household servant who had lived most of his life in London. But he was under no illusions about his likely fate if the Fenians discovered his true identity.

'You'll be tortured and shot,' Littlechild had warned him, 'and found with your hands pinioned, a bullet in your head and a card slung round your neck with the message, "This is what we do to spies". So don't get caught.'

George took two deep breaths and pushed open the door to the pub, blinking his eyes as they adjusted to the dark interior. It was a typical working men's establishment: sawdust on the floor, a minimum of basic furniture and a long bar that stretched the length of the room. The few regulars quickly scanned the new arrival before returning to their pints.

'Good day to you,' said the elderly barman, 'what'll you be having?'

'A pint of ale, if you please.'

George took his drink to a table at the far end of the bar and opened a copy of *The Freeman's Journal*, Ireland's bestselling nationalist newspaper. Pretending to read, he kept one eye on the comings and goings. Nobody spoke to him, though he caught the barman watching him a couple of times. After an hour, he left. The pattern was repeated a day later. On his third visit he had barely sat down when he felt a tap on the shoulder. He turned to see a small but solidly built young man, with long dark hair and pale skin, his small mouth set at the corners. 'Don't think I know you. Live round here?'

'Not exactly.'

'Then why you here?'

'I heard it was a good boozer.'

'It is, but I'd be careful reading rags like that, if was you,' said the man, nodding at George's paper. 'We've little time for Parnell in this place.'

'I've no time for him either,' responded George. 'To me he's a Proddie lapdog. But I like to know what the enemy's up to.'

'The enemy, is it? So you support direct action to win Ireland's freedom, do you?'

'I do.'

What's your name?'

'Tom Quinn.'

'I'm Liam Kelly,' said the young man, offering his hand. George shook it. 'So where are you from?'

'I was born in the village of Clontarf, near Dublin. You sound like a Dublin man, do you know it?'

'Not well, but I've heard of it. So when did you come over the water?'

'In the late sixties. My father came here to work as a navvy on the railways and we eventually joined him.'

'So your father's an Irishman?'

'Born and bred.'

'Then how do you explain this?' asked Kelly, wiping his hand in front of his face.

George chuckled. 'You mean my skin colour? Good question. My mother is Maltese, from Malta in the Mediterranean. She came to Ireland as a domestic servant. I'm more like her than my father.'

'Tell me about your father. Is he sympathetic to the cause?'

'He was. He died of typhus about ten years ago. But he never had the courage to play an active role. I do.'

'And what makes you think we could use someone like you?'

George frowned. 'Why wouldn't they? I'm young, fit and know how to handle guns. I could be very useful.'

'How do you know about guns?'

'I was a soldier in the British Army,' said George, using the cover story he'd agreed with Littlechild.

Liam flinched as if he'd been slapped. His right hand moved close to his jacket pocket where he was doubtless hiding a pistol. 'You were *what*?'

'I was a soldier.'

'Why would you serve the oppressors of your people?'

'Because I was desperate. It was the only work I could get. But I also thought it would be good to understand the enemy, learn how they did things.'

'And did you?'

'I think so. The Brits are physically brave – and I include the officers – but they lack the Irishman's imagination and cunning. It's not hard to second-guess them.'

Liam nodded in agreement. 'Fair point, but there are exceptions, and most of them work for the SIB. Where did you serve? Not Ireland, I hope.'

'No. Egypt and the Sudan. The first war, in eighty-two, was a piece of cake. Not so the second. The Fuzzy-Wuzzies were tough foes. I was at Abu Klea when they almost broke the square.'

'When did you leave the army?'

'Last year, at the end of my six-year term.'

'And what do you do now?'

'I have a position,' said George, 'as a valet for Lord Charles Beresford, the son of the marquess of Waterford, who lives on Curzon Street, Mayfair. He was an officer in my regiment, and offered to employ me when I left.'

Liam's eyes widened. 'Beresford, you say? Isn't he a friend of the Prince of Wales's eldest son?'

'Prince Albert Victor? Yes he is. The prince is a regular guest at dinner.'

'Well I'll be. And you're prepared to help the cause?'

'I am.'

'That's good to hear. Well thank you, Tom. I'll pass on what you've told me to those that matter and they might want to speak to you.'

'Are you not one of them?' asked George.

Liam put his finger to his lips. 'Careless talk, Tom. As I say, I'll pass on what you've said. But I warn you, they'll want guarantees.'

'What sort of guarantees?'

'The sort that tell them you can be trusted.'

'All right. How will they contact me?'

'Come back here tomorrow. Same time. If they're interested, I'll let you know. Can you do that?'

'Certainly.'

'Good. I'll see you then.' Liam shook hands and went to talk to a tough-looking man with curly hair and a broken nose.

After a decent interval, George finished his pint and left the pub, walking back up Kilburn High Street to the train station. From there he made his way to Green Park in Central London where he had arranged to brief Littlechild on his progress. But as he was entering the park, still dressed like a labourer, he almost collided with a gentleman coming out. It was the prince in his undress uniform. 'Major Hart? Is that you? What a surprise.'

'I . . . I can explain,' said George, the colour rising in his cheeks.

'There's no need,' said the prince, a knowing look in his eye. 'I've often gone incognito myself. After all, it wouldn't pay to be recognized in Green Park, now would it?'

Suddenly George understood the prince's meaning: as he dressed down when looking for male company, he had assumed George was doing likewise. George almost laughed at the irony. But it was a perfect excuse not to have to explain, so he went along with the prince's misconception. 'You're right, Your Royal Highness. It wouldn't pay at all.'

Inside the park, George found Littlechild at their pre-arranged meeting place on a bench close to Queen's Walk. George explained what had happened and asked how he should act if the Fenian leadership in London wanted to meet him.

'Don't say much,' advised Littlechild. 'Remember you're as suspicious of them as they are of you. They'll want to test your credibility, so tell them something only an employee of Lord Charles Beresford would know: such as the route into the house via the coal hatch in the rear courtyard. Explain that the coal bunker is in the cellar which the servants can access via a door in the basement. This door is always locked, but you know where the key is kept. Once they're in the basement, there is nothing to stop them making their way up two flights of stairs to the dining room on the ground floor. They'll want to check this route before they plan an assassination attempt. Once they're satisfied, you can tell them the date of the dinner. We'll be waiting to catch them red-handed.'

'Yes I can see how that would work,' said George. 'But what about the guarantees that Liam Kelly said they'd need to trust me? What might they ask me to do?'

'Who knows? But don't worry. We won't let you do anything illegal.'

George snorted. 'Is that all you've got to say on the matter?'

'What else can I say? Let's wait to hear what they ask you to do. Then we can decide on our response.'

*

Next day, George returned to The Kingdom pub in Kilburn. Liam was waiting. 'I told them what you told me. The Boss would like to meet you in person.'

'When?'

'Now. I'll show you the way. It's not far.'

'Lead on,' said George, his heart thumping at the risk he was about to take.

They went outside and Liam pointed at a covered goods wagon, its horse and driver waiting patiently. 'In that?' asked George.

'Yep.'

Liam opened the back flap and the two of them climbed inside. They sat on one of the side benches, next to each other. 'I hope you don't mind if I blindfold you,' said Liam, taking a strip of cloth from his pocket. 'Just as a precaution.'

'Go ahead.'

Twenty minutes later, the wagon stopped and Liam helped George down and into a nearby building. Their footsteps echoed as they strode across a flagstone floor. Eventually Liam stopped George and removed his blindfold, revealing a vast warehouse with rows of tea chests against one wall. Facing George were three men, two armed with pistols. The third – a stocky man in his fifties with close-cropped red hair and a long scar on his freckled cheek – introduced himself as Pat and was clearly the boss. 'Yer man here,' he said, nodding at Liam, 'says you're a former soldier who's offered to help the cause. Is that right?'

'It is.'

'And how do you plan to do that?'

George was a little surprised by how well spoken and educated the Fenian boss sounded. 'I . . . I don't know exactly,' he stammered. 'I thought you'd decide. I work as a valet for Lord Charles Beresford.'

'Your former officer?'

'Yes.'

'And you're prepared to betray him?'

'I am.'

'Why? You used to be on the same side.'

'I know,' said George, shifting from one foot to the other. 'But that wasn't by choice. I only served to put food in my mouth. And it confirmed what I'd always suspected.'

'Which is?'

'That the Brits are a cruel and heartless race, and that only by fighting fire with fire can Ireland ever be free.'

'Fine words, young Tom, but how can I be sure you're not a spy, a plant? You say you served in the British Army. You probably did. But are you still a servant of the British state, that's the question?'

'No,' said George, trying to look as affronted as possible. 'I'm not. I'm a patriot. Tell me what I can do to convince you?'

'Well, there is something I have in mind. But I'll come back to that. First I want to talk about His Royal Highness Prince Albert Victor.'

'What about him?'

'You say he's a regular dinner guest at your employer's residence?'

'He is.'

'And that you're anxious to assist the cause?'

'I am.'

45

'No matter the consequence?'

'No.'

'Good,' said Pat. 'Then you can help us kill the prince.'

George blew out his cheeks. 'I'd willingly do that. What would you have me do?'

'It's quite simple. We need advance warning of when the prince is next invited to dinner; and we need access to the house. Can you do that for us?'

'Yes, I think I can.'

'Grand. Now there's just one more thing we need before we start planning in earnest.'

'Yes?'

'We need proof we can trust you. I'm sure you understand why.'

'What kind of proof?'

'I need you to kill a copper.'

George thought he must have misheard the Fenian boss. 'Did you say *kill* a copper, a policeman?'

'I did. You all right with that?'

'I . . . I think so. I'm sorry. I don't mean to sound half-hearted. I just didn't expect this.'

'What, exactly, did you expect, Mr Quinn? You say you'll do anything for the cause. Well, killing policemen *is* part of the cause. So will you do it? A simple yes or no is all we need.'

George knew that if he hesitated he was dead. 'Yes I can do that,' he said. 'No problem. Any copper?'

'Yes, any copper will do. Just bring us his helmet and his pinkie. By Wednesday please. We'll be watching the papers to make sure you've done as you say. When we're satisfied we'll discuss future plans. You can leave any messages for us at the following safe house.' He handed George a piece of paper with a Kilburn address on it. 'They're sympathizers, but they know nothing about our work.'

As he was being taken back blindfolded to the pub, George agonized over how he could hoodwink the Fenians into thinking he *had* killed a policeman. There had to be a way – because if not his days as an agent provocateur were numbered.

He explained his dilemma to Littlechild when they met again, later that day, in Green Park.

'I think we can arrange that,' said the SIB chief. 'We'll simply fake a murder and have the press report it. We'll also get you a suitably blood-spattered police helmet and a pinkie from the morgue. When does the report of the murder need to appear?'

'By Wednesday,' replied George.

'Tomorrow, then. We'll fake the murder tomorrow, and the report will appear in the papers the day after. Then we can decide how to catch these bastards in the act.'

*

On Wednesday morning, George retrieved his copy of *The Times* from beside the front door and went straight to the table of contents on page 9. Below news stories about the opening of the Eisteddfod by Liberal leader William Gladstone, and the British Army's adoption of the new bolt-action and magazine-fed Lee–Metford rifle, was a headline that stated: 'POLICE CONSTABLE MURDERED IN EUSTON'. George turned to page 5 where the report stated:

> The brutal murder of a police constable was committed in the neighbourhood of Euston yesterday evening. The victim's body was found by a night-watchman in Phoenix Road at 11 o'clock. The throat was cut from ear to ear

and the right hand was missing its little finger, which appeared to have been severed by the perpetrator. The police constable's helmet was also missing. Sir George Warren, Commissioner of the Metropolitan Police, has condemned the attack as a 'cowardly and seemingly motiveless assault on a police constable doing his duty'. He has promised to devote all appropriate resources in an effort to catch the pitiless killer of a married man with two young children.

George nodded in satisfation. The family details were a nice touch.

He was about to close the paper when a similar news story caught his eye. It was a coroner's report into the murder of a woman in Buck's Row, just off the Whitechapel Road, in the early hours of Friday the 31st, the same night he had gone to the club in Cleveland Street with the prince and his friends. The woman had been found with her throat cut, 'terrible wounds' in her abdomen and 'two small stabs on her private parts'. She was wearing clothing of a 'common description', including a flannel petticoat with the stencil stamp of Lambeth Workhouse, and had since been identified by two women who shared her lodging house at 18 Thrawl Street, Spitalfields, as Polly Nichols, an 'unfortunate' or common prostitute. The matter was being investigated by Detective Inspector Abberline of Scotland Yard, whose only theory with regard to the murder was that 'a gang of ruffians exists in the neighbourhood, which, blackmailing women of the "unfortunate" class, takes vengeance on those who do not find money for them'. The story was additional proof, if George needed it, that the prince and his friends were ill advised to journey to impoverished and dangerous areas like the slums of Whitechapel for, as Druitt had put it, 'a bit of fun'.

'You still here?' said Lucy, descending the stairs in an emerald green dressing gown. 'I thought you had to be at the barracks for eight?'

'I do. I'm just leaving, but I thought I'd have a quick look at the paper.'

'Anything interesting?'

'Not really. Just something about the knifing of a woman in Whitechapel.'

'How awful! And there's me thinking London was safer than the Sudan. I think I've changed my mind.'

'Don't be silly. Every city has an area that's best avoided: full of cutthroats and ladies of ill repute. London's is Whitechapel. Luckily we have no reason to go there.'

'I'm very glad to hear it. Do say goodbye to Jake before you go. He's still in bed.'

George bounded up the stairs and entered Jake's bedroom. The curtains were drawn, but he could just make out a mop of black curls on the pillow. Though just seven years old, his son was tall for his age and remarkably self-reliant. Having lived all of his short life abroad – first in Natal and Egypt, latterly in Gibraltar – he loved the outdoors and was never happier than when he was camping under the stars or hunting with a .22-calibre rifle. At Gibraltar he had climbed the Rock alone and, when missing, could usually be found at the military barracks on the southern tip of the colony, where the sentries were given strict instructions to detain him until his mother arrived to collect him. He had insisted upon a replica uniform of his father's regiment for his sixth birthday and, despite the misgivings of both parents, was determined to become a 'sojer'.

George looked down at his son's sleeping form and felt his heart swell with pride, tinged with regret that his own father had never looked upon him with the same intense feelings. He also felt guilty that, even in Britain, he was doing a job that risked his life *and* that of his family. He bent down to kiss the back of Jake's head, murmuring as he did so: 'Goodbye, little man.'

'Bye, bye, Papa' murmured his son sleepily.

*

Later that morning, at his meeting with Inspector Littlechild, George was handed a battered policeman's Britannia helmet, complete with spatters of blood, and a small box containing a man's severed little finger. 'Hopefully that'll convince the Fenian chief that you've done what they asked,' said Littlechild. 'Then you can tell them that Prince Albert Victor is due to attend a dinner at Lord Charles's house a week next Wednesday. But don't forget to ask them for instructions. It's vital that we know of their intentions in advance so that we can plan accordingly. Do you understand?'

'Yes. I'm concerned, of course, for the prince's safety. Will it be necessary for him to attend the dinner, or might a "double" stand in for him?'

'No. He has to be there or the Fenians might smell a rat. But the place will be crawling with police so he won't be in any danger. I've discussed this with Commissioner Warren and we've agreed that the prince is not to be told what's happening in advance: that way he won't try to do anything stupid.'

Before leaving, George asked about the report of the Whitechapel murder that had appeared on the same page of *The Times*. Had they faked that one too, to justify the prominent position given to the police murder? 'No,' said

Littlechild, 'that one is genuine and is not an isolated incident. In fact, it's the second murder of a Whitechapel prostitute this year.'

'Is it? The report didn't mention a previous murder.'

'There was another one about a month ago: both were fallen ladies. The latest has caused a stir at CID Headquarters in Scotland Yard.'

'Why?'

'Because both were horribly cut up in similar circumstances, and it seems likely that the same person is responsible.'

*

That evening, George dropped off a letter at the Fenian safe house in Kilburn. It read: 'I've done what you asked. I'll be in The Kingdom pub until closing time.'

Two hours later, shortly before the pub was due to close, Liam walked in and beckoned him to come outside. Again he was blindfolded and taken to the warehouse where Pat and his henchmen were waiting for him. 'You've got something for me?' asked Pat.

George nodded and handed him the parcel he was holding. Pat tore the paper to reveal the policeman's bloodied helmet and, inside it, a little finger severed at the middle joint.

'Where's the rest of it?' asked the Fenian chief with a straight face.

This threw George. 'The rest? I don't know what you mean.'

'I would have thought it was obvious. This is half a finger. Where's the other half.'

'Still attached to the copper's hand,' said George, unable to decide if Pat was being serious. 'I was in a hurry.'

Pat smiled. 'Relax. I'm kidding you on. I read the report in the paper. You've done well. First time?'

'I've killed someone? No, far from it. I fought in the Sudan, remember. But it's the first time I've done it in cold blood.'

'And? Did you enjoy it?'

George knew Pat was looking for a reaction, so he kept his response matter-of-fact. 'Not particularly. It needed to be done so I did it. There was blood everywhere.'

'Occupational hazard, I'm afraid. Now tell me about the prince. Have you heard when he'll next be invited to dinner?'

'I have. The invitations have just gone out. The dinner will be held at Lord Charles's house at Eighteen Curzon Street, on Wednesday the nineteenth of this month. The prince is invited for seven o'clock.'

'How many other guests?'

'Nine: four gentlemen and five ladies. That's twelve in total, including the prince and Lord and Lady Charles.'

'How do we get access to the house?'

'There are two locked doors you need to pass through: one to give you access to the rear courtyard from the lane at the back of the house, and another, once you're into the cellar through the unlocked coal hatch, to let you into the pantry. From there it's just two flights of stairs up to the dining room on the ground floor. I know where the keys are kept.'

'Good. If you can take imprints of them in clay, we can make copies. I'll also need you to sketch a plan of the house, including stairways and, more importantly, all the exits.'

'I thought you might. So I've done that already,' said George, pulling a folded piece of paper from his jacket pocket.

Pat opened the piece of paper and looked at the sketch. 'The only problem, as I see it, is the servants. The route from the cellar passes the servants' hall and the butler's pantry. But it can't be helped. Do you know of any weapons in the house?'

'Yes. My employer has a revolver, but he keeps it in a safe in his dressing room. But that's the only one, as far as I know.'

'Good. That's all for now. We'll be in touch.'

George had been told by Littlechild to say as little as possible, but he could not resist asking: 'Can you tell me *how* you'll kill the prince? It might help if I know.'

Pat tapped the side of his nose. 'You'll find out on the night. Just get us into the building. We'll do the rest.'

5

Metropolitan Police HQ, Scotland Yard

'Ah, Major Hart, it's good to see you again,' said Sir Charles Warren as he rose from his large mahogany desk. Oddly for a commissioner of police, he was wearing the dress uniform of a colonel of the Royal Engineers, complete with campaign medals and various orders of knighthood.

George remained expressionless as he shook Warren's hand and took the proffered seat. It had been five years since their last meeting in Egypt's Sinai desert: then Warren's hair had been darker and thicker, and his girth a little thinner, even if the monocle and bushy moustache were as George remembered. The pair had been tasked with finding Professor Edward Palmer, a celebrated British archaeologist, and four companions who had gone missing a few months earlier and were assumed to have been murdered. Though George had done almost all the undercover detective work that cracked the case – slowly winning the trust of the Bedouin in his guise as an Arab trader – it had been Warren, as leader of the search expedition, who wrote the official report and took all the credit. His reward was a knighthood and the thanks of Parliament; George had got nothing, and had barely been mentioned in the press reports, an omission that he blamed on Warren's determination not to be outshone by his subordinate.

Since then Warren had led a successful military expedition to establish British rule in Bechuanaland in southern Africa that had won him further honours. But his subsequent appointment as commissioner of the Metropolitan Police had come as a shock to George, who knew from their time in the Sinai that Warren held radical political opinions – such as his support for land and parliamentary reform, and also some form of self-government for Ireland (a policy that George also had sympathy for) – that were shared by few in the British Establishment. Warren, moreover, had little practical experience of civil police work. Yet it was not the first time an army officer had been given the top job at the Met, and what probably swung it for Warren, George reasoned, was the unjustified perception that he had cracked the Palmer case. George knew the truth, of course, and it still rankled.

Since receiving the summons to the Met headquarters at 4 Whitehall Place – a jumble of Georgian neoclassical architecture better known as Scotland Yard – George had assumed that Warren wanted to talk to him about the SIB operation to foil the Fenian plot to assassinate Prince Albert Victor. He had been dreading the meeting because he feared he would be unable to keep a civil tongue in his head. But Warren surprised him by asking about an unrelated issue. 'Are you aware, Hart, of the recent murders in Whitechapel?'

'Yes, sir,' said George, his resentment all but forgotten. 'I read about one last week. Someone's killing prostitutes.'

'Quite right, and that someone has just claimed another victim. It happened in the early hours of this morning. I know what you're thinking: what's this got to do with me?

My job is to prevent the Fenians from assassinating Prince Albert Victor. Well, believe it or not, there's a connection. I've just received a report from Inspector Abberline of the CID, who is leading the inquiry into the murders, that he has a witness statement from someone who saw the prince in Commercial Street, Whitechapel, on the night of the previous murder: that of Polly Nichols in the early hours of the thirty-first of August. The witness claims to know what the prince looks like because he met him on one of his official visits to the East End Universities Settlement. He says the prince was talking to a young man. To what purpose we can only speculate.'

George thought back more than a week to the early hours of 31 August: a Friday. Where was he then? Safely tucked up in bed after an evening out with the prince and his friends. He had parted from the prince in a hansom cab outside the club in Cleveland Street, and had never doubted that the prince would keep his word and return home to Marlborough House. Until now. The prince had obviously waited for George to depart before meeting up with the others and heading to the East End. He cursed himself for taking the prince at his word, and not seeing him safely home.

'The danger,' continued Warren, 'is that people will put two and two together and come up with five. I'm not suggesting for a minute that the prince is involved in the murders, but if the rumour gets out it will do incalculable harm to the royal family. So I would appreciate it if, as well as keeping the prince safe from Fenians, you also encourage him to avoid the East End, at least until the killer is caught. His Royal Highness often visits the slums of Whitechapel in disguise as part of his work as a member of the Royal Commission on the Housing of the Working Classes. But even this is to be discouraged for the time being. Can I rely on you to do that?'

'Of course, Sir Charles. I'll make sure he stays away,' said George, seething inside that the prince had lied to him. 'If there's nothing else, I'll be on my way.'

'Actually there is,' said Warren, holding up a torn piece of paper. 'This was found at this morning's murder scene.'

He handed the paper fragment to George. It was clearly part of a letter, the heading instantly recognizable to George as his own regimental crest: a crown topping the Prince of Wales's three feathers, the motto '*Ich Dein*' (I Serve) and the initials 'X.R.H.'. Below it was written:

Knightsbridge Cavalry Barr
August 28th, '88

My dear A . . .

'Well I'll be damned,' said George. 'It must have been written by someone in the Tenth Hussars, or at least with access to regimental stationery. Do you think it was dropped by the killer?'

'Possibly. It was found right next to the corpse. Obviously we need to find the author because he will lead us to this "A" fellow.'

'Well, the author is almost certainly an officer. The bold handwriting and use of language would indicate that.'

'That was my conclusion. Any idea which officer?'

'I couldn't say without comparing their handwriting.'

'Could you do that?'

'Well, yes, I suppose I could. But why are you asking *me*? Couldn't a detective do the job just as well?'

'No, to be perfectly honest. This is an extremely delicate matter. If we were to send in a detective, the possible link between the prince's regiment and the murders would be in the papers within hours. That would both embarrass the royal family and hamper the inquiry. We need someone in the regiment to make discreet inquiries on our behalf, and you're perfect for the job. You're close to the prince and you have some experience of this type of work. I haven't forgotten what you did in the Sinai.'

Yes, thought George, it's just a shame you didn't include my role in your official report.

'We need that sort of determination to crack this case,' continued Warren. 'I know you have your hands full with the Fenians, but this shouldn't take up too much of your time. I'm under a lot of pressure, as I'm sure you can imagine. The press is demanding results, as is the Home Secretary. I was appointed by one of his Liberal predecessors and I suspect he's looking for an excuse to replace me with a commissioner more in tune with his own politics. I'm determined not to give him one, which is why I need this case solved as soon as possible. Will you help me?'

George hesitated. This was typical of Warren: he'd ask for a minor favour and, when you'd agreed, add a much trickier proposition. If you pulled it off, *he* would take all the credit; if you didn't, he'd blame *you*. He'd used much the same tactic to get George involved in the Palmer case. Now Warren was expecting him to spy not only on the Fenians but also on his fellow officers. It did not seem right. But, then again, his priority was to protect the prince, and this was a case that certainly had the capacity to harm both him and the royal family in general.

'I know it's not an easy decision,' said Warren, 'but I should tell you that there's more at stake than my career and even the reputation of the royal family. Do you know why my predecessor was forced to resign in eighty-six?'

'No. I was in Egypt.'

'It was because he failed to contain a riot by a violent mob that began in Trafalgar Square and spread to Pall Mall and Oxford Street. Windows were broken and people beaten up. Why? Because the hungry and unemployed are no longer prepared to accept the social and economic inequalities that they witness daily in the capital. I was appointed to curb both the Fenians and these large-scale working-class demonstrations. Unfortunately, despite my best efforts, the marches have become increasingly political. Last year, during Her Majesty's Golden Jubilee celebrations, demonstrators were seen on the streets of Whitechapel carrying red and black flags and singing the "Marseillaise". Many have been infected by European notions of socialist revolution and would like to see the end of both the monarchy and our system of elected governments. I have some sympathy for them. Our status as the world's greatest empire means little to the people of the East End, the majority of whom are living below the poverty line and face a daily struggle for survival. Did you know that the population density of Whitechapel is up to ten times greater than other areas of the metropolis? They're packed together like pigs in a sty, with little opportunity to earn money or feed their families. Is it any wonder that many turn to prostitution or crime, or are seduced by socialists who preach political revolution?'

'No,' responded George. 'When you put it like that, it isn't.'

'Exactly. Which is why I need to find the Whitechapel murderer before the whole East End powder keg explodes. I know it sounds dramatic, but the very future of our system of government is under threat if these brutal killings continue. Why? Because the poor of Whitechapel will conclude that we – the powers that be – don't care. That might be enough to justify rebellion. So I ask again: will you help me?'

'I don't really see I have an option, Sir Charles,' said George. 'So, yes, I'll help you. But in an unofficial capacity, and only until I've identified the letter writer and the prince is out of the picture. Then, if you don't mind, I'll concentrate all my energies on the Fenians.'

'Of course. I'm very grateful. It would obviously help your inquiries if you knew a little more about the case. So I've taken the liberty of asking one of Inspector Abberline's best detectives to brief you. His name is Detective Sergeant Jack Fletcher. He comes from a notorious Whitechapel crime family and knows the area like the back of his hand. Why he decided to go straight, nobody knows. It can't have impressed his brother, who is serving a stretch in Euston Prison for armed robbery. It's probably down to the fact that his parents sent him to a grammar school where, as far as his brother was concerned, he clearly mixed with the wrong people. We're very glad to have him on our side. He's a bit unorthodox so you should get along. Have a chat with him tomorrow and then begin your own inquiries. But if you have any luck identifying the letter writer, let me know first. Before Fletcher or anyone else. Understand?'

George nodded.

'Good. Remember: the clock is ticking and we need to catch the killer before he strikes again. Understand?'

'Yes, sir.'

George rose from his seat and turned to leave.

'Aren't you forgetting something, Hart?'

'Sir?'

'The letter. You might need it.'

*

George took the underground to Aldgate Station and headed east up Whitechapel High Street to his assignation with Sergeant Fletcher in the Three Bells pub on Commercial Street, just a stone's throw from the headquarters of the local CID. George had read and heard a lot about the grinding poverty of the East End slums, but nothing could prepare him for the grim reality.

The high street was slick with grime and soot from chimneys, and lined with innumerable hawkers and salesmen, all loudly declaiming the bargains they had to offer. But few locals seemed tempted. Instead, the men, mostly short of stature and with faces bloated by alcohol, lounged in the doors of shops and smoked evil-smelling pipes, while women in aprons were sauntering about in twos and threes, or were seated gossiping on steps. Children in tattered clothing and cloth caps were everywhere: in the gutters, in doorways and passages, and on staircases. Some were playing; others fighting over morsels that they had pulled from piles of rotting garbage. All were dirty, thin and undernourished. As George passed one house he could see a swaddled baby lying abandoned in the hallway, exhausted with crying.

Seen through the yellowish smog that seemed to settle permanently on London, but particularly the East End, the road was a jam of horse-drawn carts and vans, their drivers cursing each other and the world in general. Nowhere in sight was a horse and rider, still less the type of clean and well-dressed citizen that was so prevalent in other areas of London. For the East End, as George knew only too well, was the dumping ground for European immigrants, particularly Jews who had fled the recent anti-Semitic pogroms in Russia. Most had arrived penniless and unable to speak English, and struggled to feed themselves and their families. They lived in dilapidated tenements or terraced houses, often five or six families to a building that would previously have been occupied by one.

But the greatest indictment of the area was the smell: a noxious combination of rotting refuse, sulphur from nearby factories and stinking fumes from open drains. The locals did not seem to notice, which was hardly surprising as they lived with it all the time.

It was a relief for George to reach the Three Bells and exchange the grim odour of the street for the acrid fug of an East End pub. No sooner had he entered than a short, broad-shouldered man with red hair and pale skin came up and said in a surprisingly educated accent: 'You must be Major Hart? I'm Detective Sergeant Jack Fletcher.'

The sergeant was neatly dressed in a dark jacket, waist-coat and matching bow-tie that underlined his status as a detective who had left his lowly origins behind him. He had a glum look on his broad freckly face, as if the task of sharing the latest police intelligence with a foreign-looking army officer was not one that he relished. But orders were orders and, once the pair was seated with drinks, Fletcher proved cooperative enough.

'So far,' said the sergeant, 'there's been three killings we think are linked: Martha Turner in George Yard Buildings, just behind the High Street; Polly Nichols in Buck's Row, not far from Whitechapel Underground Station; and, yesterday, Annie Chapman in the backyard of number Twenty-Nine Hanbury Street. All were prostitutes who had separated from their husbands and were living, hand to mouth, in local dosshouses. All were knifed to death. Turner was stabbed multiple times, while Nichols and Chapman had their throats cut and their bellies torn open. Chapman had, in addition, her uterus and part of her vagina and bladder removed. In each case the sexual organs had been either stabbed or cut out, indicating a possible sexual motive.'

'Christ!' said George, his stomach turning. 'Who would do such a thing?'

'Who indeed?' said Fletcher. 'It's my job to find out.'

'Yes, of course. So tell me, Sergeant,' said George, reverting to the unfamiliar role of criminal investigator, 'were there any signs of sexual intercourse?'

'No. The post mortems found no trace of semen on any of the victims. But they did conclude that Turner and Chapman were killed by a right-handed assailant and Nichols by one using his left hand, or at least her neck was cut from right to left.'

'You mean the killer might have been facing her?' asked George.

'Yes.'

'Do the doctors who examined the bodies think that the killer has any specialist anatomical knowledge?'

'Good question and, yes, they do think it's possible. The doctor who examined Chapman's corpse, for example, thinks it would have taken the killer at least fifteen minutes to inflict the wounds, and that the mode in which the knife had been used indicated considerable "anatomical knowledge", as you put it. Certainly the killer is used to working with sharp knives.'

'And your suspects so far?'

'Where to start? We've considered everyone from soldiers to slaughtermen. After the Nichols's murder we were given credible information that a Polish Jewish boot finisher called John Pizer – better known as "Leather Apron" – was black-mailing prostitutes and assaulting them if they did not comply with his request. When we finally apprehended Pizer a couple of days ago, he told us he had had nothing to do with the murders, but had been lying low in his brother's house because he feared what the mob would do if they got to him before we did. We checked out his alibis for each of the murders, and they proved to be correct, but we're still holding him for his own safety until he can be cleared by the public inquiry into Chapman's death.'

'Anyone else?'

'Since the Chapman killing we've narrowed the field down to someone with surgical experience or used to working with sharp knives, and almost certainly insane. We're checking the records for medical students with a history of mental illness, for example, and also looking at butchers. Only today we received a tip-off from two doctors in Holloway that a Swiss butcher they knew called Jacob Isenschmid was, as they put it, "not unlikely" to have been involved in the recent murders. When we spoke to his wife, she said she had not seen him for two months, and that he was in the habit of carrying a large butcher's knife around with him, and making threats to both her and members of the public. So he's defi-nitely a possibility.'

'Interesting. Is there there anything specific that incrimi-nates the butcher?'

'Not yet. Once we have him in custody, we'll arrange a line-up in the hope that a witness can identify him. A Mrs Long saw Chapman talking to a man shortly before she was killed. I wrote down her description,' said Fletcher, taking out his notebook and turning the pages. 'Ah, yes, here it is.

She said he was a foreigner of about forty years of age with a shabby genteel appearance, of medium height, wearing a brown deerstalker hat and a dark coat. They were talking loudly, and Mrs Long overheard the man say, "Will you?" To which she replied, "Yes." Unfortunately she only saw the back of the man and doesn't think she could identify him. But a few hours later a Mrs Fiddimont, wife of the proprietor of the nearby Prince Albert pub, saw a suspicious man drinking at the bar. She described him as dishevelled and with blood on his hand and his ear. Moreover he was a similar height and wearing similar clothes to the man seen by Mrs Long. We need to know if Isenschmid is the man seen by Mrs Fiddimont,' said Fletcher, closing his notebook. 'He could be the killer.'

George was surprised by the paucity of the evidence that had been gathered so far: there were very few clues and no reliable witnesses, as far as he could judge, and an over-reliance on rumour and a sighting of a man who may or may not have been involved. The police seemed to be clutching at straws. 'One thing I don't understand. Your main suspect, the Swiss butcher, is a local working man, and yet Mrs Long described the person talking to Chapman as having a "shabby genteel" appearance. Might he have been a gentleman in scruffy clothes?'

'It's possible. Quite a few gents come "slumming" out East: for pleasure or to see how the other half lives. But witnesses make mistakes. We're keeping an open mind. Inspector Abberline is convinced the killer is a deranged local.'

'You mentioned that soldiers were among the suspects. Why?'

'Because Turner was last seen alive with a soldier. That was a couple of hours before her body was found.'

'Who was the witness?'

'A fellow prostitute called "Pearly Poll". She and Turner had met up with two soldiers in a pub and eventually went their separate ways to have sex. Turner was murdered three hours later so the soldier – or soldiers – could have been responsible. We tried to trace them but no luck so far.'

'Does she know which regiment were they from?'

'No. She was drunk at the time and couldn't remember any distinguishing marks.'

'Good heavens, you haven't had much luck, have you? One last question: who found the three bodies?'

'Turner and Chapman's bodies were both found by local residents. Nichols was discovered in the street by PC Black who, as it happens, was also the first policeman to view Chapman's body. He was filling in for the officer who usually walks that beat.'

'Thank you. I may need to speak to this PC Black and Pearly Poll. Could that be arranged?'

'Yes, of course. I've been told to give you all the help you need.'

*

Fletcher was as good as his word, arranging for George to meet PC Black at the Three Bells as soon as the constable had returned from his beat. A short handsome man with sallow skin and a light brown moustache, Black entered the pub still wearing his uniform of blue frock tunic, blue trousers and combed Britannia helmet. On the right side of his high stand-up collar was a metal clasp with his divisional letter and number: H474.

'I been told you wan' ask me few questions 'bout murders,' said Black in an accent that sounded European.

'That's right. You aren't English, are you? Where are you from?' asked George.

'Russian Poland. My family name is Cherniy, which means Black in Russian. We change it when we arrive few years ago.'

'How long have you been working as a policeman?'

'Mebbe three years. First for City police; then for Met in Whitechapel. It's easier for me.'

George asked about Polly Nichols, the second victim, and Black said he had found her as he walked his beat down Buck's Row, just off Whitechapel Road, at around 3.45 a.m. on Friday 31 August. At first he thought it was a pile of rags in the entrance to a stable yard. But as he got closer he could see it was a woman lying on her back, lengthways along the footway, her head towards the east and her hand touching the stable gate. Her skirts were raised almost to her stomach, and Black could see that her throat had been cut with two deep wounds and her belly cut open. He thought he could detect a faint heartbeat but it soon faded.

She was wearing – he said, consulting his notebook – a black straw bonnet trimmed with velvet, a reddish-brown ulster with seven large brass buttons, a brown linsey frock (nearly new and probably stolen), black ribbed woollen stockings, two petticoats, both marked 'Lambeth Workhouse', flannel drawers, and men's elastic-sided boots with steel tips on the heels.

On further inquiry, explained Black, he discovered that Nichols had last been seen alive at 2.30 a.m. in a drunken state near the Whitechapel Road by Ellen Holland who lived in the same lodging house on Thrawl Street. She was then alone, had no money and was going in the direction of Buck's

Row. Her body was identified in the mortuary by her husband, William Nichols, who had read the reports in the press. They had separated in 1881 and a year later he cut off her allowance when he discovered she was a prostitute. He had not seen her for three years.

'Any witnesses who might have seen the killer?' asked George.

'No,' said Black.

'You say you were walking your beat when you found Nichols's body?'

'I was.'

'Do you normally walk down Buck's Row? I had a quick look at it before I came down here to meet you, and it's a very narrow, dark passage backed by a row of cottages. Surely it would make more sense to patrol down the wider and better-lit Winthrop Street?'

'I do both routes. That night I choose Buck's Row.'

'So, tell me about the Chapman murder. Sergeant Fletcher tells me that, once again, you were the first policeman on the scene. Is that right?'

'Yes. Is not my usual beat. I fill in for sick colleague. Anyway, it was six in morning when carman came running up and say he find body in back yard of Twenty-Nine Hanbury Street. I follow him back and find woman between steps to upper storeys and wooden fence. Her head was towards house, her feet near woodshed. She was lying on her back, her left arm resting on her chest. Again her skirts were raised to waist and I see terrible injuries: throat cut and belly slashed open, with part of guts lying by side. Next to head I found fragment of letter that I gave to inspector. I sent for surgeon to pronounce her dead, though I knew she was. Poor lady.'

'When was she last seen alive?'

'At 1.45 a.m. by deputy of her lodging house at Thirty-Five Dorset Street. He asked for lodging money of four pence. She had none, but said she would get. She was dressed in black jacket, brown bodice, black skirt and lace-up boots – all old and dirty. She was married, but her husband left few years ago because of her drinking and whoring.'

'Thank you, PC Black. That's very helpful. Anything else I should know?'

'Yes. Two witnesses came forward and—'

George waved his hand in dismissal. 'No need. I heard about them from Sergeant Fletcher. I'm chiefly interested in what *you* saw and heard. Did *you* notice any suspicious characters on the streets on the night of either murder?'

'Every night I see bad people. But, no, I see nothing unusual. Is that all, sir?'

'Yes, I think it is. So how're you coping? It can't have been easy coming to terms with what you've seen.'

'I'm all right. I seen worse.'

'Really? When?'

'In Poland, before I leave,' said Black. 'I see terrible things. Believe me.'

*

George's next appointment was with the prostitute Pearly Poll at a café in George Street, Spitalfields, a few doors from the dosshouse where she and the first murder victim Martha Turner had shared a room. Poll – real name Mary Ann Connelly – was around forty years of age, short and shabbily dressed, yet still attractive. George explained who he was and said: 'Before we start, would you like to order something?'

'Two slices an' a cup of tea, please.'

'Is that all? Sure you wouldn't like bacon and eggs as well?'

'Go on then.'

Two helpings later, with Poll sated and grateful, George got down to business. 'I want to ask you about the two soldiers you met on the night of Martha's death. Can you describe what they were wearing?'

Poll replied in broad Cockney that they were both wearing uniform, though it sounded more like: 'They wuz bofe in uniform.'

'Colour?'

'Blue, I think.'

'Anything else?'

'They had caps. Blue with a yellow band.'

'Really?' George pulled out a recent photo of his squadron from an inner pocket. 'Like these ones?'

'Yes, I think so.'

'Anything else about their dress that you remember?'

'The one with me had a chain across his chest, like this one,' she said, pointing at one of the officers in the picture. George's heart skipped a beat. The officer was wearing a chained-pattern pouch belt over his left shoulder that was unique to the Tenth Hussars. If Poll was telling the truth, her client was either an officer in the Tenth, or deliberately impersonating one. 'Are you certain it was the same chain as this?'

'Yes. I never seen one before.'

'What did his voice sound like?'

'The one with me spoke proper, like you. Martha's had a foreign accent like many round here.'

George shook his head: an officer and a private on the hunt for Whitechapel prostitutes? It didn't make sense. 'Did you tell the police about the chain?'

'Nope. I didn't remember till you show'd me the picture.'

70

'What did the two soldiers look like?'

'Mine was tall and handsome, with dark hair and a curly moustache.'

'Waxed?'

She nodded.

'And the other one?'

'Shorter and foreign, I'd guess, with a lighter-coloured moustache. I was certain I'd seen him before,' she said, shaking her head, 'but I couldn't place him.'

'How old did you think they were?'

'Mine was about thirty; Martha's a bit younger.'

'Any other distinguishing marks?'

'Nope.'

'So, tell me again what happened?'

'Well, as I told the police, we were drinking at Satchell's, our dosshouse, when the warden asked for our night money. Well we didn't have any, we'd drunk it all, so I says to Martha, "Let's go out an' do a turn."'

'So if you hadn't gone out looking for clients, you'd have been turned out into the street?'

'Yep. That's why so many gels is on the streets at night, even with this nut on the loose. We ain't got a choice. Anyways, we got dolled up in bonnets and such, and went to the White Hart pub on Whitechapel High Street where we met the soldiers. We drunk with them for about an hour, and then mine said, "Let's get down to business." So we goes outside and parted at the entrance to George Yard. That's the last I seen of poor Martha.'

'What time was that?'

'About midnight.'

George knew from Fletcher that Martha Turner's body had not been found until 4.45 a.m., and that she had been dead for at least two hours. That still left almost three hours unaccounted for. 'So where did you go?' he asked Pearly Poll.

'Another alley nearby. I often take punters there for a knee-trembler.'

'And did you this time?'

'Nope, he changed his mind. Said he was late and had to go. Paid me sixpence, twice the rate, and ran off.'

'In which direction?'

'Back past George Yard, I think.'

'Did you think of finding Martha?'

'No, she's a big girl. Or was. Thought I'd see her back at Satchell's. But she wasn't there in the morning, and when I heard there'd been a murder I started to worry. I went to the police and that's when I was shown her body. She was covered in a sheet and looked like she was sleeping. Poor girl,' said Poll, her voice breaking at the memory of her murdered friend. 'Why her? She never hurt anyone.'

Fat tears began to roll down Poll's lived-in face, streaking her make-up. George leaned over and touched her hand. 'I'm sorry for putting you through this. It can't be easy for you. But we need to catch this monster before he harms anyone else.'

'I understand,' said Poll, dabbing at her eyes with a grimy handkerchief. 'I'll be all right. Ask away.'

'Thank you. How long did you know Martha?'

Ten years, explained Poll, and all that time Martha had been working as a prostitute. Prior to that, Martha had been married to a foreman at a furniture packer, and they had had two children. But both died young of scarlet fever and, in her grief, Martha had taken to drink. This was the cause of her husband leaving her, though for a time he gave her an allowance of 12 shillings a week. She later lived with a carpenter, but again the relationship was ruined by Martha's drinking and her refusal to stop selling her body. Pearly Poll's background was similar: a broken marriage, followed by destitution and a drift into prostitution as the only means to survive. 'The East End is full of girls like us,' she told George. 'Living like animals and selling our bodies for a night's kip. It's no life.'

George returned home to Hammersmith thoroughly depressed. The police investigation into the Whitechapel murders had made little headway, and Fletcher and his superiors were, it seemed to him, pinning all their hopes on the Swiss butcher being the man responsible. What if it wasn't him? What then? He couldn't help thinking that the investigation would have been more advanced if the victims had been middle class. But they were lower class and, even worse, prostitutes and heavy drinkers. It mattered little that, like so many of their kind, they had previously led respectable lives and been forced into prostitution by factors beyond their control. It was enough to turn George into a social reformer. If there was one thing that he, a man of mixed race, could not stomach, it was blind prejudice towards those who were different, often through no fault of their own.

He felt relieved that *solving* the Whitechapel murders was not his chief responsibility. Yet his task was difficult enough: to try to identify the author of the letter found at the Chapman murder and, if possible, exonerate the prince. But to do that he would have to spy on his brother officers – not an undertaking he relished, and one complicated by the fact that the writer of the letter might have been involved in the earlier Turner murder. Or was that too literal a reading of the evidence? After all, Martha could easily have picked up another client after she and the private had had sex. There was certainly time for her to do that, and if she had, then the private could not have killed her. Either way, the soldiers needed to be identified and questioned. Pearly Poll could do the unmasking, but how to organize an identity parade for the whole regiment, or at least those off duty that evening? The colonel would oppose it tooth and nail unless there was more evidence, and if it did take place it would make it next to impossible for George to carry out his own discreet inquiries about the letter.

He resolved to voice his concerns to Fletcher – who seemed a solid enough fellow, if not a particularly inspiring detective – at their next meeting.

As for Warren, he did not trust his motives for a moment. The commissioner had talked dramatically about revolution if the murders were not solved. Was that realistic? George doubted it very much. What he did expect to happen if the killer remained on the loose, however, was that the senior policeman in the capital would lose his job. That, of course, was Warren, and George knew enough of the former soldier's ruthless ambition to realize that he would do anything, and use anyone, to further his career. He had done it before, in the Sinai, to George's detriment. This time, George vowed, it would be different.

6

George knocked on the door of the adjutant's office.

'Come in.' Captain the Honourable Edward Berkeley looked up from his paperwork as George entered. 'How can I help, Major Hart?'

'I need some regimental writing paper.'

'Oh, that's easy. You can buy it in the canteen. There are two options: a cheap lightweight version that is popular with the men; but officers tend to use the white laid quarto with a raised letterhead. It's more expensive, of course, but worth it. You can also get it in the Post Office in Rutland Gardens, opposite the main gate.'

'You mean it's sold to members of the public as well as soldiers?'

'Well, yes. Though I can't imagine why they'd want it if they haven't served in the regiment.'

'Yes, quite,' said George, fully aware of the implications. If the writing paper was easily available to the public, it might prove next to impossible to discover who had authored the torn letter. Unless, of course, it *was* written by an officer and he could make the link by comparing the handwriting. 'Well, thank you for that. There's one other thing you could help me with. I've been meaning to look over the reports that my squadron officers compiled for the last inspection in the spring. In fact, could you give me the inspection reports of all the officers? I'd be interested to know how mine compare.'

'Yes of course, sir,' said the adjutant, reaching up to a shelf behind him and bringing down a thick file. 'All the reports are in here.'

'Thank you.'

George took the file back to his office and started working his way through the handwritten reports, comparing the writing to that on the letter fragment. He had checked roughly a third of the reports with no match when he came upon one headed: 'Captain HRH Prince Albert Victor, Officer Comdg E Troop'. He looked from the report to the letter, and back again. My God, thought George, his chest hammering, the capital letters 'C' and 'A' are almost identical. The prince might well have written the letter. But slow down. What did that prove? He would certainly know who the letter was written to, but that wouldn't necessarily link him to Chapman's murder. Not at all. Trying to stay calm, George worked his way through the remaining reports, but the handwriting in none of the others was a match. He closed the file, put the letter and the report in his tunic pocket, and was about to get up from his desk when in walked the prince.

'Good morning, sir.'

'Uh, good morning, Your Royal Highness,' said George, a little flustered. 'What is it?'

'I wanted to ask you about the squadron field day next week.'

'Of course. Well do take a seat.' George's mind was racing. Even the thought that the prince might have some connection, however innocent, to the Whitechapel murders was shocking to him. Yet that seemed to be the case, and it was vital, he realized, that he heard the prince's side of the story. 'Before we talk about the field day,' said George, 'there are a couple of things I need to ask you.'

'Yes, sir?'

'Well, first off I've been informed by the police that you were spotted in Whitechapel in the early hours of the thirty-first of August. Apparently you were talking to a young man. That was the night you promised me you'd go home to bed. Yet it seems you changed your mind and accompanied your friends to the East End after all. Is that right?'

The prince reddened. 'Um, well, yes I did,' he said at last. 'I thought you'd disapprove so I didn't tell you. We weren't there long.'

'How long?'

'An hour or two.'

'What were you doing?'

'Oh, you know, this and that. We go there for a bit of entertainment, as I told you that night.'

'What sort of entertainment?'

'I'm sorry, sir,' said the prince, finally losing patience. 'But I don't see what this has to do with you? I was off duty. It's a strictly private matter.'

'Only it isn't. May I remind you that you're an officer of the Tenth *and* the heir apparent, and that both roles have certain responsibilities.'

'Such as?'

'Such as not being seen with a young man on the streets of Whitechapel in the early hours of the morning. Think of the potential scandal for both the regiment and the royal family if this got into the papers.'

'It won't.'

'How can you be so certain? You were recognized the other night by someone who could easily have taken that information to the press rather than the police.'

'Then why didn't they?'

'Because something far more sinister happened that night: the brutal slaying of a homeless prostitute called Polly Nichols in a backstreet near Whitechapel underground station. You must have heard about it?'

'Yes, it was all over the papers. Nasty business.'

'A similar murder took place on the seventh of August, in the early morning following the bank holiday, and a third in the early hours of last Saturday, the eighth of September. The police are convinced all three are linked. Which is why I need to know if you were in Whitechapel on either of those dates?'

'What *exactly* are you suggesting, sir?' said the prince testily. 'That I'm involved in some way?'

'No, of course not. But I am worried about how the press will react if they discover that the heir apparent was in the East End when the murders were committed. So I ask again: were you there?'

'I might have been. I'm often there with Harry, Jim and Monty. I don't know.'

'Think back to last Friday night?'

'Last Friday? Yes I was there. We all were. But we went our separate ways and didn't stay too late.'

My God, thought George, this doesn't sound good. 'How late?'

'Two in the morning.'

'You're certain?'

'Yes.'

'What about the night of the sixth and seventh of August?'

'No idea. How can you expect me to remember that far back?'

'One last question,' said George, taking the torn letter from his inside pocket and handing it to the prince. 'Did you write this?'

The prince examined it. 'It *looks* like my writing. But my Ks are not quite so angular. Observe.'

He wrote out the word 'Knightsbridge' on a separate piece of paper. The 'K' was indeed more rounded than the one in the letter.

'Yes I see,' said George. He knew the prince might be shamming. After all, the 'K' in the report was remarkably similar to the one in the letter. But he wanted to believe him because the alternative was too awful to contemplate.

'Why do you want to know if I wrote the letter?' queried the prince. 'Where did you get it from?'

George hesitated. He feared that if he lied, he would lose the prince's trust which, in turn, would make it impossible to act as his bodyguard; but if he told the truth, he'd be giving a potential suspect – however unlikely – confidential information. He chose the lesser of the two evils. 'The police found it next to the body of the most recent victim. They think the murderer might have dropped it and, because it has our letter heading, asked me to make some discreet inquiries.'

'Why you?'

'Because many years ago I worked on the Palmer case in the Sinai with Sir Charles Warren, the police commissioner. He was a soldier back then.'

'So Warren asked you to find out who wrote the letter?'

George nodded.

'And you suspected me?'

'No, not at all. You were the last person I suspected of *any* involvement. I was actually trying to rule you out. But when I compared the handwriting to that of all the other regimental officers, yours was the closest match.'

'It may be close, but it's not my writing. Which probably means someone is trying to implicate me in some way. It's a horribly worrying thought, and why they would do it I've no idea. Sorry.'

'No, I'm sorry,' said George, more than a little relieved that the prince was denying any involvement. 'But I had to ask. One more thing: I hope it goes without saying that you should steer well clear of Whitechapel for the foreseeable future. Can I trust you to do that?'

'Of course.'

'Thank you,' said George, more than a little relieved that the prince had both denied any link to the letter and was not unduly outraged that he had asked the question in the first place. Yet to keep the prince's trust from now on, he knew, would be like walking a tightrope. 'Now what did you want to ask me?'

*

That evening George arranged to meet Sergeant Jack Fletcher in Whitechapel to exchange notes. First he told Fletcher about his conversation with PC Black, observing that it was odd that on the night of Nichols's murder he had chosen to patrol down Buck's Row instead of the more accessible Winthrop Street. He then mentioned Black's throwaway remark about having seen much worse sights than the two murders in his native Poland. 'Do you have any idea what he might be referring to?'

'No. I heard he was a Polack, but no details. I expect he was just boasting.'

'Yes, I'm sure you're right.'

George then related his conversation with Pearly Poll, and the revelation that she and Martha Turner went off with an officer and a soldier from the Tenth Hussars – or someone pretending to be – shortly before Martha's murder.

'Any idea who they are?' asked Fletcher.

'No. You've heard the descriptions. The officer was tall and handsome, with dark hair and a dark waxed moustache, about thirty years old; the soldier slightly younger and shorter, foreign looking and with a lighter-coloured moustache. It's not a lot to go on and could describe any number of men in the regiment, if indeed they are soldiers. We can't hold an identity parade for the whole regiment.'

'Why?'

'Because it's impractical: we've got more than five hundred men. Also, the colonel would never agree to it. If the police insist, it will be all over the press within hours, a scenario the commissioner is keen to avoid.'

'I see. What about the torn letter? Have you made any progress with that?'

'A little,' said George. 'But I can't say yet because Sir Charles asked me to tell him first.'

'I understand,' said Fletcher. 'It might not matter because Inspector Abberline thinks we have our man.'

'Go on.'

'Remember the Swiss butcher called Isenschmid we were looking for?'

'Yes.'

'Well he was arrested two days ago and taken to the station in Commercial Street. Yesterday he was positively identified by Mrs Fiddimont as the man who came into her pub on the morning of Annie Chapman's death with blood on his hands.'

'Did she indeed? Well, that's very good news.'

'Yes, it is. Inspector Abberline is convinced he's the killer. He certainly fits the profile. He's not right in the head and carries a large butcher's knife on his person. He's threatened to kill his wife and other members of the public, and has no alibi for the murders.'

'What do you think?'

'I don't know. It could be him. What concerns me is that we don't have any solid proof and, until we do, it would make more sense to keep an open mind. Then again, I'm just a lowly detective sergeant and not paid to disagree with my betters.'

'So what next?'

'We'll keep looking for evidence and hope that he confesses.'

'And if he doesn't?'

'It's not necessarily a problem because he'll be kept under lock and key anyway in a mental asylum.'

'And what if he isn't the killer? What then?'

'Then the murders will continue, and we'll know for certain.'

*

Next morning, George returned to Scotland Yard to speak to Commissioner Warren. It was not a conversation he was relishing. He had been tasked with exonerating the prince from any connection to the Whitechapel murders. Yet his initial inquiries had, if anything, only served to highlight a possible link to the Tenth Hussars in general, and the prince in particular. He would start, he decided, with the vital information he had learnt from Pearly Poll that she and Martha Turner were with an officer and a soldier from the Tenth a few hours before the latter's death.

But as he spoke he could tell by the way Warren was polishing his monocle that he was hardly listening. 'I appreciate,' said George in conclusion, 'that the obvious course of action would be to hold an identity parade for the whole regiment. But that won't be easy. There are more than five hundred officers and men, and—'

George was cut short by a dismissive wave of Warren's hand. 'You don't need to worry about any of that,' said the commissioner. 'We think we have our man.'

'Do you mean Isenschmid?' asked George.

'Yes. How do you know about him?'

'Fletcher told me.'

'Ah, yes of course. Well, you'll know why we suspect him. Now we think we have proof because he's been positively identified by a Mrs Fiddimont as the man who came into her pub on the morning of Chapman's murder with blood on his hands and clothes.'

George wanted desperately to believe that the Swiss butcher was responsible because that would exonerate the prince. But it all sounded a little too convenient and, like Fletcher, he was yet to be convinced. 'With respect, Sir Charles,' he responded, 'that still doesn't necessarily connect Isenschmid to the murders. There could be any number of reasons why he had blood on his person. He's a butcher, after all. And why, just an hour and a half after the killing, would the individual responsible stop for a glass of ale in a pub barely four hundred yards from the scene of his crime? It doesn't make sense.'

'We're not talking about a sane man, Hart. Isenschmid is mad, he has a history of violence against women, including his wife, and, most compelling of all, he's a pork butcher by trade and often carries sharp knives on his person. His wife told us she threw him out of their home in July because of his bizarre behaviour. He's been seen a number of times with his butcher's apron on and his knife and steel hanging from his belt. He's our man – Abberline is certain of it, and I have complete confidence in him.'

'What about the letter, and Pearly Poll's sighting of the two soldiers from the Tenth? Don't they together hint that a soldier, or soldiers, are involved in some way?'

'That's one interpretation. Another is that the letter and the soldiers have nothing to do with the killings. After all, Turner was with the soldier a full three hours before she was killed. She could have seen a number of other men in that time.

'Yes, of course. But we now know that Turner was last seen alive with a man from my regiment; and a letter with my regiment's crest was found next to Chapman's body. You have to admit: that's quite a coincidence.'

'Let it be, Hart,' said Warren. 'Abberline is satisfied he has his man and that he will soon find evidence to put the issue beyond doubt. They're searching the man's rooms as we speak.'

'And if they don't find any evidence?'

'They will, I'm certain of it. Meanwhile, there will be no more murders because Isenschmid is off the streets and will remain so.'

'Sir, with respect, I think it's far too early to close down these other avenues of inquiry. You haven't even asked me if I managed to identify the letter writer.'

'Well did you?'

'I think so. It was not the result I was expecting, but the closest match by far was to the handwriting of His Royal Highness Prince Albert Victor.'

'The *prince*? Are you certain?'

'Yes. He denied it was his writing, but the similarity is uncanny.'

'You spoke to him?'

'Yes.'

'And told him what?'

'I told the truth. That I'd been tasked by you to identify the author.'

'And he denied it was him.'

'Yes.'

'And you think he's lying?'

'I don't know. Maybe someone copied his handwriting to implicate him. But it is curious,' said George, half enjoying Warren's evident discomfiture, 'that he was in Whitechapel on the night of both the Nichols and Chapman murders.'

'He told you that?'

'He did.'

'This is madness,' said Warren, shaking his head. 'Have you thought about what you're saying? The prince *can't* be involved. He's the heir apparent, for God's sake. Even if he did write the letter, that's not proof that he had anything to do with the murders, is it?'

'Of course not, sir. But he might know the killer. You said as much when you asked me to find the author of the letter.'

'What I said was that the author might help us to identify the mysterious "A". But do we even know that "A" is the murderer? We don't. My hunch is that the letter is a red herring. It's too far-fetched to imagine that the killer accidentally dropped a letter addressed to himself. My suspicion now is that it was planted to put us on the wrong track.'

'I suppose that's possible, sir.'

'Yes it is. Now look, Hart, I asked you to keep the prince's name out of this, and you've done the exact opposite.'

'Well, sir, it wasn't deliberate. I was hoping to rule him out. But there it is.'

'Yes, and there it will remain. Do you have the torn letter on your person?'

'I do.'

'Can I have it?'

George pulled it from an inner pocket and handed it over.

'Thank you. Now I want you to forget all about the letter, the prostitute's sighting of the two soldiers and the prince's part in all of this. Isenschmid is our man; so you can get back to your original – and much more important – task of protecting the prince from the Fenians. The ruse to catch them in the act is planned for next week, isn't it?'

'Yes sir. Next Wednesday.'

'Good,' said Warren, rising from his seat to signal that the meeting was over. 'Best of luck with it all. And thank you for helping out with this Whitechapel matter. Your work didn't have quite the outcome I'd hoped, but you did your best and I'm grateful. Until next time.'

*

As George travelled home on the underground, he felt increasingly uneasy about Abberline and Warren's eagerness to pin the blame on Isenschmid and ignore the evidence that suggested a link between the killer on the one hand, and the prince and his own regiment on the other. Even if it was manufactured, it still indicated a guiding hand who might know or have access to the prince. It made sense that Warren would want to solve the case as quickly as possible. He himself had said he was under immense pressure from both the Home Secretary and the press to find the killer, and that the consequences for failing to do that might even be the overthrow of the government by East End revolutionaries (not that George believed that was likely). But putting the wrong man behind bars wouldn't solve anything. The murderer would go free and, as likely as not, the killings would continue. So why was Warren so convinced the Swiss butcher was responsible? Was someone with influence over Warren trying to divert suspicion from the prince and his entourage?

Arriving home, he decided to ignore the duke's instructions and talk everything over with Lucy. He found her enjoying some autumnal sun on the lawn behind the house. 'You're back early,' she said drowsily from her deckchair. 'Is anything the matter?'

'There's something I need to discuss with you. Where's Jake?'

'He's at the park playing with a friend. What is it?'

George knelt by Lucy's chair and took her hand. 'This isn't easy to say, so I'll just come out with it. I haven't been entirely honest with you about the reason we returned to Britain. I joined the Tenth Hussars because I was asked by the Duke of Cambridge to act as an unofficial bodyguard to Prince Albert Victor.

'I can't go into too many details. But suffice to say that he needs to be protected from both his own sexual proclivities and Fenian assassins.'

'Not both at the same time, I hope?!'

'Please, Lucy, this is a serious matter. The police have intelligence that the Fenians want to assassinate the prince, and to counter this threat I was instructed to travel incognito to Kilburn and pose as a Fenian supporter. I think the subterfuge has worked and we're in the process of baiting a trap that will lead to their arrest. But what I really want to talk to you about is my second task: to prevent the prince from becoming involved in a homosexual scandal.'

'The prince has sex with men?'

'Yes, and he's not alone among men of his education. But in his case the danger of blackmail is obvious. Anyway, it was my job to keep him out of trouble and unfortunately I failed. Recently, despite promising me he would stay away, the prince made a number of forays into Whitechapel to meet men. Now it may be a coincidence, but at least two of those occasions coincided with the brutal murder of a prostitute by an unknown assailant. There is, moreover, some evidence linking the prince, or someone impersonating the prince, to the scene of one of the murders. But all this has been brushed under the carpet by Sir Charles Warren, the commissioner, who is now convinced that the murderer is an insane Swiss-born butcher who was spotted drinking in a nearby pub a few hours after the crime was committed. Something isn't right, which is why I wanted to discuss this with you.'

Lucy drew her hand away. 'I can't believe you didn't mention any of this before?'

'I'm sorry, but you have to understand that this is my work, and I was sworn to secrecy, partly to protect the prince, and partly to protect you and Jake. I know I've lied to you, but I told myself it was justified because the less you knew, the safer you'd be.'

Lucy got up from the deckchair, her eyes narrowed. 'How dare you suggest your lies made us safer? In truth you've put us both in mortal danger. At least if you'd told me what you were up to, I could have armed myself and protected Jake. What if the Fenians come looking for you?'

George tried to reassure her that they couldn't know his address.

'Couldn't they? What if they followed you home?'

'That's not possible. I've been extremely careful. They can't know where I really live. Anyway, you're confusing the issue. My reason for telling you all this is because I'm perplexed by Warren's obsession with a suspect who, in all probability, has nothing to do with the murders. It's as if he's deliberately shifting attention from the prince.'

'I thought that was your job?'

'To protect him? It is. But not if he's party to murder.'

'You don't seriously think he might be?'

'I'm not sure what to think. It seems entirely out of character, but some people you never really know, do you?'

'No.'

'Look, I know you're angry, and you've a right to be. But I should say in my defence that one of the reasons I agreed to protect the prince was because the duke made me a generous financial offer.'

'Which was?'

'A pay increase, a three-hundred-pound bounty for taking the job and an extra thousand pounds if I succeeded in keeping the prince safe for a year. Given our money problems,' he said pointedly, 'it was hard to refuse.'

'What are you suggesting? That I'm to blame for our financial difficulties?'

'No, I'm not saying that at all. I'm equally responsible. I'd love to be able to promise you that I'll never gamble again, but I doubt I could keep that promise. But you must also accept your share of the responsibility.'

'Now hold on just a minute. You think that by spending

money on the odd luxury – for us and for Jake – I've given you no option but to take a job that puts all of us in danger. Is that what you mean?'

'No, you're twisting my words. I'm saying we've both been too profligate and this job was a chance for us to get back on our feet.'

'I can't believe you're equating your gambling to my occasional purchase of curtains or a gown. There is no comparison.'

George held his hands up. 'I don't want to argue. What's done is done. My concern now is the prince and his possible involvement in the Whitechapel murders. Do I listen to Warren and forget all about it? Or do I go above his head with my concerns?'

The question was met with stony silence. 'Please, Lucy. I really need your help with this. We can always solve a problem if we put our heads together; we've done it in the past. I know I haven't always been a constant in your life. But it's different now. I'm not the person I was. I love you and Jake with all my heart; I'd never do anything to put either of you in danger.'

'You already have. Don't you understand that? I'm sorry, George, I'd love to help you work this out. But Jake's safety is much more important to me; which is why I think it best if I take him to stay with my parents in Devon until this all blows over.'

'But it could take weeks, even months. I can't do without you both for that long.'

'You'll survive. You have before, and I'll feel better knowing Jake is safe. You should too,' she said, before striding past George and back into the house.

He thought of following her, but knew from experience that her temper took a considerable time to cool. It was, he now knew, a mistake to come clean about the prince. It had only caused her unnecessary worry. He didn't think that worry was justified, because the Fenians had no history of targeting their enemy's families. But she felt it, as a mother, and he had to respect that. On the other hand, if he couldn't talk such things over with her, what was the point of their marriage? Was the duke right after all? he asked himself. Was it a mistake for him to marry someone 'beneath' him, from a lower social class? Did they see things so differently? Or was this the type of disagreement that any married couple could have? He didn't know. He didn't have the experience to know, and it almost made him weep to think that the only person he could have discussed such intimate issues with was his old schoolfriend Jake Morris, his son's namesake, who had died so tragically at Isandlwana at the age of twenty. He thought of Jake most days, and missed him dreadfully, but never more than at this moment.

7

Chiswick Mall, west London

'What the hell am I going to do now?' muttered George as he approached Harry Wilson's chummery in Chiswick. He had been invited to another dinner with the prince and his set, but his immediate concern was no longer the Whitechapel murders but money. Before leaving with Jake for Cornwall, Lucy had admitted that the monthly rent of £20 was unpaid and that she needed some cash to cover her travel and expenses. When George asked her what she had done with her allowance, she told him she had spent most of it on a new dress so that she could look her best for her parents. A furious George gave her all he had in his pocket book – £20 – and wondered how he would cover the rent. The £300 bounty he had been paid by the duke had been swallowed up by his debts, and he still owed more than £1,000. He could in theory pay that off if he succeeded in his task, but he needed money to live on, and even his increased salary was not enough. One obvious solution was to resort to his old vice of gambling. He had promised Lucy he wouldn't, but then she had hardly kept to her side of the bargain.

All thoughts of money, however, were soon relegated to the back of George's mind by the prince's opening comment at dinner. 'You may find it hard to believe, gentlemen,' said the prince, with a little shake of his head, 'but a suspect in the Whitechapel murders case is sitting amongst you this evening.'

'Eddy, please,' said his host, 'it's not a joking matter.'

'I'm deadly serious,' said the prince.

'So who is it then?'

Before the prince could answer, a smiling Stephen interjected: 'I hope you don't mean me.'

'Or me,' added Druitt, frowning.

'No, neither of you. I'm referring to myself.'

'You?' they said, almost in unison.

'Yes me. Apparently they found a fragment of a letter beside the last victim with handwriting that closely resembles mine.'

'Who found the letter?' asked Wilson. 'The police?'

'Yes.'

'And they told you this?'

'No,' said the prince. 'George did.'

All eyes turned to George 'Is this true?' asked Stephen.

George shifted uncomfortably in his seat. 'Yes, in a sense. I was asked by Commissioner Warren, who I worked with a few years ago, to investigate a link between the torn letter and our regiment, the Tenth Hussars. I checked the handwriting against that of all the officers and it does look similar to the prince's.'

'It might look similar,' said the prince, 'but it's not mine. I think I'd know.'

'So what exactly is the problem, George?' asked Druitt. 'Eddy says it's not his handwriting. Don't you believe him?'

'Look,' said George. 'I'm not accusing the prince of anything. He's certainly not a suspect. But there are certain coincidences that need to be cleared up.'

'Go on,' said Stephen.

George shook his head, a pained expression on his face. 'I'm really not comfortable discussing this.'

'Well I am,' said the prince, 'and I'd like you to explain to my friends why you felt the need to warn me off Whitechapel.'

'All right,' said George, his hands raised in surrender. 'I will. It's not just the letter. The prince was seen in Whitechapel on the occasion of the second murder, on the thirty-first of August, and he himself told me he was also there, as were all of you, on the night of the most recent killing.'

'Which,' said Druitt, 'is proof of what exactly? That we're *all* involved? Honestly, George, does Eddy strike you as a murderer? Do the rest of us?'

'Well no, of course you don't.'

'What if one of us *was*?' said Stephen. 'I really don't see what all the fuss is about. To my mind the killer is doing Whitechapel a favour.'

George narrowed his eyes. 'What exactly do you mean?'

'What I *mean* is that the place is infested with pox-ridden whores, selling their wares for just a few pennies, and London would be a better place without them.'

'Are you seriously suggesting that this brutal killer is to be applauded, even encouraged?'

'Well, I'm not losing any sleep over the death of a few prostitutes. They wouldn't be at risk if they weren't on the streets at all hours.'

George frowned. 'Do you have any idea how desperate these women are? Many only sell their bodies to pay for a night in a cramped dosshouse. They're to be pitied, not condemned.'

'Well, if you feel like that, George,' said Stephen, 'I suggest you switch from the British to the Sally Army. Then you can devote your life to saving whores, because they won't save themselves.'

George could feel his temples throbbing with indignation. He longed to challenge Stephen's harsh misogyny with a few home truths. But he held his tongue and the awkward silence was broken by Harry Wilson. 'I don't know why we're all getting so worked up. I read somewhere that the police already have a suspect in custody.'

'Do they?' asked Druitt. 'Who?'

'Can't remember his name. But he's definitely Swiss by birth and a butcher by trade.'

'Well, we'll soon know if it's him,' said Stephen.

'How so?' asked Wilson.

'Why, if the killings stop, of course.'

After dinner, the prince suggested a few hands of whist and George was enthusiastic. He had become a fine whist player in Gibraltar and saw an opportunity to win a few pounds off his friends. He also hoped that a game of cards would thaw the frigid atmosphere. He was wrong on both counts.

As only four players were needed, Wilson opted out, leaving the prince to partner Stephen, and George with Druitt who, it turned out, was not a particularly skilled card player. He even needed reminding that the purpose of whist was to win a majority of the thirteen tricks available per hand, with the players following suit unless they had a void when a trump could be played. The real skill of whist was to remember which cards had been played, and to anticipate which were still held in which opponent's hand. The prince was brilliant at both, combining a phenomenal memory with an unerring ability to play the right card at the right time. He and Stephen, as a result, won the first hand nine tricks to four and the second eight to five, giving them a game-winning score of 5-0 (each trick over six scoring a single point).

And so it went on. George and Druitt won the occasional hand, but never by more than a single trick, and the game was ultimately taken by their opponents: 5-2, 5-1 and 5-0 (again). After this last humiliation – by which time the losing partnership was down £20 each (the agreed bet being £10 per game) – George called it a night. As he didn't have any cash he wrote out an IOU, batting aside the prince and Stephen's offer to forget the debt. 'A gentleman,' declared George, with more conviction than he felt, 'should always pay his dues.'

Inwardly, however, he cursed himself for losing yet more money he didn't have.

Fortified by his victory at cards, Stephen suggested another trip to Hammond's in Cleveland Street. But George was adamant that he was going home and, this time, Druitt and the prince sided with him. 'I'll just stay for a nightcap with Harry and Jim,' said the prince. 'Then straight to bed.'

'All right then,' said George, hopeful that the prince had learnt his lesson. 'I'll walk with Monty as far as Hammersmith.'

On the way, Druitt apologized for his poor showing on the card table. 'But I have to say, George, that even if I was a better player, I'm not sure it would have made a difference. The prince is a demon at whist. It's just about the only thing he excels at. As for the Whitechapel murders, I don't care which way the evidence points. The prince has nothing to do with it. I know him too well. He's not capable of such bestiality.'

'How long *have* you known him?' asked George.

'Oh, about four years. Unlike the others, I was up at Oxford. But I met Jim and Harry at the Inns and playing cricket, and they introduced me to the prince. We've become close friends. He was very supportive when my father died and, again more recently, when my mother was committed to an asylum.'

'I'm sorry to hear about your parents,' said George. 'That must have been hard.'

'Losing my father was. But my mother hadn't been right for years and, to be honest, her incarceration was as much a relief as anything else. She could appear perfectly normal for weeks on end; and then suddenly she'd become a different person, violent and aggressive. A bit Dr Jekyll and Mr Hyde, you might say, but definitely more of the latter in recent times.'

'Where is she now?'

'In Brook Asylum in Clapham.'

'Do you ever visit her?'

'Rarely. It's too painful. She rants and raves and is not the woman I remember. I was devoted to her.'

'My condolences. But tell me, Monty, why does Jim have such a visceral hatred of women?'

'I think you're exaggerating a little.'

'Am I? Think of the verse in the poem he read out to us a couple of weeks ago about a woman he encounters in the Backs in Cambridge: "I did not like her: and I should not mind/ If she were done away with, killed, or ploughed." It's pretty strong stuff. And this evening he as good as admitted his belief that the Whitechapel victims are getting what they deserve.'

'I don't think he went quite that far.'

'Don't you? He said he "wouldn't lose any sleep" over their deaths.'

'Yes, but that's not quite the same.'

They had reached the entrance to Hammersmith Underground Station, where they would go their separate ways. Before taking his leave, George asked: 'I know the prince is close to his mother, but do you think he likes women, as a species I mean?'

'No, not really. He's always been pretty suspicious of them, so it didn't help when he caught the clap from a harlot in Singapore. He was prescribed silver nitrate by his doctor when he returned to this country, but it still took more than a year for the symptoms to disappear.'

'What were the symptoms?'

'Not nice,' said Druitt. 'I remember him telling me that it was extremely painful to pee, and that he kept noticing a white discharge. He was furious that it took so long to clear up, and used to call the woman in question every name under the sun. Jim's response was that it would teach him to steer clear of women. I don't think he needed much encouragement. He often described the *demi-mondaines* who sought to usurp his mother as "temptresses luring his father to disaster". I think it's fair to say he regards most women as schemers, and mistrusts them intensely.'

*

As George made his way home, he tried to make sense of Druitt's comments about the prince and Stephen: the former disliked and mistrusted women; the latter hated them. Such revelations hardly made either of them murderers, as Druitt himself had stressed. Yet it sounded suspiciously like a mixed message. If Druitt was really trying to convince George of the prince's innocence, why mention the fact that His Royal Highness had earlier caught the pox from a Singapore prostitute? It didn't make sense, and he had to wonder at Druitt's motive.

8

18 Curzon Street, Mayfair

George checked his pocket watch. It was 6.50 p.m., just ten minutes before the prince and the other nine guests were due to arrive for dinner. He and Inspector Littlechild, both hold-ing revolvers, were observing the door of the dining room from the darkness of the servery opposite. The servants had been told to avoid their hiding place, and instead to bring the various dinner courses directly from the kitchen in the basement.

It was impossible to know exactly when and how the Fenians would try to kill the prince. On delivering the impression of the keys to the Fenians a few days earlier, George had tried to find out more. But their leader Pat had remained tight-lipped, simply telling George to make sure that he had the evening off and was not in the house during the dinner party. Littlechild's assumption was that an assassin or assassins would enter the house during dinner and try to kill the prince with firearms. To prevent this he had posted armed men throughout the house, with some dressed as servants and more watching both entrances outside. Their orders were to apprehend the Fenians as soon as they had entered the house and their intention had become clear. George and Littlechild were stationed opposite the entrance to the dining room in case the would-be killers got that far. But it was an insurance policy that Littlechild, for one, did not expect to need.

At one minute to seven, the doorbell rang, and the first guests were let in by a footman and shown upstairs to the first-floor drawing room where Lord and Lady Charles were waiting to receive them. Both host and hostess were aware of the Special Irish Branch operation and happy to cooperate. As a serving soldier and veteran of many wars, Lord Charles was used to handling weapons and had hidden a small pistol in the waistband of his dress trousers. Lady Charles had a more personal reason for taking revenge on the Fenians: a few years earlier they had stabbed to death her brother, the newly appointed chief secretary to Ireland, as he walked to the Viceregal Lodge in Phoenix Park, Dublin.

The next guest to arrive was the prince, his unmistakable voice carrying up the corridor from the entrance hall to George in the servery. He tapped Littlechild once on the shoulder, their pre-arranged signal for the appearance of the royal guest. By 7.20 all ten guests had arrived and were drinking champagne in the drawing room. 'So far, so good,' whispered Littlechild to George. 'Now we wait.'

George, however, could not relax. Since entering the servery an hour earlier, he had felt a strange sense of foreboding. Not the usual fluttering in his stomach that all soldiers experienced prior to combat. But rather a nauseous feeling that something wasn't right, and that Littlechild's confident assumption that an assassin would try to shoot the prince would prove to be a horrible miscalculation. What then, George asked himself, were the alternatives?

He couldn't think and, as the minutes ticked by, his sense of panic increased. He was running out of time when, suddenly, the answer came to him: they could have planted a bomb!

George himself had assumed, from the few comments that the Fenian leader had made to him, that the assassins would use the copied keys to enter the house *during* the dinner party. But what if they had come earlier to plant a bomb? And if so, where would they have left it? The obvious place was the dining room, as the prince would spend most of the evening there. Yet, as George knew, it contained little furniture apart from a large mahogany table and chairs. A much easier place to hide a bomb was the drawing room, with its sofas, Ottomans and baby grand piano. Did the Fenians have the sophistication to time a bomb to explode during the hour the guests were having drinks? George doubted it. That left a bomb needing to be triggered inadvertently by . . . what?

The sound of laughter drifted down the staircase from the drawing room above. Then the dramatic opening notes of Beethoven's Fifth Symphony could be heard. *Dit, dit, dit, dah.* Someone – probably Lady Charles – was playing the piano. *Dit, dit, dit, dah.* My God, thought George, that's it: they've planted the bomb in the piano with a detonator attached to the keys. If it's mercury based it will take just seconds to explode once the right key has been pressed. 'There's a bomb in the piano,' he hissed at Littlechild. 'I'm sure of it!'

Without waiting for a response, George ran from the servery and down the corridor to the main staircase, praying he would make it in time. He took the stairs two at a time, almost colliding with a footman coming the other way with a tray of empty crystal glasses, a couple of which toppled to the floor and shattered into tiny pieces. 'What the . . .?' shouted the servant.

Ignoring him, George tore up the second and third flights. He was just yards from the top when the door to the drawing room, directly opposite him, exploded outwards in a storm of noise, flame and flying splinters. George was lifted off his feet and hurled backwards, landing heavily and painfully on the second landing, his head striking the polished wood floor with a crack. For a second or two he lay there stunned, his ears ringing and his vision obscured by a cloud of plaster dust. He briefly checked for injuries and was relieved to find only minor lacerations to his face and a lump on the back of his head. His body felt bruised and battered, and he was tempted to just lie there until help arrived. But the sound of cries and moans from the floor above forced him to his feet.

He looked around for his pistol but there was no sign of it, and no time to look. So he hobbled back up the stairs unarmed, steeling himself for the grim sight he knew awaited him. A bloodied figure, missing his right jacket and shirt-sleeve, staggered through the jagged hole that had been the door to the drawing room. 'Please help!' he implored George. 'My wife is badly hurt.'

George rushed past him and into the shattered room, where a thick pall of smoke and dust made it hard to navigate. He moved towards the sound of a woman's cry, and found her lying in a foetal position, a pool of blood spreading beneath her. 'Help is on its way,' said George. 'Where is the prince?'

She lifted a hand and pointed to the far end of the room where the piano had stood. Oh God, thought George, he must have been listening to the music. He can't have survived.

He moved slowly through the gloom, bumping into a couple of prone bodies before reaching the piano. Only a part of the keyboard and a single leg remained. Beyond it was the headless trunk of a woman whom George knew, from the fragments of her emerald evening gown, to be Lady Charles. Just a few feet away was the blackened, badly mutilated body of her husband. The stench of nitroglycerine and burnt flesh was almost overpowering. George gagged.

There was no sign of the prince, so George moved back down the room, checking the bodies as he went. A couple were still breathing, though badly wounded. Just beyond the fireplace, partly protected by the chimney breast, lay an unconscious male figure in uniform on its back. It was the prince. George knelt down and checked his wrist pulse. It was strong and regular. Thank God, murmured George. As he checked for injuries, two gunshots rang out from a lower floor, then two more.

'Who the hell is shooting?' yelled George. 'We need help up here.'

He was answered by a fusillade of shots. It had to be the Special Irish Branch men, he decided, but who were they shooting at? Surely not the Fenians? They'd used a bomb partly because that method made it easier to avoid detection. Why would they send men as well?

'For Ireland!' came a cry in an Irish accent from the ground floor.

Christ, thought George, it *is* the Fenians. They don't care about losing men. Their only thought is to kill the prince and they've sent a follow-up team to make certain. I need to find a weapon, and fast.

He thought of retrieving his revolver on the stairs, but knew there wasn't time. What else? He remembered that Lord Charles had hidden a small pistol in his waistband. It must still be there. He ran to the house owner's mangled corpse, praying that the small two-shot Remington pistol wasn't damaged. He found it on the floor next to Lord Charles, blood-spattered but seemingly intact. Grabbing the pistol, he could hear rapid footsteps on stairs. 'Stop him,' shouted a voice that sounded like Littlechild's.

He swivelled towards the door, cocking the pistol's hammer with his thumb as he did so. A stocky man with long dark hair appeared in the doorway. George instantly recognized him as one of the Fenians he had met in the ware-house. The man was armed with two six-shot pistols; even allowing for a few discharged bullets, he still outgunned George who, to even the fight by shortening the range, strode forward.

Recognizing George as the household servant who had set up the hit, and assuming he was coming to help, the assassin shouted, 'Where's the bloody prince? Is he finished?'

George lifted his pistol and took aim.

'What the fuck are you doing?'

Boom. The low velocity slug passed slightly to the left of its target and struck the wall behind in a puff of plaster dust. George cursed.

The Fenian responded with three shots in quick succes-sion. All missed, though George could feel the shock wave of one pass uncomfortably close to his right cheek as he threw himself behind a wrecked sofa. The floor was slick with blood.

'That's right, hide you bloody turncoat! Show your face again and you're a dead man.'

George could hear the Fenian moving and knew it wouldn't take him long to identify the prince in his high-necked blue and gold dress tunic. He had to do something. Peering beneath the sofa, he could see the legs of the Fenian as he moved from body to body, barely fifteen feet away. He was getting closer to the fireplace. It was now or never. Holding the pistol at arm's length, with his left hand steadying his wrist, he drew a bead on the Fenian's thigh and fired.

'Aaargh!' screamed the Irishman as he crumpled to the ground. 'My leg!'

Bullets thudded into the sofa, causing George to seek cover behind a nearby corpse. More shots rang out: at least half a dozen, one after the other. He must have a third weapon, reasoned George.

'I think I got him,' said a voice from the doorway. 'Major Hart? Are you all right?'

'Yes,' responded George. 'Who is that?'

'Sergeant Mitchell, Special Irish Branch. I was guarding the front entrance and heard gunshots.'

'Is the Fenian dead?' asked George, rising gingerly from behind the sofa.

'Yes I think so,' said Mitchell, a short man with bushy red mutton-chop whiskers. 'I put two bullets into him after you slowed him down. Where's the prince?'

'By the fireplace. He's unconscious but alive, or was when I checked him a minute or two ago.'

'Thank God! I'll get help,' said Mitchell, holstering his pistol and turning to leave.

George called after him. 'Do you know if Inspector Littlechild is alive?'

'He is. He took a bullet in his leg, but not before shooting this one's associate. You look a little battered yourself. Wait here. I won't be long.'

As George started to walk towards the prince, he lost his balance and had to clutch some furniture to stay upright. He felt sick, and realized it must be delayed concussion from the fall. He lay down, amidst the bloody carnage of the explosion, thanking God that he had kept going long enough to save the prince's life.

*

'I've read the report, but I want to hear from the horses' mouths. What happened?' asked Sir Charles Warren.

George looked across at Inspector Littlechild. They were seated in front of Warren's desk, Littlechild with his wounded leg supported by a footstool. It had been three days since the attempt on the prince's life, and both were still coming to terms with their injuries – albeit relatively minor in George's case – and the nearness with which the Fenians had come to succeeding. Though outwardly fine, George kept suffering memory recall and migraines – typical symptoms, a physician had assured him, of a traumatic head injury.

'Well, sir,' began Littlechild, 'we thought we'd prepared for every eventuality. I posted armed men at all the entrances, and had another four inside the building. I didn't want to flood the building with men for fear of alerting the Fenians. As a final precaution, Major Hart and I were stationed in the servery opposite the dining room. What we hadn't accounted for was—'

'A bomb in the drawing room?'

'Yes sir.'

'Never mind that it's the Fenians' weapon of choice,' said Warren, his voice dripping with sarcasm, 'and that the drawing room was the obvious place to hide such a device.'

'I know, sir. But we thought we'd arrested all their best bomb-makers, and that they'd try to kill the prince with personal weapons.'

'You thought, but you couldn't know for certain.'

'No, sir, but all the signs from the Fenians themselves were that they would send a shooter on the night.'

'Which they did.'

'Yes, sir, but only to make certain.'

Warren stroked his bushy moustache. 'I've a good mind, Inspector, to relieve you on the spot for dereliction of duty. It was down to your cockeyed plan that the Fenians were able to plant the bomb in the first place. If they'd succeeded in killing the prince, you'd already be out of a job. Fortunately for you he survived the blast and Hart was on the scene quickly enough to foil the gunman.'

The commissioner turned to George. 'What made you suspect a bomb, Major?'

'I don't know, sir. I just had a feeling something wasn't right. Then when I heard the opening bars to Beethoven's Fifth it came to me. The bomb was hidden in the piano. I doubted I would get there in time, but I had to try.'

'Yes, indeed. Well, the attempt almost cost you your life; but more importantly it put you in a position to save the prince's, and for that I and the rest of the Metropolitan Police, not to mention the royal family, are eternally grateful. Her Majesty the Queen and Their Royal Highnesses the Prince and Princess of Wales have all asked me to pass on to you their deep sense of gratitude.'

'Thank you, sir.'

'You'll both be pleased to hear the prince is recovering well. By great good fortune he had retreated to the fireplace just moments before the blast and was protected by the large chimney breast. He was knocked out by a piece of flying debris but otherwise uninjured. Most of the others in the room were not so lucky. The final toll is nine dead – including Lord and Lady Charles, two servants and two policeman – and five badly injured, two of whom have lost limbs. We killed two of them, but it's an awful butcher's bill for a botched operation. We must do better in future.'

'Yes, sir,' said Littlechild, relieved he still had a job.

'The official statement we've given to the press is that the explosion was caused by a domestic gas leak. We don't want the Fenians to gain any publicty from this outrage, particularly with regard to the prince. For that reason he is not on the list of guests attending the dinner, and any newspapers inquiring about his absence from public life will be told he's recovering from a minor fall from his horse. It therefore makes sense, Major Hart, for you and the prince to leave London while the dust settles. Is there somewhere private you can go?'

'Let me speak to my commanding officer Colonel Anson. He has a country house on the North Yorkshire moors. The press will never find us there.'

'Very good. I'll assign a couple of detectives to keep an eye on you while you're there. The Fenians may have missed their target this time, but they'll certainly try again, so do make certain you're on your toes.'

'I will. On a separate matter, sir, may I ask if you've made any progress with the Isenschmid case? When we last spoke you said you were endeavouring to find additional evidence to tie him to the Whitechapel murders.'

Warren frowned. 'I *also* told you, Major Hart, that we had the case well in hand and that you were to concentrate on your primary task of protecting the prince. So you have, and I hope you will continue to do so. As for Isenschmid, our inquiries are continuing.'

'So you've found nothing *yet*?'

'Hart,' intervened Littlechild, 'that case is really none of our business.'

'As I said,' continued Warren, 'our inquiries are continuing. Goodbye, gentlemen.'

9

69 Alnwick Grove, Hammersmith

George turned the key in the lock and opened the front door. On the hall floor was a scattering of letters, most of them bills. He opened one – addressed to 'Mrs George Hart' – and discovered a demand for payment from Lucy's milliner on New Bond Street to the tune of 8 guineas for two hats. My God, thought George, she knows perfectly well we're strapped for cash, yet she's happy to order hats at *4 guineas a piece*. What was she thinking?

He ignored the other letters, assuming they were from creditors: most had their business addresses on the back flap and had been posted in either West London or Gibraltar. One was different. Handwritten, its postmark was E1, the East End. Tearing open the envelope, he found a brief note from Sergeant Fletcher, asking to meet him at 4 p.m. that day at the Three Bells pub in Whitechapel. No explanation.

George arrived early and ordered a pint of pale ale. He was dressed in working men's clothes and, despite his height and looks, blended easily enough into the pub's typical clientele of manual labourers and prostitutes. The latter were laughing and drinking as if the previous three murders of their fellow night-walkers had never occurred. Perhaps they know something I don't, mused George.

A tap on the shoulder heralded the arrival of Sergeant Fletcher who sat down opposite George, a rueful smile on his face. 'Thank you for agreeing to meet me, Major Hart,' said Fletcher. 'I feel embarrassed to admit this, when I consider my last words to you, but I need your help with the case.'

'So no luck then, Sergeant, with proving the Swiss butcher was responsible? I asked Warren and he would only say that inquiries were "proceeding".'

'And so they are, Major. But there's been an important development that, if genuine, would point the finger in an opposite direction. Yesterday we received a letter written in red ink and purporting to come from the killer. It was originally sent to "The Boss" of the Central News Office in Bridge Street, Westminster, and bears a London East Central postmark. At first the editor thought it was a hoax. But after two days he changed his mind and forwarded it to Scotland Yard. They passed it on to us. Here's a facsimile.'

George took the copy and began to read:

Dear Boss

I keep on hearing the police have caught me but they won't fix me just yet. I have laughed when they look so clever and talk about being on the <u>right</u> track. That joke about Leather Apron gave me real fits. I am down on whores and I shant quit ripping them till I do get buckled.

He stopped reading and looked away, his heart thumping. 'Is something the matter?' asked Fletcher.

'There might be,' said George. 'I'm not sure. Let me read the rest of it.'

Grand work the last job was. I gave the lady no time to squeal. How can they catch me now. I love my work and want to start again. You will soon hear of me with my funny little games. I saved some of the proper <u>red</u> stuff in a ginger beer bottle over the last job to write with but it went thick like glue and I cant use it. Red ink is fit enough I hope <u>ha</u> ha. The next job I do I shall clip the lady's ears off and send to the police officers just for jolly wouldn't you. Keep this letter back till I do a bit more work then give it out straight. My knife's so nice and sharp I want to get to work right away if I get a chance.

Good luck.

Yours truly

Jack the Ripper

Don't mind me giving the trade name

PS Wasn't good enough to post this before I got all the red ink off my hands curse it. No luck yet. They say I'm a doctor now <u>ha</u> <u>ha</u>.

George read the letter a second time and was convinced of a resemblance between its handwriting and that on the torn note found next to Chapman, particularly the capital letter 'B' and the lower case 'd'. He no longer had a copy of the torn note, but he remembered it well. He looked up at Fletcher. 'There's something I think you should know. The officer whose handwriting most closely resembled the note found next to the Hanbury Street victim was none other than His Royal Highness Prince Albert Victor. When I put it to him, he denied it. But I can see a definite similarity to the writing on this letter.'

'The *prince*? You think *he* wrote this letter. But that would make him the killer, or at least someone pretending to be. It's not possible. He's a member of the British royal family, for God's sake. They just don't do this sort of thing.'

'That's what I keep telling myself. But we can't rule him out entirely. There are just too many coincidences. The other possibility – and one, frankly, that I'd welcome with open arms at this point – is that someone is trying to incriminate him.'

'That seems more likely to me,' said Fletcher. 'Because if the prince is the killer, why would he send such an obvious clue? Wouldn't he at least try to disguise his handwriting?'

'Yes, you might have thought so.'

They discussed whether the new letter was genuine and agreed that it might be. The problem, explained Fletcher, was that Abberline and Warren were convinced it was a fake, probably made up by a journalist who wanted to sell more copies of his newspaper. They were still clinging to the idea that Isenschmid was responsible, and Fletcher couldn't understand why.

'But what if he isn't?' said George. 'What if this "Jack the Ripper" *is* the killer? He's bound to kill again.'

'Exactly,' replied Fletcher. 'Which is why I need your help, Major Hart. Officially the case is closed – or as good as. Most of the detectives have been assigned to other duties. I'm one of the few still working on it. My job is to find more evidence to incriminate Isenschmid. The problem is: there isn't any. When I mentioned his name to my contacts in the Underworld, they just laughed and said we were heading up a blind alley. The Swiss is well known for his knife-wielding antics, but no one takes him seriously. He's all bark, they say, and no bite. If they're right, the real killer is still on the loose and it's down to us to do something.'

'Us?' said George. 'I'd love to help, sergeant, I really would. But I've been warned off the case by the commissioner.'

'But you said yourself, Major Hart, that the prince might be involved; or possibly someone who knows him. You've got to help me. I won't forgive myself if more women die and I've done nothing.'

George thought about Fletcher's words: 'or someone who knows him'. *That must be it. Someone is trying to implicate the prince by impersonating his handwriting. Pray God that's what is happening, because the alternative is too horrible.*

Fletcher could see George hesitating. 'Don't take this the wrong way, Major Hart, but there might be one extra incentive for you to get involved. You mentioned before that you were pressed for cash. Well, an anonymous individual has just put up a reward of £2,000 for information leading to the capture and conviction of the Ripper. As a policeman I can't claim it. But if you help me catch the person responsible, I'll make sure the money goes to you.'

George would probably have agreed to help Fletcher anyway. The more he thought about the prince's possible involvement, the more determined he was to prove him innocent. But the possibility of a large reward was not unwelcome. 'All right,' he said. 'I'll do what I can. It's not because of the money. My duty is to protect the prince, and if I have to trap the killer to do that I'm ready and willing. But I won't deny the cash will come in handy. Very handy in fact.'

Fletcher smiled, showing a full set of slightly tar-stained teeth. 'Thank you. I was beginning to think I'd have to do this on my own. Righto, let's review what we know so far,' he said, opening his notebook and thumbing through the pages. 'Here we go. We're looking for a killer who, according to the post-mortems, is used to handling sharp knives and has a certain amount of anatomical knowledge. It's possible, therefore, that he might be a doctor or medical student, and therefore a gentleman. He likes to mutilate, particularly the sexual organs, which implies that he has a hatred of the female sex and is probably insane, or at least suffering from a homicidal or erotic mania. Agreed?'

'I'm not entirely sure what those terms mean, but, yes, he's undoubtedly not right in the head.'

'Good. Now the only *reliable* sighting of the probable killer was by Mrs Long, the last person to see Chapman alive at five-thirty in the morning of the eighth of September. The man with Chapman had his back to Long and so she couldn't see him clearly. But she remembered that he had a dark complexion and was wearing a brown deerstalker hat and a dark coat. He looked to her to be over forty years of age, a little taller than the deceased – who was just five feet tall – and was probably a foreigner. His appearance was "shabby genteel", which could mean a gentleman down on his luck or someone pretending to be one.'

'Didn't Long mention a brief conversation?'

'Yes. She remembered that the pair were talking loudly, and were close against the shutters of number Twenty-Nine. The man said, "Will you?", and the woman answered, "Yes". They seemed to her to be sober. That's it.'

'Is she certain it was Chapman she saw?'

'Yes, she identified her in the mortuary the following day. There's no doubt.'

'It's not a lot to go on, is it?' commented George. 'As for

Long's description, how could she possibly know how old the man was if she couldn't see his face? The only telling details she gives are height – not tall – dress and complexion: dark and foreign-looking. The height aside, it could be me.'

Fletcher laughed, adding: 'But definitely not the prince: both the height and colouring are wrong for him.'

'True. But it's not unlike Pearly Poll's description of the soldier Martha Turner went off with when they parted on the night of Turner's death. He, if my memory serves, was late twenties, short and dark, foreign-looking and with a light brown moustache. Apart from the age – which Long might be wrong about because she didn't see the killer's face – it could be the same person.'

'Yes. And if it is, that brings Pearly Poll's officer and your regiment back under suspicion.'

'And also, I hate to say it, the prince,' said George with a shake of his head. 'Pearly Poll described the officer as about thirty years old, tall, dark-haired and handsome, with a dark waxed moustache. That description is not unlike the prince.'

'True, but it's also not unlike plenty of other men about town.'

'Yes, I suppose you're right. But were they in Whitechapel on the occasion of at least two of the murders, and possibly all three? And are they all misogynists? The prince has a number of homosexual friends who hate women; and he himself, I was told by one of them, dislikes and mistrusts them.'

'Do you know why?'

'Well, one of the reasons is that he caught the pox off a Singaporean whore when he was touring the Far East, and it took more than a year of treatment to clear up. Apparently he also resents the many royal mistresses who are trying to take the place of his beloved mother. She's one woman he *does* have time for; but then I doubt he regards her as typical.'

'So he doesn't like or trust women. Is that enough of a motive to murder in such a bestial fashion?'

'Well, no, not in a man of sane mind. But it's not always easy to tell. Syphilis *can* lead to madness. Though I have to say I've got to know the prince quite well in the last month or so, and I haven't seen any evidence of mental instability. My best guess, as things stand, is that he's being set up. After all, he's bound to have met some pretty unsavoury characters on his jaunts to Whitechapel and elsewhere.'

'I agree. I think it's highly unlikely he's involved. In any case, most of what you've told me is speculation and hearsay. What we need is hard evidence.'

'Of course. So, Sergeant, how do you suggest we proceed?'

'Well, sir, here's one thing at least. Earlier today I received a tip-off from a contact I trust in the Underworld. He says he has important information relating to the murders, so I've agreed to meet him at seven p.m. today in the King's Arms in Thrawl Street. I'd appreciate it if you'd watch from a distance as my support. I'd normally take along another detective, but as the case is officially closed I can't tell Abberline what I'm doing.'

'No, I can see that. All right, I'll do it.'

*

George quickened his step as he passed the hordes of hawkers and salesmen on Commercial Street, their rough stalls illuminated by the glare from shops and public houses. Competing for space on the broad pavement was a seething mass of people, eager for entertainment and sustenance from the profusion of cook-shops, gin palaces, assembly rooms, mission halls and shooting galleries. George was astonished to see so many women on the streets of Whitechapel after dark, and if some prostitutes had heeded the commissioner's advice not to ply their trade at night, it had not been for long. For here they were, easily recognizable by their heavily rouged faces, gathered in little groups under street lamps and on street corners, looking for business.

Further on, George could see a crowd gathered round a boy without legs. Some were laughing; a few offered words of pity and a copper or two. Then, just beyond a man loudly declaiming the 'everlasting' quality of corduroy trousers for just nine and sixpence a pair, was a waxwork show of the recent murders, complete with gruesome pictorial details. 'Roll up, roll up,' shouted the bowler-hatted proprietor, 'come and see lifelike representations of the Whitechapel murderer and his foul deeds.'

Despite the obvious bad taste, and the fact that, as far as the public were aware, the perpetrator was still on the loose, this lurid attempt to profit from the recent horrors was extremely popular with women, many with babes in arms, who were jostling to pay the entry fee of two pennies so they could see the ghastly objects within. This public appetite for gore – never better exemplified than by the huge crowds that used to watch public executions before they ended in the 1860s – had never ceased to amaze George who, having seen his fill of bloodshed on the battlefield, had no wish to view it by choice. He was almost relieved when the next major draw on Commercial Street proved to be a fire and brimstone preacher, promising damnation to all who wouldn't repent their sinful lives and follow the path of righteousness. Not all his large audience was convinced. 'Never heard nobody go on like 'im in all my days,' said one old lady in

George's hearing. 'I declare there ain't no chance for none of us.'

Turning right into Wentworth Street, the change of atmosphere was palpable in a narrow road that was quiet and oppressively dark. Children scurried in the shadows. From one staircase came the sound of a scuffle and high-pitched shrieks. 'You hit me! Jest you hit me!'

The challenge must have been accepted because it was followed by the thud of fists on flesh, and more oaths. Then a child screamed. 'You let that child alone or you'll get this rock on your head!'

This was too much for George and he headed for the staircase. But as he reached its entrance a woman emerged, dragging a small child by the hand. 'Are you all right?' asked George.

The woman stopped. Her hair was dishevelled and her right eye a little swollen. 'Do I knows you?' she asked suspiciously.

'No. Not at all. I was passing and heard the commotion. Do you need any help?'

'Help? From you?' She laughed. 'Much good that would bloody do. You going to come back tomorrow to sort my man out, are you? And the day after? And the one after that? No, I thought not. So best leave well alone, eh?'

She walked away, child in tow, leaving George to see the sense of her words. A single intervention was not enough, and might even do more harm than good. He was late, in any case, so hurried on his way. As he turned left into George Street he realized he was just yards from where the first 'Ripper' victim – he found himself using the name – had been killed in George Yard Buildings. It was darker even than Wentworth Street, and George could see how easy it would be for the killer to go about his grisly business in such unlit and unpopulated back streets. The only sign of life on Thrawl Street, first right, were the lights from a large building that George assumed must be the King's Arms. He was right.

Dodging past an amorous couple partially blocking the entrance, George entered the smoky confines of the saloon bar and ordered a pint. At a table in the far corner of the bar he could see Sergeant Fletcher talking to his contact. The plan was for George to observe from a distance, so he remained at the bar in case he was needed. 'Hello handsome,' said a voice to his left.

George turned to see a young blonde woman smiling at him. She was tall and remarkably pretty, with dark blue eyes and even white teeth, and, had her clothes been more fashionable, she would not have looked out of place in a West End drawing room. But like many of the women of Whitechapel, she was dressed in a cheap brown linsey frock, with only a red shawl to give it a dash of colour. Evidently proud of her curly golden hair that reached to her waist, she wore no bonnet. Yet if George had been in any doubt as to her occupation, he was soon disabused. 'Buy me a drink, mister?'

'And what do I get in return?'

'Anything you like, though it'll cost extra.'

George ordered her a half-pint of pale ale and, once she'd taken a gulp, asked her why she was still plying her trade. Wasn't she afraid?

'No,' she replied, wiping the foam from her Cupid's bow lips. 'People here, most of them, think the madman's either locked up or left town, possibly on a ship. Anyways, I'm not fearful. I always carry a chiv in case a customer gets testy. I've waved it a few times, but never serious. You look a nice gent: doubt I'd need it with you. So how about it?'

George laughed. 'Are you propositioning me? I thought it worked the other way round?'

'Usually does,' she said with a grin. 'But it ain't often I get talking with a young man as handsome as you. Come on. You won't be disappointed.'

'No, that's not why I'm here. In any case, I'm happily married.'

'Is you now?' she said. 'Well, so is most of my customers. Tell you what, I'll only charge you half my rate, just as long as you keep mum. Can't have people thinking I'm a charity.'

'It's a kind offer, but no.'

'You're a Jack, ain't you?'

'A what?'

'A Jack. A detective. But even if you is, you should know that some of your colleagues take advantage, especially coppers on the beat.'

'What do you mean?'

'I mean they want sex for nothing.'

'And you agree?'

'What choice have we got? If we say no, it's a night in the blooming lock-up and no grub. Now is you coming with me, or not?'

'Not. But I do have something for you,' said George, holding up a shilling. 'Take this and go home. This is no time to be roaming the streets.'

She chuckled. 'Money for old rope! Thanking you. I'll be off, then,' she said, finishing her half-pint. 'Till next time.'

'Yes, next time. Before you go, what's your name?'

'Mary Kelly.'

'Good to meet you, Mary Kelly. Look after yourself.'

She smiled broadly. 'I will.'

Once the prostitute had left, George turned his attention back to Sergeant Fletcher's conversation with the criminal. It got heated at one point, and eventually the criminal left the pub. Fletcher finished his drink and also left.

They met in a street nearby, as agreed beforehand. 'What did he say?' asked George.

'He said that the word on the street is that we shouldn't be looking for a single murderer, but rather two men working together: one keeping a look-out while the other one does the business. It makes sense to me: why else would the killer have taken the risk of going into the back yard of Hanbury Street, or even into the George Yard Buildings, without someone keeping watch? There's only one exit from each and, if someone had surprised him, he would have been caught like a rat in a trap.'

'How do you know you can trust this man?'

'I can trust him. He's one of my brother's associates, and has been running the gang since Walter was put away. I've known him since I was a kid.'

'Where does he get his information?'

'The gang has look-outs all over the East End. They hear and see things. But they'll never testify, for obvious reasons.'

'Did he say anything else?'

'Yes, he said we've got the wrong man in custody. The culprits, according to him, are still at large, and one has local knowledge.'

'Surely if they know all this they can tell us more? Do they know their names?'

'He said no. When I pressed him, he lost his temper. Said he'd told me everything he knew.'

'Fine,' said George. 'Let's say your brother's associate is right: the killer has an accomplice and is still on the loose. How does that help us?'

'Well, it rules out Isenschmid for starters. We suspected as much and now we have some corroboration. And it confirms Pearly Poll's story that two people might be involved. But other than that, we're still very much in the dark. Talking of which, I know it's late, but as we're here why don't we spend an hour or two walking the streets, looking for someone who matches the descriptions given by Mrs Long and Pearly Poll? You never know, we might strike lucky.'

George agreed and they split up: Fletcher covering the area north of Whitechapel High Street and the Whitechapel Road, and George the roads, lanes and pubs to the south, including Commercial Road. At one point George saw at a distance a man who appeared to be wearing a deer-stalker. But by the time he crossed the road the man had disappeared. It was just after 11 p.m. when he entered the Bricklayer's Arms on Settles Street, just north of Commercial Road. It was packed with prostitutes and working men, and George ordered a drink at the bar. As he was sipping it, a woman squeezed into the gap beside him and asked in a foreign-sounding voice: 'You want company?'

George turned to see a handsome, middle-aged woman smiling at him. She was nicely dressed in long, fur-trimmed black jacket, brown velveteen bodice and black skirt. Her curly black hair was peeping out from under her black bonnet, and round her neck she wore a checked scarf, knotted on the left side.

'No, I'm fine,' replied George, 'but I'll buy you a drink so we can talk.'

She frowned. 'It's not talk I want,' she said in a voice slurred by drink. 'Just money for a bed.'

George couldn't help noticing the woman's very pale skin and large light grey eyes, and wondered how such a nice-looking foreigner had stooped to such depths. 'Stay a while, and I'll give you money for a bed. Where are you from?'

'I live in dosshouse in Flower and Dean Street.'

'No, I mean originally. Where were you born?'

'Sweden. My father was farmer.'

'So why come to England?'

'I came to work for a family in Kensington. Then I married. But it didn't last so here I am.'

'Is there nothing you can do but this?'

'I sew a little, but not enough to get by. Why all these questions?'

'I would have thought that was obvious,' said George. 'The streets are hardly safe for people like you.'

She snorted in derision. 'You mean the murderer? He's long gone. There hasn't been a killing for weeks.'

'What if I told you the police think he's still at large?'

'Is that what *you* are? A copper?'

'No, but I—'

She raised her hand. 'I don't care. I need money not chat.'

Looking beyond George, she spotted another possible customer and made the decision to move on. 'I'll take my chances. Goodnight.'

She walked to the far end of the bar where a man was standing with his back to George. He was tall and wearing a dark cutaway coat, black bowler hat and a red scarf round his neck. George could see him handing her a red rose. Minutes later they were kissing and cuddling, and then they left to ribald cries from other drinkers: 'Don't go with him! That's "Leather Apron" getting round you.'

George debated whether to follow them, but decided against it. After all, there were thousands of prostitutes on the streets of Whitechapel and he couldn't guard them all. Five minutes later he began to regret his decision. There was something about the behaviour of the man she was with that struck George as not normal. He seemed too sure of himself, offering her a flower and kissing her in the pub. George drank up and went outside. Inevitably there was no sign of the couple. He made a half-hearted attempt to find them by scouring nearby streets and alleys, even disturbing one amorous couple as they rutted against a wall. He didn't recognize the woman and, having made his apologies, George moved on. An hour and a half later – just after 1 a.m. – he was walking up Berner Street, a thoroughfare of two-storey slums not far from the Bricklayer's Arms, when he heard a cry from the opposite side of the road. He ran across and saw a dark-haired man, about forty years of age, gesturing frantically from the entrance to a yard. 'Call the police!' he shouted in an East European accent. 'It's too horrible.'

'I am the police,' said George, flashing his SIB warrant card. 'What's happened?'

'On the right, by the wall. See for yourself,' said the man, handing George his candle. 'I almost ran her over with my pony and cart. I think she's dead.'

The tall yard gates were open. Beyond them was a narrow passageway that led to the yard, bounded on both sides by brick buildings. Close to the one on the left, a short distance from the entrance, George could see a dark shape. As he got closer, the candle illuminated a woman's body. He came across her boots first, just visible from beneath her voluminous black skirts. The body lay on its left side, with its right arm resting on the belly and its left arm extended. Its head was turned towards the wall. The dark clothes looked familiar to George, but the clincher was the check silk scarf round the woman's neck. It was identical to the one the Swedish prostitute was wearing. It had to be her.

George picked up her left wrist to take the pulse. It was still warm, the hand clenched round a small white paper bag. He pressed firmly with two fingers. There was no heartbeat. So he checked for injuries and could see none, until he lifted the woman's chin and revealed a gaping cut from ear to ear, two inches wide and at least six inches long, still leaking blood into a large pool beneath the body. He winced and turned away.

'Is she dead?' asked the man who had hailed him.

'Yes.'

He looked back at the victim. Her eyes were still open and their grey colour left George in no doubt that it was the woman he had spoken to. Given the absence of other injuries, he concluded that the killer must have been disturbed. He quietly berated himself for leaving the prostitute to her fate. He had sensed something was wrong when she left with the tall man in the cutaway coat. Other people in the pub had jokingly warned he was 'Leather Apron'. How ironic, and how tragic, that their mirth had been all too accurate. He clenched his fists tightly as he imagined the battering he would inflict if he ever got hold of this cowardly killer – or was it killers? – of women.

By now a small knot of people had gathered round George and the body, most of them emerging from the International Working Men's Educational Club that ran along the left of the passageway. They were soon joined by a police constable, found on his beat in nearby Commercial Road. 'Everybody get back,' said the constable as he shone his powerful bull's-eye lantern on the body. 'You might get blood on your clothes and disturb the crime scene.'

George stood up. 'Who are you, sir?' asked the constable.

'I'm Major George Hart. I work for the Special Irish Branch,' said George, flashing his warrant card. 'I met this woman barely an hour ago in a pub. She left with a smartly dressed man but I didn't get to see his face.'

'The Special Irish Branch, you say,' said the constable. 'Now what would you be doing in Whitechapel? Well, you can tell Inspector Abberline. I've just sent a colleague to collect him from the Commercial Street Station.

A sleepy-looking police surgeon was the next to arrive on the scene. Having examined the body, and found some warmth in the face and body, he pronounced the time of death from loss of blood at between 12.46 and 12.56 a.m., the latter estimate just a few minutes before the body was discovered.

George was about to leave when a stout, bowler-hatted man with impressive mutton-chop whiskers strode into the yard. The police constable at once saluted. 'Evening, Detective Inspector. The victim was found at one a.m. by Mr Louis Diemschutz, here,' said the police constable, pointing to the man George had spoken to. 'He's the steward of the building behind us, the International Working Men's Club, and lives with his wife on the premises. He was returning from the market at Crystal Palace where he sells jewellery.'

'Have you taken his statement?' asked Abberline, his gentle voice more reminiscent of a bank manager than a hard-bitten detective.

'I was about to, sir.'

'Good. But first shut the gates. I want the yard sealed off.

'Yes sir.'

'Then take the details of everyone here. I also want them checked for bloodstains.'

'Sir.'

Abberline noticed George kneeling by the body. 'And who are you, sir?'

'I'm Major George Hart. I work for Inspector Littlechild of the Special Irish Branch.'

'In what capacity?'

'I'm not at liberty to say, Inspector, but Littlechild will vouch for me.'

'I hope you're right. What are you doing in Whitechapel?'

George decided to come clean. 'As well as working for Littlechild, I'm a serving member of the Tenth Hussars and was asked by Sir Charles Warren to look into the provenance of the torn letter found next to the Hanbury Street victim. It was written on our regimental paper.'

'Ah, yes, I remember the torn piece of letter. We quickly concluded it was an irrelevance. So why are you still involved?'

'Because it didn't make sense to me that you would pin all your hopes on the Swiss butcher Isenschmid being the killer. Even my relatively limited knowledge of the case raised the possibility of an accomplice, and the fact that someone with links to the military might be involved. So I decided to carry out some unofficial inquiries of my own and, I think you'll agree, this evening's melancholic events have proved that I was right to do so.'

Abberline snorted with contempt. 'So, let me get this straight, Major Hart. You're a soldier not a detective, yet you presume to know how to go about solving a murder inquiry better than a man like me with twenty-five years' experience of policing? Is that correct? Moreover, you ignore the commissioner's instructions to leave well alone, and just happened to be wandering the streets of Whitechapel when you came across the body of the latest victim? It sounds highly suspicious to me.'

'I didn't come across the victim. I was hailed by Mr Diemschutz, here,' said George. 'He found the body.'

'But you were obviously in the area? It strikes me, Major Hart, that you have some explaining to do.'

Just then, Sergeant Fletcher arrived on the scene. 'Evening, Inspector,' said Fletcher to Abberline. 'I was walking home down Commercial Street when I heard the commotion. How terrible that the killer is still at work.'

'Yes, it is unfortunate. But it doesn't necessarily mean the Swiss butcher is innocent,' said Abberline, defensively. 'They could have been working in tandem.'

'Possibly, sir, but I wouldn't put money on it. The butcher strikes me as a deranged loner. I can't see him cooperating with another killer. I might be wrong. But either way we have more work to do. May I ask why Major Hart is in attendance?'

'He says he was carrying out his own inquiries because, like you, he didn't believe that Isenschmid was the killer. He was one of the first on the scene. My own feeling is that—'

Abberline was interrupted by a police constable, who rushed into the yard, shouting: 'Inspector! Inspector!'

'Calm down, Constable. What's the matter?'

'There's been another murder, sir.'

'Where?'

'At Mitre Square in the City. We've just received word from Bishopgate Police Station.'

Abberline turned to Fletcher. 'Sergeant, how far is Mitre Square?'

'About half a mile, sir. But it's beyond our jurisdiction.'

'I know that. But if it's the same killer we have to investigate. Let's go. You too, Major Hart.'

IO

Mitre Square, City of London

A brisk six-minute jog-trot down Whitechapel and Aldgate high streets brought Abberline, Fletcher and George to the site of the second murder, a small, stone-cobbled square just within the eastern boundary of the City of London. All three were breathing heavily as they entered the south of the square via a carriageway off Mitre Street. It was a dark and desolate location, bounded on three sides by warehouses and dilapidated dwellings, and illuminated only in its north-west corner by a single gaslight.

To their right, on a broad pavement that backed onto some empty houses – the darkest part of the square and a favourite spot for prostitutes and their clients – the trio could see a group of policemen with lanterns clustered round a dark figure on the ground. As they got closer, the horror of the scene became apparent: the victim was lying on her back in a pool of blood, her feet facing the carriageway and her clothes up round her chest, exposing a gaping red wound in her white belly which had been cut open from breastbone to groin. George could see that, in addition, the woman's throat had been cut, her face savagely slashed, and part of her grey intestines were lying across her right shoulder. He felt nauseous and looked away. He'd seen many similar, if not worse, sights on a battlefield, and they hadn't affected him like this. But that was kill or be killed. This was different. This was butchery, pure and simple, of innocent women on the streets of London, the beating heart of the British Empire. It was hard to believe it was happening, and harder still to stomach.

'Who are you?' asked a tall, austere-looking man in a tailored frockcoat and top hat, his ginger beard and distinct accent betraying his Scottish roots.

'Inspector Frederick Abberline of the Met's CID. I'm leading the inquiry into the Whitechapel murders. We've just come from a separate murder scene in Berner Street. Another prostitute. Her throat was cut but she wasn't badly mutilated. It's possible that the two murders were committed by the same person or persons. If they were, the killer was probably disturbed in his butchery, hence the need for a second victim.'

'Yes, we heard about the murder in Berner Stret, which is why I asked my desk sergeant to get a message to you. I'm Inspector James McWilliam of the City's Detective Department. This poor thing,' he said, pointing at the victim, 'was found by a constable on his beat at 1.45 a.m. He'd come through the square a short time earlier, at about 1.30 a.m., but found it empty, which means the murderer must have done his devilish work in under fifteen minutes, possibly even less. Another constable came into the square down a narrow passage in its northeast corner at 1.40 a.m. but saw nothing untoward and retraced his steps to Duke Street. The killer and his victim were surely in the square at that time and must have only narrowly avoided detection. One thing is certain: he's getting bolder. The City is crawling with police. I've sent detectives in all directions to search for suspects and ask if anyone saw anything.'

'Any clues?' asked Abberline.

'Yes,' said McWilliam. 'Watkins found this by the body.'

He handed Abberline a brown paper evidence bag. The inspector took out a small gold button and held it up to the light. 'It looks like it's decorated with a military crest,' said Abberline. 'It has a crown, feathers and the letters "X.R.H.".'

George's heart skipped a beat. 'Can I see that?' he asked.

Abberline showed him the button. There was no doubt.

'Do you recognize it?' asked McWilliam.

'I do, unfortunately,' said George. 'It's the regimental crest of the Tenth Hussars. The button is from the cuff of an officer's tunic.'

'And you are?'

'Major George Hart of the same regiment.'

'He's helping us with our inquiries, Inspector,' said Abberline to McWilliam. 'With that in mind, could I request that we keep this button? This is clearly another Ripper murder and, as all the others occurred in Whitechapel, including the one just a couple of hours ago that may or may not be connected, we'll continue to take the lead on this. I hope that's acceptable to you. If not, the Home Secretary will have to adjudicate.'

'No, that's quite all right. You keep the button.'

McWilliam had barely finished speaking when another constable ran up, gasping for breath. 'Inspector,' he said to McWilliam, 'we've just had word from Commercial Street Police Station that one of their men has found a suspicious message written in chalk on a door jamb in Goulston Street in Whitechapel.'

'What does it say?'

'Something about Jews not being blamed, sir. It didn't make sense to me. And there's something else.'

'Go on.'

'On the ground below the message, the constable found what looks to be a piece of bloodstained apron.'

'Are you certain it's blood?' asked Abberline.

'Yes, sir, it appears to be; and not all of it was dry.'

'Which means,' said Abberline, 'that if the rag was left by the murderer, the blood is from the most recent victim, this poor soul.'

All eyes looked down at the dead woman's clothes, some of which had been cut away from her body. There, beside the torn remnants of her old green alpaca skirt, grey petticoat and brown linsey dress bodice lay a piece of white apron, spattered with blood. It appeared to have been cut with a knife.

'It must be the same apron,' said Abberline to McWilliam. 'He probably used it to clean his knife and hands, and then dropped it as he headed back to the East End. I'd better get over there. Do you mind if I take this piece of apron with me? Then I can compare the two and see if there's a match.'

'That's fine. Take it. Just keep me informed. I'll let you have a copy of the post-mortem as soon as the examination is complete.'

'Thank you. But I'd be grateful if you'd let my divisional police surgeon, Dr Phillips, attend the post-mortem. He has conducted the same for a number of the victims and might be able to draw some conclusions.'

'Gladly. Tell your man to go to the mortuary on Golden Lane. An ambulance will take the body there shortly.'

*

As Sergeant Fletcher knew the quickest route, the one probably taken by the murderer, he led George and Abberline out of the northern side of Mitre Square by the narrow passage that emerged onto Duke Street. From there they worked their way through a tangle of dark and deserted back lanes to Goulston Street, a nondescript thoroughfare of slaughterhouses and dilapidated tenements that were mostly occupied by Jewish immigrants. The walk of just under a quarter of a mile took them four minutes.

The address given by the constable was a tenement called the Wentworth Model Dwellings at numbers 108–119. As they neared its entrance they saw, waiting for them, the Polish-born constable Tom Black, wearing civilian clothes and clearly off duty.

'You again, Black!' said Abberline. 'What happened?'

'I meet friend in pub in Wentworth Street,' said Black, in his distinctive broken English, 'and on way home I see apron here in doorway. So I call for copper on beat, tell him to inform station and stay to guard. Other men join me. I find like this.' He pointed to the ground behind him where, illuminated by Fletcher's lantern, they could see a scrunched-up piece of white apron that was stained with smears of blood and what looked like a trace of faeces.

'You haven't touched it?' asked Abberline.

'No, sir.'

'Good.'

Abberline took the piece of apron he had brought with him out of an evidence bag. Then he knelt down to compare it to the piece on the ground, spreading out both so that he could observe their shapes. The one he had brought with him was bigger and with a string attached. It was missing a corner that was the same shape as the piece Black had found.

The clincher came when Abberline turned both pieces over and found they had been patched, and that the borders of the repair corresponded exactly.

'It's the same apron,' said Abberline, before turning to Black. 'Where's the message?'

Black pointed to the right side of the open archway where, at shoulder height, they could see five lines of writing on the fascia of black bricks:

> The Juwes are
> The men That
> Will not
> be Blamed
> for nothing

'Well I'll be blowed,' said Abberline, crouching close to the message, as if searching for clues. 'Any idea what it means?'

'It's hard to say, sir,' said Fletcher. 'It seems to be saying that Jews are not the sort of people who will tolerate being blamed for something they didn't do. If written by the killer, he may be trying to say he's embarked on his killing spree because of a real or intended offence to his race. Or it could, on the other hand, be an attempt to point the finger at Jews by saying they always refuse to take the blame, even when they're guilty of something.'

'So it was either written by a disgruntled Jew or a Gentile trying to blame Jews? For my money it's the latter. Why would a Jew implicate himself?'

'Well, sir,' said Fletcher, 'deranged people can do strange things. It might be a defiant gesture.'

Abberline looked at George. 'Hart, what do you think?'

'I agree with Sergeant Fletcher. It might be a Jew crowing about what he's done; but it might just as easily be a deliberate smokescreen.'

'Yes,' said Abberline, 'well, either way, it needs to be scrubbed off as soon as possible. Recently there's been a lot of bad feeling against the Jews of Whitechapel, as we saw with the hue and cry over "Leather Apron". If this becomes public knowledge, it could lead to riots against Jews and even murder. We can't risk that.' The inspector turned to the off-duty constable. 'Black, I need you to go to the station and fetch a sponge and a bucket of water.'

'Me?' questioned Black. 'I not at work.'

'Not at work!' barked Abberline. 'Two murders have been committed tonight, and you're refusing to help? A policeman is never off duty, remember that! Now go!'

A contrite Black nodded his compliance and set off for the nearest police station on Commercial Street.

'Fletcher,' said Abberline, 'you might as well check the stairways for marks or evidence. While you're at it, knock on some doors and see if anyone saw or heard anything.'

'Yes, sir,' said Fletcher, before disappearing through the archway, his heavy boots clattering on the stone stairway.

Left alone with Abberline, George tried to make sense of all that had happened that evening. The killer had struck again, as he and Fletcher suspected he would, and even Warren would have to concede that either Isenschmid was the wrong man – the most likely scenario – or that he had not been acting alone. But if, as George believed, Isenschmid wasn't responsible, who *was*? It seemed increasingly likely to him – given the witness statements provided by Pearly Poll and Mrs Long, and the information from the gang boss – that two killers were involved, and that he had probably seen the back of one of them in the pub with the first of that evening's victims. He tried to visualize what the man looked like, and could only remember that he was tall and wearing a cutaway coat, bowler hat and red scarf. Could it have been the prince? Crucially George had not seen his face, and his failure to act on his suspicions and follow the couple out of the pub would, he knew, haunt him to the end of his days. But there were two vital extra clues: the gold officer's button, which put the suspicion back on the officers of his regiment, and the message on the wall in front of George. Whether its content was a deliberate smokescreen or not, it had probably been written by the killer or his accomplice, and it was vital that it be preserved.

George was about to say as much to Abberline when a closed carriage drew up and Sir Charles Warren got out. He looked tired and irritable, with dark smudges under his eyes. 'Well, Detective Inspector,' he said to Abberline, 'what have you got to say for yourself? I've been informed that two prostitutes were killed tonight in circumstances very similar to the earlier murders. Yet you assured me we had the man responsible under lock and key.'

'I thought we did, sir,' replied the contrite inspector. 'But we shouldn't jump to too many conclusions: maybe he was working with tonight's killer?'

'Do you really believe that?'

'I'm keeping an open mind, sir.'

Warren noticed George. 'Major Hart? What on earth are you doing here? The last time we spoke you were about to accompany Prince Albert Victor to the North Yorkshire moors.'

'We went, and now we're back.'

'And your presence here is explained by what, exactly?'

George was tempted to tell Warren everything he now knew, particularly the mounting number of clues and hints that suggested a possible link between the prince and the murders. But his memory of the commissioner's duplicitous dealings with him in the Sinai, plus the man's willingness to dismiss the earlier hints of a soldier's involvement and pin the blame on an unlikely suspect like Isenschmid, were together convincing George that Warren was not to be trusted. So he gave the commissioner the same explanation he had given to Abberline, adding that he might have caught sight of the killer in a public house shortly before the first murder.

'In that case,' said Warren, 'you'll need to give a statement to the inspector or one of his men. But I don't appreciate the fact that you have disobeyed my instructions and, had it not been for our past association, I would certainly be taking disciplinary action against you. I trust that, in future, you'll leave the sleuthing to Abberline and his men and concentrate on your own duties. Do I make myself clear?'

'Yes sir.'

'Good, because I won't say it again. Now where's this message?'

George pointed to the door jamb and Warren took a moment to decipher the writing. 'What an odd message!' he said, shaking his head. 'I'm particularly intrigued by the word "Juwes".' He turned to Abberline. 'Tell me, Inspector, is that a Yiddish word?'

'I'm not sure, sir. Constable Black would know better than me. Here he is now,' said Abberline, gesturing to the end of the street, where Black had just appeared, dutifully carrying a bucket and sponge.

'Why would Black know?' asked Warren.

'Because he's a Jew and speaks Yiddish.'

'And the bucket? What's that for?'

'I asked Black to fetch a bucket and sponge so that we can erase the message. Given the excited state of the population, and particularly in the East End, I think it highly like that such a message would provoke an onslaught on the Jews that would cost lives and property. Do you agree, sir?'

'I do,' said Warren. 'The East End is a tinderbox and such a message might provide the spark.'

The commissioner turned to address the approaching Black. 'Well done, Constable. But before you obliterate the message, I want to ask you about the word "Juwes". Is that the way you would spell it?'

'No, sir.'

'So what is the word in Yiddish?'

'Yidden, sir.'

'Have you seen this word "Juwes" before?'

'No, sir.'

'Very strange. All right, Constable, go ahead.'

Black lifted the dripping sponge from the bucket and stepped forward.

'Wait!' said George.

Black looked at Warren for direction. The commissioner frowned. 'Hold on, Constable. What is it, Hart?'

'I think you're making a mistake, sir. There's a high probability the message was written by the killer; if it was, it's vital to the case. A comparison of the handwriting might prove that some of the other notes are genuine. Can't we just guard it until a photographer arrives?'

'No, Hart, we can't. There isn't time. It's just getting light and soon the public will be on the streets. If they see this there will be hell to pay for the Jews round here.'

'Can't we cover it up?'

'No. That won't do. It's visible to all who pass this spot, and couldn't be covered up without the danger of the covering being torn off. It's my responsibility to preserve the public order, and given the recent strength of feeling against the Jews, inflamed by the suspicion in the press that a Jew was "Leather Apron", and the fact that this is a Jewish neighbourhood, I can't with all conscience leave this writing a minute longer. If I do, there's a strong likelihood that Jews will be attacked, property wrecked and lives lost. The best we can do is take a duplicate.'

'Sir,' said George, 'please reconsider what you're about to do. Once this writing is erased there's no going back.'

'I've said all there is to say on the matter. Get rid of it, Constable.'

Thus sanctioned, Black slopped the dripping sponge on the door jamb and rubbed until there was no trace. 'All done, sir.'

'Good. Abberline, I expect your report on my desk by this afternoon. I must go straight to the Home Office and explain to Mr Matthews that, contrary to my assurances, the killer is still on the loose.'

11

George was pouring coffee in the front parlour when the door knocker was rapped twice in quick succession. He opened the door to find the reassuringly squat form of Sergeant Fletcher, a sheepish grin on his broad freckly face. 'I apologize for not coming earlier,' said the detective. 'I've been busy taking witness statements. Can I come in?'

'Yes, of course,' said George, leading the way to the front parlour.

'Coffee?' he asked his guest.

'Don't mind if I do.'

'Sugar?'

'Three lumps.'

George arched his eyebrows. 'Three?'

'Yes, please.'

Fletcher took a sip of the steaming coffee and nodded. 'Just right. Can't stand it when it's bitter. Reminds me of the medicine me mum gave me as a child. Anyway, down to business. I'm here to talk about the murders and I have to say, Major Hart, I'm mystified. I truly am.'

'As am I,' said George, 'but can you be more specific?'

'Yes, sorry. I'm mystified by Inspector Abberline's behaviour. He's a first-class detective. The best we have. Before moving to Scotland Yard he worked for fourteen years as the head of the local CID and knows the East End and its villains as well as anyone. He's usually meticulous and even-handed in his work. Yet, from virtually the moment he was assigned to this case by Warren, he clung to his pet theory that a local madman was responsible: hence his willingness to believe Isenschmid was the culprit. Only now that two more unfortunates have lost their lives is he prepared to accept that someone else is involved. But he still won't exonerate Isenschmid entirely.'

'Strange,' said George, shaking his head. 'When did he take over the case?'

'Shortly after the second murder, that of Polly Nichols. At first he kept an open mind about who might be responsible, and was keen to follow up the last sighting of Martha Turner with a soldier. This became even more of a priority when the torn letter with your regimental crest was found by Chapman's body. But then we arrested Isenschmid, after a tip-off, and Abberline seemed to lose interest in any other line of inquiry.'

'Why do you think that was?'

'I don't know. I can only conclude that he was following instructions from his superiors.'

'The head of the CID or Warren himself?'

'Definitely Warren. No one else would have had the authority. But what I can't work out is why the commissioner would be so short-sighted.'

There was a slight pause, broken by George. 'We know that Warren was and is under huge pressure – from both the Home Secretary and the public at large – to solve the case.

But that doesn't explain why he was so quick to believe that Isenschmid was the killer. The evidence against the Swiss was purely circumstantial and very tenuous. Unless . . . unless . . . No, it couldn't be that.'

'Couldn't be what?'

'Well, I know this is unlikely. But is it beyond the realms of *all* possibility that Warren suspected who the real killer or killers might be and was trying to cover up the fact?'

'Why would he do that?'

'I don't know, exactly. This is pure speculation. But what if one of the killers was a man of influence whose identity had to be kept secret as a matter of national importance.'

'Someone like the prince?'

'Yes, someone like that, though I still struggle to believe *he*'s a murderer. I don't believe in elaborate conspiracies as a general rule. The truth is usually much simpler, and more a case of happenstance. But in this instance it does seem possible that there's been some kind of a cover-up; a closing of the ranks, if you will, to protect a person or even an institution.'

Fletcher took another sip of coffee. 'I think I need something stronger. Do you have whisky?'

'Of course,' said George. He retrieved the bottle from the sideboard and poured two slugs into the coffee cups.

Fletcher gulped some down. 'That's better,' he said, wiping his lips. 'I get what you're saying, Major Hart, I really do. But isn't it possible that Warren's behaviour is less conniving than you think? Believe me, it's not that unusual for senior officers to convince themselves that the first viable suspect is responsible for a crime. It might be wishful thinking, but it happens when the pressure to solve a case becomes acute, as in this instance. In any event, like you I still can't believe that a grandson of Her Majesty is involved. It's surely more likely that someone is trying to incriminate the prince. The question is: who and why? If it is a third party, it might explain why one of your officer's buttons was so conveniently "left" beside the second victim the other night. I find it hard to believe it was left there by accident; if it was, it was very negligent of the killer. Are we to believe, in any event, that the killer would be foolish enough to wear his own uniform as he wielded his knife? Would it not be covered in blood?'

'Fair point. Then again,' said George, 'don't forget that two of the original suspects were seen wearing their uniforms. As for the button, couldn't it have been lost in the struggle? It seems incredible, I know, but if the prince is in any way connected to the murders, even as a dupe for the man or men actually responsible, that might explain why Warren seems determined to muddy the waters. Do you believe the reason he gave for wiping clean the chalk message in Goulston Street? That he did it to protect the local Jewish community?'

'No, I do not,' said Fletcher. 'It's a concern, no doubt, because Jews have been under suspicion since the papers mentioned we were after "Leather Apron". But it's not a big enough concern to justify the destruction of vital evidence: if the message been photographed, we could have compared the handwriting with the torn letter and the "Ripper" note. Warren made certain that could not happen.'

'Exactly.'

'But if you're right, Major Hart, and Warren *is* protecting someone of influence by muddying the waters, how does all this end?'

'It ends when *we* unmask the killer or killers. Who else is going to?'

'I think we can safely say it's killers, plural. My brother's associate was right: the Ripper has an accomplice.'

'I agree, but why the certainty? Do you have new information?'

'I do. Since the double killing, three credible witnesses have come forward. One provides pretty clear evidence that two men are acting in concert.'

'Go on.'

'I'll come on to the witness statements in a moment. I can also tell you that the victims have been identified,' said Fletcher, taking out his notebook and reading from it. 'They are, respectively, forty-five-year-old Elizabeth Stride, born in Sweden and known as "Long Liz", and Catherine Eddowes, forty-six, originally from Wolverhampton in the Midlands. Both are prostitutes who live at two separate dosshouses in Flower and Dean Street, Spitalfields. There's no indication that they knew each other.

'As for the witnesses, the first is a police constable, William Smith, who at half past midnight on the thirtieth saw a man and a woman – he's pretty sure it was the first victim, Liz Stride – standing on the pavement of Berner Street, opposite the entrance to Dutfield's Yard. Smith describes the man as about twenty-eight years of age, five feet seven inches tall, wearing a dark overcoat and trousers. He was wearing a brown deerstalker hat and appeared "respectable" looking. He was holding a newspaper parcel, about eighteen inches in length and six or eight inches wide.'

'Interesting,' said George. 'Go on.'

'The second witness is a Hungarian Jew called Israel Schwartz. He's the most important, in my view. Schwartz says he saw not one but two suspicious characters near Stride at around 12.45 a.m. One of them was standing with Stride

– who he later identified in the mortuary – in the gateway to Dutfield's Yard. He thinks he was about thirty years old, five feet five inches tall, with a dark complexion, dark hair and small brown moustache. He was broad-shouldered and dressed in a dark jacket and trousers, and a deerstalker, and was probably the same man that Smith identified. As Schwartz approached, this man threw the woman down to the floor, causing her to scream three times in muffled tones. Not wanting to get involved, Schwartz crossed to the opposite side of the street where another man was standing. He was around thirty-five years old, five feet ten inches tall, with dark hair and dressed in a dark overcoat, wearing an old black hard felt hat with a wide brim. Soon after throwing the woman to the ground, the first man shouted the word or name "Lipski" to the second man. Or at least Schwartz thought he was addressing the second man. As Schwartz walked briskly away, he was followed for a time by the second man, causing him to break into a run. He eventually got away.'

'My God,' said George, 'it does sound like they were acting together. What about the third witness?'

'He's another Jew, a cigarette seller called Joseph Lawende. He claims that shortly before the second murder, he saw a couple standing at the corner of Church Passage, leading to Mitre Square. The woman was wearing a black jacket and bonnet, as was the second victim Catherine Eddowes; the man he describes as, and I quote, "of shabby appearance, about thirty years of age and five feet nine inches in height, of fair complexion, having a small dark moustache, and wearing a red neckerchief and a bowler hat".'

George nodded. 'Well, that makes sense. The taller man with the dark coat, red neckerchief and black bowler that

Schwartz saw with Stride must be the same person that I saw in the pub, and that Lawende saw with Eddowes. Which means that the smaller man with the dark complexion, wearing a deerstalker, who was seen by the policeman and Schwartz, and with Chapman by Mrs Long, must be his accomplice. They could be taking it in turns to proposition the victims, and even to kill them.'

'Exactly. But that's not how Commissioner Warren and Inspector Abberline see things. They're downplaying the significance of the button and don't see the witness statements as definite proof that two men *other* than Isenschmid are involved. Instead, Warren in particular seems fixated by Schwartz's claim that the killer shouted the word "Lipski".'

'What does "Lipski" mean?'

'Israel Lipski was an umbrella salesman of Polish-Jewish descent who was hanged last year for the poisoning and murder of a pregnant Jewess, and the last name is often used in the East End as an insult. It seems to me there are three possibilities. Firstly, the murderer and his accomplice are Gentiles, but wrote the chalk message and shouted out "Lipski" to implicate Whitechapel's many Jewish immigrants. Or, they could have been directing the insult at Schwartz, an obvious Jew, to scare him off. The second possibility is that the murderer was mocking his accomplice, who is a Jew, while he himself is a Gentile, or even vice versa. And, thirdly, both the murderer and his accomplice are East End Jews, and are trying to throw us off the scent by the double bluff of implicating their own people. I think, on reflection, the second option is the most likely, but it's impossible to know. Warren favours the third, but with the twist that a single Jew was acting alone: again, as you say, he seems to be determined that no shadow of suspicion should fall upon anyone but a local, and a Jewish local at that. Which is why he's ordered house-to-house inquiries of the Jewish neighbourhoods and the dosshouses. He wants us to find out how many men live in each house, and what they've been up to recently. Do they stay out late? Is there a history of mental illness? What he won't accept is the possibility of two men acting in concert.'

'No, and by extension he's ruling out a murderer from beyond the Whitechapel area, thus ensuring the finger of suspicion doesn't linger on anyone of gentle birth. I'm not so convinced. The evidence that two people are responsible is mounting, and there's nothing to say that one or both are not from a more salubrious part of town. Anything else I should know?'

'Yes. The killers must have been disturbed during the first murder in Dutfield's Yard. But they made up for that in Mitre Square by mutilating Eddowes' face beyond recognition, cutting her throat, disembowelling her, and removing her left kidney and most of her uterus. They also cut off the lobe of her left ear. Ring any bells?'

'Yes, indeed. The Ripper's letter threatens to "clip" off the ears of his next victim and send it to the police "just for jolly". Well, he's done the first part.'

'Exactly so, Major Hart. And there's more. Yesterday the "Boss" of Central News received another message from Jack the Ripper on a postcard. It mentioned a "double event", the fact that number one "squealed" a bit, and that he had not time to, and I quote, "get ears for police". Given that the card was almost certainly written on the thirtieth, it's very unlikely that anyone but the murderer would have known that, according to Schwartz, the first victim did indeed cry out.'

'So you think it's genuine?'

'I do,' said Fletcher. 'And you should also know that the City doctor who conducted the post-mortem thought that the mutilation gave no particular evidence of anatomical knowledge, but could rather have been committed by any person who, and I quote again, "had been a hunter, a butcher, a slaughterman, as well as a student in surgery or a properly qualified surgeon". He also commented on the ritualistic nature of Eddowes' wounds: the piece of intestine, two feet long, placed between the body and the left arm; the matching triangular emblem cut into her cheeks, and the corresponding nicks to her eyelids. I mentioned these details to Inspector Abberline but he didn't seem interested.'

'Did you say triangular cuts on each cheek?'

'Well, not a simple triangle as such, more like two open triangles laid across each other.'

'How extraordinary. Have you ever come across anything similar?'

'On a corpse you mean? No, I haven't.'

George got up and fetched a pencil and paper from the sideboard. 'Can you show me what the cuts looked like?'

Fletcher sketched a woman's head, nose and eyes, and on each cheek drew two sides of inverted right-angled triangle, overlaid with a more acute angle. The shape looked familiar, but George couldn't place it. Then a thought came to him. 'Wait here.'

He left the room and returned seconds later with a book.

'What's that?' asked Fletcher.

'It's called "Freemasonry from the Great Pyramid of Ancient Times". It was given to me by my brother officers in the Sixtieth Rifles, some of whom were members of Masonic lodges. I imagine they hoped I would join. I never got round to reading it, but your sketch reminded me of the symbol on the front cover. Look.'

Fletcher looked from the book to his sketch and back again. The similarity was obvious. 'My God, it's not a triangle at all. It's the Masonic square, overlaid by a compass, the classic Masonic emblem.'

'It seems to be, doesn't it? The actual cuts on the cheek can't have been that precise, but it's too close to be a coincidence.'

'So are we to assume the murderer of Eddowes, at least, is a Freemason?'

'Not necessarily. He might be impersonating a Freemason. But if he's the genuine article, that could explain why Warren is so keen to obstruct the inquiry. I remember him telling me in the Sinai that he had once been the grand master of a lodge of Freemasons in Singapore. He must still be a member.'

'He is, as are many coppers. Abberline, for example. He tried to get me to join. He described Freemasonry as an ethical brotherhood – non-political and non-religious – that does a lot of work for charity. But I know from other coppers who've joined that it's a misogynistic secret society that looks after its own. You're right about one thing, Major Hart. If the killer is a Freemason, Warren and Abberline might well try to prevent that fact from becoming known.'

'At the risk of letting the killer or killers continue their grisly business?'

'I don't know about that. I doubt they'd be a party to murder. But they might try to shield a fellow Mason from *public* justice, and that's bound to hamper the inquiry.'

'Then we must prevent that from happening. In the meantime, I'll keep a close watch on the prince and try and discover if *he* has any links to Freemasonry. If you can keep me up to date with the inquiry, that would be much appreciated. Can you do that?'

'Of course.'

*

'Come in, Your Royal Highness,' said George, waving the prince into his office at the barracks. 'How're you feeling? No lasting effects from that horrific business in Curzon Street last month, I trust?'

The prince strode up to George's desk and saluted. 'I'm fine, sir,' he said, a broad smile on his face. 'Thanks to you. Or at least, I am physically. I have the odd nightmare, but I imagine that's to be expected.'

'It is, I'm afraid. I've had them for years. The shock of combat, or any grim experience, seems to trigger them. They lessen over time. Do sit down, there's something I need to ask you.'

Taking off his cap, the prince sat opposite George. As always, he was beautifully turned out in his tailored uniform and looked the picture of health. It was hard to believe that just a few weeks earlier he had narrowly escaped an assassination attempt; or that he might in any way be connected to some of the most brutal murders ever committed on British soil. 'Ask away, sir,' said the prince, twisting the end of a waxed moustache.

'Forgive me,' said George, 'this is not a military matter. I've been approached by a friend of my mother's, who is a Freemason. He wants to know if I'm interested in joining his lodge. I know nothing of these matters and thought you might be able to enlighten me.

The prince raised one eyebrow. 'You know *nothing* of the Masons, sir?'

'What I mean to say is that I know no more than any outsider.'

'Well, you're asking the right person. I've been a Mason for a number of years and would heartily recommend it.'

George felt strangely conflicted. He liked the prince and was hoping against hope that he was not a Mason, thus removing one possible link to the murders. But he was also determined to catch the killers and if the prince, unlikely as it seemed, was one of them, then so be it.

'Would you mind telling me, Your Royal Highness, how you got involved?'

'Why, through Papa, of course. He's been grand master since seventy-five, and arranged for my initiation four years ago. The link between the royal family and Freemasonry goes all the way back to Frederick, Prince of Wales, in the early eighteenth century. Why, even my grandmother the Queen is grand patroness of the Craft.'

'I had no idea. What about our chief and your cousin, His Royal Highness the Duke of Cambridge. Is he a Mason?'

'No, he isn't. It may be that his – how shall I put it? – unconventional family life disqualifies him from membership. We Masons, after all, are assumed to be respectable people, following some reputable calling, and of generally good morals and personal behaviour. We're not expected to be angels, of course – that is hardly a description that is suitable for Papa – but what is known of us must, on the whole, be to our credit.'

'I see,' said George. 'It seems the public reputation is more important than the private. But I still don't understand the point of Masonry and why it might be in my interest to join what is, to all intents and purposes, a secret society. Can you enlighten me?'

'Gladly. But first let me tell you what Freemasonry is *not*. It is not a political society, a religion, or even a trades' organization, despite its descent from the Freemasons of the Middle Ages who built all our churches and castles. Instead it admits men of all political views, religions and social classes; though, as I say, they must be respectable.'

'That sounds reasonable.'

'Yes, and another thing it is not is a *secret* society. Such bodies tend to conceal their purpose and aims, and the identity of their members. We do not. Once a year, every lodge sends a full list of its members to the clerk of the peace. Moreover, we freely proclaim our aims and objects. We have some secrets, of course, but they are chiefly to do with practice and ritual, and have no sinister application. Does that make sense?'

'Yes, I think it does. What, though, are these aims you mention?'

'To practise the three grand principles of Brotherly Love, Charity and Truth. The first two are self-evident. The last signifies an unswerving honesty of thought and deed to ourselves, our neighbours and our God.'

'It all sounds very laudable. Is it also fair to say that one Mason will always help another, and that the Masons in general look after their own?'

'Yes, I think it is.'

'Even if a Mason has committed a crime?'

'Ah,' said the prince. 'Well, now you're entering murky waters. Of course a criminal cannot become a Mason. But what if a Mason commits a crime . . . what then? Should he be handed over to the authorities and tried by a court of law? Yes he should. What I suspect *actually* happens is that his fellow Masons rally round.'

'Do you mean they'd try to cover up his crime?'

'No, I don't think they'd go that far. But they might help with mitigation, and suchlike. You do ask some odd questions. Take it from me: Freemasonry is a force for good. Masons respect the law, and any help they give each other is usually above board.'

'I understand,' said George.

'So, you'll join us? I could put you forward at my lodge, if you want.'

'That's very good of you to offer, Your Royal Highness. Let me think it over.'

'Of course. Is there anything else?'

'Yes, as it happens, there is. You've read in the papers, I'm sure, that two more murders were committed in Whitechapel the other night.'

'Yes, I heard about them. Horrible, simply horrible.'

'Now I have a question to ask you, Your Royal Highness, that I hope you won't find impertinent. Since the discovery of the torn note with the regimental crest, Sir Charles Warren has been anxious to ensure that not even the tiniest ray of suspicion should fall upon you, for obvious reasons. So he's asked me to get an assurance from you that you were not in Whitechapel at the time of the recent murders. Presumably I can give him that assurance?'

'Of course you can. I was at home, if memory serves. It was early last Sunday, wasn't it? Yes, I was definitely at home. I haven't been back to Whitechapel since you warned me off.'

'You're certain?'

'Yes, of course I'm certain. I'm not a fool. And, I have to say, I resent the imputation from the commissioner, and from you, that I might in any way be involved.'

'Neither of us thinks you were,' said George. 'On the contrary, we're looking for proof that you were not, because that will end all speculation. So, to that end, is there anyone who can vouch for your whereabouts on Saturday evening and Sunday morning?'

'Yes, as it happens. There is. I was at The Osiers with Harry, Jim and Monty. They'll vouch for me.'

'Excellent. Thank you, Your Royal Highness. That will be all.'

The prince rose and saluted. In doing so, he revealed that his right cuff was missing a gold button. George's jaw fell open. He'd meant to ask about the button but had forgotten all about it. Probably he didn't want to know the answer – but there it was, staring him in the face.

'Is something the matter, Major Hart? You look as if you've seen a ghost.'

'No, w-well yes, actually,' he stammered, heart racing. 'You're missing a button.'

The prince looked sheepish. 'Yes, I know, sir, I'm sorry. I only noticed it was missing after I'd left Marlborough House this morning. I'll get it fixed this very day.'

Once the prince had left, George put his head in his hands. His job was to protect the heir apparent and, until now, despite mounting evidence to the contrary, he had wanted to believe that this charming, likeable man could not be a brutal murderer. But the prince's missing button, while still short of absolute proof, was yet another indication that he might be involved in some capacity. Slowly but surely, with each passing day, his faith in the prince's innocence was being eroded. He needed to know for certain.

*

Returning home that evening, George found a letter with an E1 postmark on the floor of the hall. He tore it open and read:

With regard to Prince Albert Victor's forays into Whitechapel, I suggest you ask the Pole Aaron Kosminski. He lives with his sister and brother-in-law at 3 Sion Square, Whitechapel. He knows the prince.

There was no signature. George wondered who had sent the note and for what purpose. His immediate thought was that the author was a crank and that to take the letter seriously would be a waste of time. Then again, how would a crank know about the prince's 'forays' or that he, George, had been investigating them? It had to be someone he knew, and who knew his address. He resolved to show the letter to Sergeant Fletcher and ask his advice.

Next day he did just that, asking: 'Where is Sion Square?'

'Just south of the junction between Whitechapel High Street and Whitechapel Road, and not far from Dutfield's Yard where Liz Stride was murdered.'

'Who do you think sent the note?'

'I don't know,' replied Fletcher. 'Perhaps someone who suspects the prince and Kosminski are up to no good, or is simply trying to get them into trouble. Either way, we need to pay Kosminski a visit.'

12

Sion Square, Whitechapel

It was raining as they entered the west side of Sion Square, off Union Street, and walked towards the lower numbers that backed onto Whitechapel High Street. To their right, in the centre of the square, was a small, well-tended communal garden, guarded by iron railings, and lined on three sides by neat, terraced two-storey red-brick houses, their windows clean and their doorsteps scrubbed. 'Good neighbourhood?' asked George.

'Not bad for Whitechapel,' responded Fletcher. 'Most of the residents are Jewish tradesmen.'

They stopped outside number 3 and knocked. The door was opened by a pretty woman with a broad face and high cheekbones. She looked nervous. 'Can I help?' she asked with a foreign accent.

Fletcher stepped forward, showing his identity card. 'We're detectives from the Metropolitan Police's CID, inquiring into the Whitechapel murders. We're checking on the recent movement of all males who live in the area. Can you tell me your name and the names and occupations of all the men who live here?'

The woman blinked rapidly. 'Have we done something wrong?'

'No, no. There's nothing to worry about. We're just making inquiries. Your name please?'

'Betsy Abrahams. I live with my husband Woolf, a tailor, and daughter Rebecca.'

'How old is your daughter?'

'Six.'

'Does anyone else live here?'

'No . . .' she said, before adding, 'but my brother is staying for short time.'

'His name?'

'Aaron Kosminski.'

'Occupation?'

'He cuts hair.'

'Is he here now?'

'No, he's out walking.'

'Well, could we come in? We'd like to ask some more questions and have a look around.'

They were shown into the simply furnished front parlour and seated round a small table. 'Tell me about your family history, Mrs Abrahams,' said Fletcher. 'When did you come to this country?'

Betsy explained, in halting English, that she'd arrived in England seven years earlier, having emigrated with her family from their native Polish Russia. They had been living in cramped conditions in a small shtetl near Lublin, within the Jewish Pale of Settlement, but were forced to flee by violent anti-Semitic pogroms. They had seen terrible things and were lucky to get out with their lives, she explained, but Aaron was the worse affected. Ever since, he had been withdrawn and moody.

'Has he ever been violent?' asked George.

'No, no,' said Betsy, shaking her head firmly. 'Definitely not. He once got excited and shouted. But it wasn't serious and I calmed him. He wouldn't hurt his family.'

'Did he threaten you?'

She looked wary, as if worried her brother would get into trouble. 'No, not really,' she said at last.

'What do you mean "not really"?'

'I mean we all lose our temper. It's normal.'

'Has he ever threatened you or your family with a knife?' asked Fletcher.

Betsy frowned, as if the question was ridiculous. But her delay in answering was telling. 'No, he has never done that.'

George and Fletcher looked at each other. 'Has he ever been in trouble with the police?' asked George.

She shook her head. Before they could ask more questions, the front door opened and the subject of their conversation appeared. He was short and powerfully built, a handsome young man with dark hair and a dark brown moustache. Both George and Fletcher were struck by how similar he was to the descriptions given by Smith and Schwartz. George introduced himself and Fletcher as CID detectives and said they were investigating the Whitechapel murders. Kosminski looked alarmed. 'Why do you want to speak to me?'

'We're not accusing you of anything. We'd just like to know where you were on the nights of the recent murders: sixth/seventh and thirtieth/thirty-first of August, seventh/eighth and twenty-ninth/thirtieth September?'

'I don't know exactly. I was here I think.'

'Can anyone verify that?'

'Yes I can,' said Betsy. 'He was home on all those dates. He stays here at night. Rarely goes out.'

It seemed odd to George that she could be so certain without checking a diary or some other written record. 'You know that for sure?' he asked.

'Yes.'

'And you'd be prepared to make a formal statement to that effect?'

'Yes.'

'Good. We'll do that in a moment. I have one more question for Mr Kosminski,' said George, turning to face the young Pole. 'Have you ever met His Royal Highness Prince Albert Victor?'

Kosminski hesitated, looking to his sister for guidance. She nodded her head imperceptibly. 'Yes,' he said after a long pause.

'In what capacity?'

'I cut his hair.'

'You cut his hair?' said George, momentarily nonplussed.

'Yes. I first met him in Trumper's barber's shop in West End where I worked. He was customer. When I lost my job for being late, he wanted me to keep cutting his hair and would visit me in East End.'

'He would come to Whitechapel to get his hair cut?'

'Yes.'

'Whereabouts exactly?'

'Here.'

'You cut his hair here, in this house?'

'Yes. My sister and brother-in-law work in day so the house is empty.'

'When was the last time you saw him?'

'A few weeks ago. I don't remember the day.'

'Do you have an appointment book?'

'No. He sends a note with the date and time. I confirm by post.'

'Do you have the last note?'

'No. He told me destroy them.'

George changed tack. 'How would you describe your relationship with the prince? Are you friends?'

'We are friendly enough. He likes my haircuts.'

'Do you ever socialize together? Meet for a drink?'

'Well . . . uh . . . maybe.'

'Well do you or don't you? It's a simple question.'

'We have done it a few times.'

'So you're friends.'

'Maybe.'

'We'll take that statement now, Mrs Abrahams,' said George. 'But before we leave, do you mind if we take a look round the house?'

'No. Please do.'

Thirty minutes later, having searched the house and found nothing, George and Sergeant Fletcher conferred in a nearby pub. 'What do you think?' asked George.

'I don't know what to think,' said Fletcher. 'It all seems a little convenient that you were sent the note about Kosminski. Then again, he does match the description of one of the possible killers, is friendly with the prince and lives in Whitechapel. He's also something of a loner who has threatened members of his family. Who knows why. He may have become unhinged after witnessing the pogroms. Terrible things were done to Jews, by all accounts: rapes, murder, you name it.'

'Yes, and don't forget that his given name begins with "A". If the prince *was* the author of the torn letter, then he might have been writing to Kosminski to arrange their next meeting.'

'You asked if they were friends, Major Hart. Do you think they might be more than that?'

'Are you asking if they're lovers? It's certainly a possibility. Why else would the prince meet Kosminski for a drink? But try telling your superiors that the prince and the pauper routinely meet for a haircut and sexual relations and they'd laugh in your face.'

Fletcher chuckled. 'They would indeed, sir.'

'The real question is, of course, are they murderers? As you say, Kosminski matches the descriptions given by various witnesses of the last man seen with Martha Turner, Annie Chapman and Liz Stride; whereas the prince could be the taller man with a dark moustache who was seen with or near Turner, Stride and Eddowes. He's also linked to the Turner, Chapman and Eddowes murders by his handwriting and his regiment, the Tenth Hussars. When I last saw the prince he was missing a button from the cuff of his tunic. That button matches the one found beside Eddowes.'

'Why didn't you tell me this before?'

'I was going to. I got sidetracked by the letter naming Kosminski. But you know now. Do you have a local map?'

Fletcher shook his head. 'But I know where to get one. There's a stationer's at the end of the street. Wait here. I won't be long.'

'Can you also get a pencil and a piece of string?'

Fletcher was about to ask why, but thought better of it. Instead he nodded and headed for the door. George was still trying to mull over the horrifying possibility that the prince might be a murderer when Fletcher returned with all three items and spread the map on the table.

'All right,' said George, 'now I need you to mark the murder sites and also Kosminski's address.'

Fletcher did so, using the pencil.

'So,' said George, scanning the map, 'four were committed north of the Whitechapel Road; and just one – Stride's in Berner Street – to the south. Is there any difference between the neighbourhoods to the north and south of the Whitechapel Road?'

'Yes,' said Fletcher. 'I would say there is. The area to the south where we are – chiefly Leman Street and Commercial Road – is mostly law-abiding, clean and relatively respectable. Many of the inhabitants are Jews. The streets to the north, on the other hand – I'm talking about streets like Dorset, Flower and Dean, Thrawl and Wentworth – are among the most squalid in the capital, infested as they are with dosshouses, prostitutes and petty criminals.'

George traced his finger from Mitre Square in the City to Buck's Row off the Whitechapel Road. 'What is the distance between these two locations?' he asks.

Fletcher checked the map's scale. 'Just under a mile.'

'That's the biggest gap between any two murder sites,' said George. 'Now, if I mark the mid-point between Mitre Square and Buck's Row, and use the pencil and string to draw a circle with a radius of half a mile – ' he paused to complete the action – 'like this, you can see that all the other murders took place within this area. Note, too, that Kosminski's dwelling in Sion Square is not far from the centre of the circle. So my question is: do most murders take place reasonably close to the perpetrator's home?'

'In my experience, yes. A habitual murderer will usually maraud out from home, killing as opportunity allows. As his home is in the respectable bit of Spitalfields, it makes sense that he ventures north of the Whitechapel Road to kill.'

'What about Stride? She was killed south of the divide, just a few streets from Kosminki's house. Why would he take such a risk?'

'Opportunity, I don't know . . .'

'His sister says he couldn't have done it.'

'Well she would, wouldn't she? She's family and could be lying to protect him.'

'So what next?'

'Well,' said Fletcher, 'I agree with you that it's all highly suspicious, but the evidence we have so far to implicate either the prince or Kosminski is circumstantial at best. We need more concrete proof, but how to get it? I just don't know.' He thought for a moment. 'There is something obvious we could do.'

'Go on.'

'As a green detective I was told by my boss, Inspector Lyall, that the simplest solution is often the best. So, with that in mind, why don't we tail the pair of them for a week or so, watching their respective movements at night. I'll keep an eye on Kosminski; you do the same for His Royal Highness. That way we'll know if they get up to mischief.'

'Yes,' said George, 'and we'll also know if they don't. It could be a complete waste of time. What if another murder takes place while we're tailing them?'

'Well then, we'll know they're not involved.'

'Yes, I suppose that's something. All right, let's give it a try for a week or two.'

*

George and Fletcher did just that and, for a while, there was nothing to report: the prince stayed away from Whitechapel and Kosminski hardly ventured out from 3 Sion Square. Then, late one evening, George was waiting near the main entrance to Marlborough House when he saw the prince emerge in dark, nondescript clothes, hail a hansom cab and head east. He quickly flagged down a separate cab and instructed the driver to follow.

George's driver almost lost sight of the prince's cab in heavy traffic in Trafalgar Square. But thereafter there were few wheeled vehicles on the road and it was a simple task to keep within twenty or thirty yards of the other cab as it continued east along Fleet Street and into the City, passing St Paul's Cathedral and Mitre Square, the site of the most recent murder, and on into Whitechapel. It finally came to a halt outside a pub on Gowers Walk, south of Commercial Road and not far from Kosminski's house in Sion Square. George waited inside his own cab while the prince got out, paid his driver and went inside the pub. He then got down and made his way to a darkened courtyard opposite the pub where he could observe the comings and goings without attracting attention. It reeked of urine, and worse, but that suited George because it would deter other loiterers.

George had been in position for barely five minutes when Kosminski arrived from the direction of his house and entered the pub. Moving cautiously, George crossed the deserted road to sneak a look through the pub's window. The main bar was full of drunken revellers and, for a time, George could not see the prince and Kosminski among them. Had they left through another door? he wondered. But then a thickset man vacated the bar with a tray of drinks, revealing the pair on stools beyond him. They were deep in conversation, their heads as close as conspirators.

Turning back to his hiding place, George almost collided with Fletcher. 'Hell's teeth!' he hissed. 'Don't creep up on me like that.'

'Are they both inside?' whispered Fletcher.

'Yes. We can wait over there,' said George, indicating the courtyard. 'If the prince leaves first, I'll follow him. You do the same with Kosminski.'

An hour later and George and Fletcher were warding off the autumn chill by tapping their toes and rubbing their arms. A number of people had left the pub but their quarry had not. George was considering a trip to a nearby café for a cup of tea when the pub door opened and Kosminski emerged. He paused briefly to don a flat cap and then headed in the direction of his home. Fletcher followed at a discreet distance. Soon after, the prince exited the pub and headed north towards Commercial Road. After a short pause, George set off after him. But he had covered barely a few yards when a man walked out from a side alley and barred his path. He was holding a pistol.

'Remember me?' said the man in a thick Irish accent. 'You're a hard man to find.'

George's heart began to race. Squinting in the gloom he recognized the long dark hair and pale skin: it was Liam Kelly, the young Fenian from the pub in Kilburn. He felt sick. This must be revenge for the foiled assassination attempt. But how on earth had Liam found him in Whitechapel? Had he discovered his address and followed him from home? The only minor consolation for George was that Liam hadn't recognized the prince. He considered drawing the two-shot Derringer from his shoulder holster. But, before he could do so, Liam leant forward, put his hand inside George's coat and recovered the gun. 'Move,' he said, nodding down the street.

As George began walking, he tried to imagine why the Fenian hadn't shot him already. Perhaps they wanted to interrogate him first and then kill him. Or did they intend for him a slow and painful end to avenge their comrades? Either way they would not allow him to live. His only hope, he realized, was escape – and the sooner the better. He knew from his army training that guards are at their least vigilant when they first take a prisoner. So he waited until he was told to turn left and, half hidden by the corner of a building, he swung his right arm back in a blur of movement, catching Liam flush on the temple. The Irishman staggered backwards. But before George could close, he recovered and re-pointed the gun. 'You'll pay for that,' he said, wiping a trickle of blood from his mouth. 'The boss man wanted you taken alive. But I'll say you tried to run.'

Liam cocked the hammer and George knew he had just seconds to live. Instinctively he raised his right palm to deflect the bullet. It was a last futile gesture. He could see himself lying lifeless on the pavement. He thought of Lucy and his son Jake; of his mother and even the man he thought must be his father; of his friends Jake and Ilderim. All the people he'd loved. He wondered how it had come to this, shot down in the street by a young Irish fanatic. The Fenian's forefinger whitened as it pulled on the trigger.

'Don't shoot him, Liam!'

The Fenian hesitated. Out of the dark strode Mary Kelly, the pretty young prostitute George had given a shilling to on the night of the double killing. 'Don't kill him, Liam!' she implored. 'I know him.'

'Stay out of this, Mary. He's an undercover copper who pretended to support the cause. He set us up and cost us two good men. Now he's going to die.'

'I don't know about that. All I know is he was good to me. Gave me a shilling so I could get a bed for the night. Please don't shoot him. He's a good man.'

While Liam hesitated, Mary moved between him and George, her palms out.

'Get out the way, Mary!'

She shook her head.

'Move or I'll shoot you too!'

'No. Despite all that's happened, you wouldn't shoot your own sister.'

'Wouldn't I? You asked for it!'

'Police!' came a shout from their left. 'What's going on?'

They could see a light fast approaching. Liam fired first at the policeman and then at George, the bullet thwacking into the wall near his head in a puff of red brick dust. Then Liam ran off.

'Police!' shouted the constable as he gave chase. 'Stop!' But his pursuit was half-hearted – he was unarmed, after all – and he soon lost track of his quarry in the maze of dark alleys. He returned to find George comforting Mary, who was still shaking. 'Is she all right?' asked the policeman.

'Yes. She'll be fine. Thank you, Constable,' said George, 'your arrival was very timely.'

'Glad to help. Now, if you don't mind accompanying me to the station on Commercial Street, I need to take a statement.'

'Can it wait until tomorrow? My friend is a little upset and I'd like to get her back to her room.'

The policeman frowned. 'I'm sure you would, sir, but first I need that statement.'

'I don't think that will be necessary,' said George, taking his SIB identification card from his pocket and showing it to the constable. 'I've been working undercover and that man must have guessed who I am. He's a Fenian. Nothing for you to worry about. Do I make myself clear?'

'You do, sir. Anything I can do to help?'

'You've done quite enough already. Goodnight, Constable.'

'Goodnight, sir.'

Once the policeman had gone, George took Mary into the pub for a brandy. Seated at a corner table, her hands still shaking from the shock of the near fatal encounter with her brother, she poured out her life story: how she had been born in Limerick, Ireland, and moved with her family to Carmarthenshire when she was just eight. A headstrong girl, she had clashed repeatedly with her drunken father and was just fifteen when she met and moved in with a young Welsh collier. A year later they married and it seemed, for a time, that she would live modestly but happily in the mining village of Garnant in the beautiful Amman valley, just north of Swansea on the edge of the Brecon Beacons. But her husband Rhodri – five years her senior – was killed in a roof fall, and from that date, in 1882, her fortunes had plummeted. First she went to live with a cousin in Cardiff who introduced her to prostitution. From there she moved to London and, after a brief and unhappy stint as a charwoman, worked in a high-class bordello in the West End.

'Most of them treated me well,' said Mary as she remembered happier times. 'I had bonnets to wear and rode around Knightsbridge in a horse and carriage. One gentleman even took me with him to Paris. But all good things . . .'

She explained how she had eventually drifted to Whitechapel, living first with a mason's plasterer called Joseph Fleming, and then with her current partner, Joseph Barnett, in a single room at 13 Miller's Court, off Dorset Street. But after Barnett lost his job, Kelly returned to prostitution. Objecting to her habit of bringing back to the room both clients and fellow prostitutes, Barnett had recently moved out.

She had only seen Liam, her younger brother, once since she'd left home. That was a couple of years earlier, when he'd tracked her down to Whitechapel and tried to get her to

give up prostitution. He told her he was a Fenian dedicated
to achieving a united Ireland, and that if she helped them by
seducing senior policemen for them to murder, she would be
given money and a place to stay. 'I refused,' said Mary. 'I told
him, "I can't be a whore and a party to murder!" He was
furious.'

'I bet he was,' said George. 'But you made the right decision. If you'd done what he asked, you'd have paid the price
sooner or later.'

Mary nodded as she took another sip of brandy. 'That's
my story. What about you? Liam said you're an undercover
copper. So I was right all along.'

'Yes. You were. The reason your brother was trying to kill
me is because I recently infiltrated his group of Fenians and
foiled a plot to kill a member of the royal family. Two of the
Fenians died in the attempt and, not surprisingly, they want
revenge.'

'I see. But why are you here?'

'In Whitechapel? Because I'm helping the CID catch the
killer known as Jack the Ripper.'

'And are you close to catching him?'

'Yes, I think we are. I can't go into details, for obvious
reasons, but we have some suspects. I was tailing one of them
when your brother intervened.'

'Why don't you just arrest him?'

'Because we don't have any real evidence. It's all circumstantial, meaning it suggests the person is the culprit but
wouldn't prove his guilt in a court of law. What we need is
proof: a murder weapon, a piece of the killer's clothing, that
sort of thing. Or we need to catch him in the act.'

Mary paused to think. 'I've an idea,' she said at last. 'I'll
help you catch the Ripper if you give me some money.

Enough to leave London and start a new life. You can use me as bait.'

'How do you mean?'

'Well, you know who you think he is and what he looks like. Give me that information and, if I meet him, I'll take him back to my place and you'll be waiting to pounce. Easy.'

George had to admire Mary's courage; but he also knew that such a desperate course of action might end in disaster. 'No,' he said, shaking his head firmly, 'absolutely not. It's far too dangerous.'

Mary tried to persuade him, saying she was happy to take the risk. But he would not be swayed. 'I appreciate the offer, Mary, I really do. But you've done enough for one night.' He looked at his watch: it was just before midnight. 'It's late. Let's drink up and I'll walk you home. It's the least I can do.'

They finished their drinks, left the pub and, with Mary leading the way, walked up Church Lane to Whitechapel High Street, where the earlier throng of late-night carousers and street vendors had thinned considerably. As they turned right up Commercial Street, a garishly painted middle-aged prostitute recognized Mary and called out: 'Hello girl! Looks like you've done all right for yourself!'

'Ignore her,' said Mary. 'She's just jealous.'

A couple of hundred yards later, Mary turned left into Dorset Street. It was a typical Spitalfield slum: dark and dirty, and largely comprised of tenements or common lodging houses, the latter offering beds for fourpence a night. Situated just behind the street were several narrow courts, mostly inhabited by prostitutes. Mary lived off one called Miller's Court on the north side of the street, directly behind number 26. She stopped outside the narrow stone-flagged passage, just three feet wide and twenty long, that led to her door. 'This is my place. I've a furnished room off the court that costs me the princely sum of four and six a week. Want to see it?'

The right side of Mary's face was bathed in the yellow glow of a nearby gas lamp. A half-smile played on her lips and, to George, she looked extremely attractive. 'Well? Are you coming or not?'

He was tempted. Lucy and Jake's sudden departure had left him smarting, and a bit of female company was just what he needed. No one need know. But just as quickly he came to his senses. 'I-I . . .' he stammered. 'No, I'd better not.'

'In that case, give us a kiss. Least you can do.' She put her hands on his arms and stood up on tiptoes, her lips reaching for his. He responded with the demurest peck on her lips, conscious that his willpower was fading fast.

'That it? I got better kisses from my dad!'

George chuckled. 'I trust you did *not*! But, yes, sorry, I really must go, and thank you again for what you did. It was very brave.'

'It was nothing. He wouldn't have shot his own sister.'

'You sure about that?'

She laughed. 'No. But I don't think he would. We're blood, after all.'

Her words took him back almost nine years, to that moment in the fort at Kabul when Major FitzGeorge, a man George suspected was his first cousin, had threatened to shoot him if he didn't hand over a valuable jewelled clasp. He had thought of mentioning their probable kinship, but chose not to because he didn't think it would have made a difference. Was he right? Or was Mary right? Was blood thicker than water?

Mary interrupted his musings. 'Is something the matter?'

'Er, no nothing,' said George. 'I'll be going, but if you . . .' He paused, trying to think of the right words.

'If I what?'

'If you need any help, ever, I'll gladly give it.' He reached into his inner pocket, pulled out a calling card and gave it to her. She turned it towards the gaslight and read:

Major George Hart VC
69 Alnwick Grove
Hammersmith
London W14

'George Hart, eh?' said Mary. 'That's a nice name. But what does VC mean?'

'You don't know?'

'I wouldn't be asking if I did.'

'It means I've been awarded the Victoria Cross for "conspicuous bravery" in the face of the enemy.'

'What enemy?'

'Afghan tribesmen.'

'Never heard of them. So you're a hero, are you?'

'Something like that.'

'Well that makes two of us. Goodnight George Hart.'

'Goodnight.'

13

69 Alnwick Grove, Hammersmith

Jack Fletcher arrived early and George told him, over coffee, about the dramatic events of the night before: the appearance of the armed Fenian bent on revenge, the intervention of his sister and their narrow escape. 'The end result,' concluded George, 'was that I lost track of the prince. What about you? Did you discover where Kosminski went after leaving the pub?'

Fletcher nodded. 'He went straight to his sister's house on Sion Square. I waited outside until all the lights were out. Then I went home. I'm sorry that I wasn't there to help you, Major Hart. I had no idea you were in mortal danger.'

'How could you have known? The main thing is that I emerged with my skin intact, thanks to the Fenian's sister. Now let's get back to this Ripper business. We've seen with our own eyes that the prince and Kosminski are close. But are they murderers? That's the question. They certainly fit the descriptions and it would be easy to assume that the reason for their meeting last night was for Kosminski to warn the prince that the police knew of their friendship. Did he also suggest that, for the foreseeable future, they needed to stop meeting?'

'The thought did cross my mind,' said Fletcher. 'But we also need to consider another development in the case. Inspector Abberline has just received the contents of a brown paper parcel that was originally sent to Mr George Lusk, the head of the Whitechapel Vigilance Committee, at his home address in Mile End.'

'I haven't heard of this Vigilance Committee. What is its purpose?'

'As it sounds: to keep a watchful eye out for the Ripper. The members are all local tradesmen. Lusk, for example, is a builder. They're public-spirited men who mean well. But to us they're a bloody nuisance as they constantly roam the streets at night, looking for suspicious activity, and it's hard to tell them from the actual murderers. Anyway, Lusk was sent this package which contained a short letter, allegedly from the murderer, and half a female kidney.'

'A what?'

'A female kidney.'

'Wasn't one of the victims found with part of her kidney removed?'

'Yes, Catherine Eddowes. She was the second of the two victims on the thirtieth.'

'Has the kidney been tested?'

'Yes. Abberline sent it for examination by Dr Thomas Openshaw, curator of the Pathological Museum at the London Hospital, who declared that it belonged to a female, was part of the left kidney and showed signs of damage from alcohol abuse. Like a lot of prostitutes, Eddowes was known to be a heavy drinker. Openshaw was also of the opinion that the woman probably died at the same time the Mitre Square murder was committed. So it's possible – in fact

175

probable – that it's Eddowes' missing kidney, and that the writer of the letter is the killer. The other reason for thinking this is that the renal artery is about three inches long: two inches remained in Eddowes' body, while attached to this kidney is the remaining inch. I think it's genuine.'

'Do you have a facsimile of the note?'

'Yes,' said Fletcher, taking a folded piece of paper from his pocket and handing it to George. It read:

From hell

Mr Lusk
  Sor
  I send you half the
Kidne I took from one women
prasarved it for you tother piece I
fried and ate it was very nise I
may send you the bloody knif that
took it out if you only wate a whil
longer
  Signed   Catch me when
you can
Mishter Lusk

George could see that the spelling, grammar and punctuation were very poor, as if it had been written by someone barely literate – but was that deliberate? It certainly didn't resemble in any way the handwriting on the Ripper letters and the note found beside Chapman. 'Where was the parcel posted?' he asked.

'We can't be absolutely certain because the postmark is too indistinct. The only letters that *are* decipherable are "OND", which obviously denote "LONDON". But as it was only franked once, it was probably posted in the district in which it was received: the Eastern District. Lusk's address is 1 Alderney Road, Mile End, just down the road from the killings.'

'Yes,' said George, 'and not far from Kosminski in Sion Square. My guess is that the writer is pretending to be more uneducated than he actually is. Then again, Kosminski is a foreigner by birth and his English is not good. So what next? If we continue to keep tabs on the prince and Kosminski, it could take weeks for them to make their next move. And what if it's not them?'

'Then the real killers will strike again, but at least the prince and Kosminski will be exonerated. Meanwhile my colleagues in the CID are making half-hearted inquiries at best, so it really is up to us. We need to find a way to lure the killers from the shadows. But how?'

After a pause, Fletcher said: 'What if one of us dressed up as a prostitute?'

'Are you serious? I'm over six feet and you don't have the looks. Sorry, but it's true.'

'You clearly haven't seen the state of some of the ladies on the streets. As for my phiz, they won't even notice in the dark.'

'No, it would never work with one of us as bait.'

'What about using a real prostitute?'

George thought of Mary's offer, but again rejected it without telling Fletcher. She was a brave, spirited girl who deserved better than the hand-to-mouth life of a prostitute. But he couldn't bring himself to put her in such mortal danger. 'No,' said George, firmly. 'There has to be another way.'

*

George was still wondering what that might be when, later that day, he encountered the prince at the weekly regimental riding school in Knightsbridge. 'Afternoon, sir,' said the prince, bringing his horse to a halt in front of George and saluting smartly. 'I hope I won't let you down today. I've been working hard to improve my drill.'

George returned his salute. 'I'm glad to hear it.' He looked around. There was no one in hearing distance. 'There's something I need to ask you on an extra-regimental subject.'

The prince nodded. 'Go ahead, sir.'

'A contact in the Whitechapel CID tells me that someone who resembles you was spotted in Gowers Walk last night. Was it you?'

The prince hesitated for just a moment, and as he did so George scanned his face for signs of nervousness or anxiety. But there was no rapid blinking, no perspiration, nothing. Instead the prince looked him in the eye and said: 'No, sir. It wasn't me. I haven't been to Whitechapel for weeks. Nothing has changed since you last asked.'

My God, thought George, *you're a cool one. If I didn't know you were lying, I'd be completely fooled. But I do, and sooner or later you're going to have to tell the truth.* He was tempted to confront him then and there. But he chose not to because he knew they couldn't prove the prince had done anything wrong. 'I'm glad to hear it,' said George at last. 'Please keep it that way for the foreseeable future.'

A couple of hours later, as George was about to leave his office for home, he was handed a note from HRH the Duke of Cambridge. 'My dear Major Hart,' it read, 'there is something I would like to discuss with you as a matter of urgency. Please come to my private residence at 6 Queen Street, Mayfair, at 9 p.m.'

George thought back to the last time he had visited the commander-in-chief at home in the spring of 1879. The note summoning him had contained remarkably similar language to this latest one, and the evening had ended with him agreeing to a request by Lord Beaconsfield, the Prime Minister, to undertake a secret mission to Afghanistan to locate the Prophet's Cloak and head off a holy war. *I just hope*, he said to himself, *that the bombshell the duke is intending to drop this time is not quite as momentous. Might it even be a personal matter, with the duke finally coming clean about my paternity?* George doubted it, but even the prospect made him nervously excited.

With just enough time to return home and change, George took a hansom cab from Kensington to Hammersmith. He found a letter, with Lucy's distinctive left-leaning handwriting, waiting for him on the doormat. He felt his heart beating as he ripped open the envelope and pulled out a single sheet of writing paper. It read:

Dear George,

I've composed this letter many times in my mind, but each time I've delayed writing it in the hope that I'd hear from you first. But there has been no word from you.

I want you to know that I hated leaving when I knew you needed my help and, more importantly, were doing work that was highly dangerous. But that's exactly why I had to go. My first loyalty as a mother will always be to Jake. Your actions put both of us at risk and that, for me, is unacceptable.

Please don't think I'm trying to avenge myself for your abandonment of me in Cape Town and again in Pietermaritzburg. I'm not. You came back for me, eventually, and that's all that matters. I love you deeply. But a mother's love for a child is different: it's boundless and unbreakable, or at least it is for me. So when I was forced to choose between your welfare and Jake's, I didn't hesitate.

That doesn't mean the decision wasn't painful – it was and is. I'm sorry I had to go, but I hope you understand why. I'm also sorry for adding to our financial worries by my occasional bout of excessive spending. But I don't accept that I'm 'equally responsible', as you put it, for our financial difficulties.

Barely an hour goes by without me wondering if you're safe and well. I pray to God you are, and that it isn't long before your work in London is done, and we can be reunited as a family.

Jake, you won't be surprised to hear, is the apple of his grandparents' eyes. He climbs the same trees I used to, and swims in the same river, though the water is much colder than I would have put up with! He even snared a rabbit. I felt that was a good omen for what you're doing. I hope I'm right.

Please write when you have a moment.

All my love
Lucy

As George reached the end of the note, a single tear fell onto and smudged Lucy's name. It was a beautiful letter that had moved him intensely, and never more so than when he read Lucy's declaration of her boundless love for Jake. His mother had given him much the same kind of love, and it had been the rock he had clung to as a young, fatherless boy. Jake had always known both parents, but for long passages of time, when George was on campaign, he too had had to make do with just a mother.

George vowed to spend less time away from home in the future and, in the meantime, do everything he could to catch those responsible for the Whitechapel murders. Then, and only then, could he relinquish his duties in London and return to his family.

*

It was just before nine when George reached the Duke of Cambridge's double-fronted townhouse in Mayfair. The door was opened by a footman who told George that the duke was delayed and would be home in half an hour. In the meantime, added the footman, would Major Hart follow him up to Mrs FitzGeorge's rooms on the second floor because the lady of the house wished to speak to him?'

'Lead on,' said George. He had long wanted to meet the woman who bore many similarities to his mother, not the least of which was that they had both fallen in love with the same man. George knew from snippets in the press that the duke had met the then Louisa Fairbrother, the daughter of a Bow Street printer, at a ball the Duchess of Sutherland gave to celebrate Queen Victoria's marriage to Prince Albert in the winter of 1840. She was then a celebrated actress and an accomplished dancer, famed for her classical beauty, raven hair and elegant deportment. They eventually married in secret in 1847, by which time they already had two sons and Louisa was pregnant with a third. Needless to say, neither this illegal marriage – all royal princes had to receive the permission of the monarch to marry – nor its illegitimate offspring had ever been acknowledged by the Queen who, officially at least, pretended that Louisa did not exist. Yet

Mrs FitzGeorge, as she was known, was said to have borne her exclusion from high society with equanimity, preferring the cosy domesticity of her life with the duke in the house he had bought for her in Mayfair.

George had heard that her one fear was that the duke would eventually leave her for another woman. This hadn't happened, though the duke had had affairs with a number of women who included, George now believed, his actress mother Emma Hart. After more than forty years of marriage, Mrs FitzGeorge's health had begun to fail and she was said to be mostly bedridden, which explained why George was being taken up to her suite of rooms on the second floor, and not to the spacious drawing room on the first.

Passing first through a small sitting room, they entered a simply furnished but beautifully decorated bedroom with theatrical scenes covering the walls. Mrs FitzGeorge was lying in bed, an open book in her right hand. Though pale and drawn, and, George estimated, at least seventy years of age, she was still an extraordinarily handsome woman with high cheekbones and green, almond-shaped eyes. 'Major Hart,' she said, extending her hand in welcome, 'I'm so glad finally to make your acquaintance.'

George took her hand – small and delicately shaped – and kissed it.

'I know you've come to speak to my husband,' she continued, 'but I couldn't let the opportunity pass without telling you how sorry I am.'

'Whatever for?'

She puffed out her cheeks. 'It's hard for me to admit this, but I've been the cause of much of your unhappiness.'

'Unhappiness? I don't understand.'

'I wouldn't let your father acknowledge you. I was jealous.'

'My father? You're saying – admitting – that my father is your husband the duke?'

'That's exactly what I'm saying. He had a brief affair in Dublin with your mother. I put an end to it; but not before you'd been conceived. I acted because I was jealous of your mother's beauty, and protective of my own sons. But it was unfair on you, and for that I'm truly sorry.'

George sat there, stunned. He had long suspected the duke was his father; but finally to have those suspicions confirmed, by someone who knew, and in such a frank and open manner, was quite a shock.

'Why are telling me this now?'

'Because I don't have long to live, and need to settle my accounts before I leave this earth; and because I know the duke is proud of your achievements, and would love to be able to tell you. He can't, of course. But I can, and now I have.'

'Did you send the note summoning me here?'

'No, the duke did. But I heard he'd been delayed and took the opportunity to speak with you. I hope you don't resent me for it.'

To gather his thoughts, George walked across to the window and looked out into Queen Street. Apart from a couple of carriages, and a smartly dressed couple heading in the direction of Piccadilly, it was empty. 'No,' he said, turning to face her. 'I don't resent you. You did what you felt you had to do. My mother would have done the same.'

'Thank you for saying that. You have every right to be bitter. After all, it was because of me that you grew up without a father; without even knowing who your father is. He's a good man, you know. He just finds it hard to demonstrate his goodness to his family, let alone the world.'

'Did you know he'd set me certain tasks to achieve when I was eighteen?'

'Not at the time. He told me later.'

'It seems an odd way to show affection: to bribe your unacknowledged son to do well.'

'Yes, I suppose it does. It was his way of keeping an eye on you, and of keeping you on the straight and narrow. I have to say it seems to have worked. Our three sons, on the other hand, have done nothing but disappoint him.'

'I met your eldest, Colonel FitzGeorge, in Afghanistan. We didn't see eye to eye.'

'I'm not surprised. Harry was always more interested in money than duty. He left a perfectly good job in the army in eighty-three to write for the press and speculate in the City. In neither has he been a success. Recently he married a divorcee. It's as if he's trying to antagonize his father.'

George scented a whiff of hypocrisy: the duke, after all, was hardly in a position to criticize his son's marriage arrangements, given his own unorthodox union with an actress who had produced five children by three different fathers (including the duke). But he held his tongue.

'I've kept you long enough. My husband will soon return and I don't want him to know we've spoken. I just wanted to apologize for what I've done, and to wish you good luck for the future. You sound like the sort of person who considers adversity a challenge. I admire that trait very much – perhaps because I possess a trace of it myself. Goodbye, George Hart,' she said, taking his hand and giving it a squeeze.

'Goodbye, Mrs FitzGeorge.'

Minutes later, George was standing beside the fireplace in the first-floor drawing room, ruminating on his conversation with Mrs FitzGeorge and nervously excited at the prospect of seeing the man he now knew to be his father. He accepted he was the same person who had got out of bed that morning, with the same prejudices, insecurities and foibles. Yet in one important sense *everything* had changed: his sense of identity. No longer was he a fatherless bastard without connections and history, on the male side at least. He now knew that he had ROYAL BLOOD running in his veins. It was hard to take in and he felt strangely light-headed. *I'm a great-grandson of mad King George III, for God's sake*, he mused, *not to mention the first cousin once removed of the current sovereign Queen Victoria. I'm a member, albeit unrecognized, of the British royal family!*

Such happy thoughts were still swirling through his head when the duke walked in. Not in uniform for a change, he was wearing a grey three-piece suit, white shirt and yellow silk tie. 'I'm sorry to keep you, Major Hart. Drink?'

George looked intently at his father's smiling face with its fleshy cheeks, bulbous nose and bushy white whiskers, and found it hard to see a resemblance to his own. Yet it seemed to be a kind face, and gave George hope that in time they could forge the type of relationship that would make up for the past. 'Thank you, sir. I think I will.'

'Whisky?'

'Please.'

Once they were both seated with their drinks, the duke spoke. 'I asked you here because I've been hearing disturbing rumours that you think Eddy might be connected in some way to the murders in Whitechapel.'

George was taken aback, though on reflection he realized he shouldn't have been. 'May I ask, sir, the source of the rumours?'

'You may indeed. I heard them from Commissioner Warren. He told me that Eddy had been seen in Whitechapel on the night of one of the murders, and that part of a letter written on Tenth Hussars' notepaper was found next to one of the bodies. As Warren had worked with you before, and knew you were Eddy's minder, he asked you to do your best to keep Eddy out of the story. Yet you failed to prevent him from returning to Whitechapel and, worse, you began to suspect him of some sort of involvement in the killings. Is that true?'

'It's a bit more complicated than that, sir. I told the commissioner that, in my opinion, the author of the torn letter was probably an officer of the Tenth, and he asked me to try and identify him by comparing the handwriting with that of my fellow officers. I did so, and the closest match – in fact it was almost identical – was with the prince's hand. When I challenged the prince, he denied it.'

'I'm sure he did. How could you think, for even a moment, that he has anything to do with this?

'At first I didn't, sir. I kept hoping I'd find proof that he couldn't be involved. But it's not just the letter. The prince told me that he was in Whitechapel on at least one other occasion when a prostitute was murdered, and possibly more. A witness to the first killing said that a few hours before the murder she and the victim met two soldiers, one of whom was an officer who matched the prince's description.'

'She said that?'

'No, she just described him.'

'Was the officer the last person seen with the victim?'

'No, the soldier was. But it's possible they were acting in concert. I know this is all supposition, but there is other evidence that points to the murderer having an accomplice.'

'Is there anything else that links the prince to the murders?'

'Yes. A letter purportedly sent from the murderer – and signed "Jack the Ripper" – contained handwriting similar to that of the prince. Then there's the gold button from the cuff of an officer's tunic of the Tenth Hussars that was found next to the last victim. A couple of days later I noticed the prince was missing a similar button.'

'Did you ask him about it?'

'Yes. He said he couldn't remember when and where he'd lost it.'

'And you're inferring from all of this that Eddy, who will one day be King-Emperor, is a murderer? I simply don't believe it. He may not be the sharpest tool, but nor does he have the capacity to kill. He doesn't even like the sight of blood, for goodness' sake!'

'I'm not saying he's a murderer. We simply don't know, yet, and it's possible that he's being set up by someone else. It's a huge mystery that we've yet to solve. But you have to admit, sir, that it all looks very suspicious.'

'It's certainly suspicious. But what possible motive could Eddy have for murdering prostitutes?'

'I've asked myself the same question and I don't have an answer. The best I can offer is that he seems to dislike female prostitutes. I was told by one of his friends that he caught the pox off a lady of the night in Singapore, and that it took him over a year to get rid of it. The same friend said that he regarded most of the *demi-mondaines* in his father's life as temptresses and schemers.'

'And so they are. But it's one thing to dislike such women; quite another to butcher them.'

'Yes. I agree with you entirely, sir. It doesn't seem to make any sense.'

'I take it you've given all this information to Warren? What did he say?'

'To be perfectly honest, sir, I haven't told him everything.'

'Why ever not?'

'Because, to be frank, he's been less than straight in his dealings with me in the past – when, for example, we worked together in the Sinai – and for a long time was uninterested in any indication that the prince might be involved. Until the last pair of murders, he was convinced that a deranged Swiss butcher was solely responsible.'

'Might the Swiss still be one of the culprits?'

'No, not in my opinion. He was under lock and key when the last murders occurred on the thirtieth of September. In any case, the evidence against him was virtually non-existent and he does not match any of the descriptions given by witnesses of the possible killer. Yet the evidence was enough for Warren, and the detective inspector leading the inquiry, to close down all other avenues of inquiry, particularly those that might have focused on the prince. When I told Warren that the prince was the probable author of the torn letter, he said he was convinced the letter was a red herring and that I was to forget all about it.'

'What if he's right? You said yourself it's possible the prince is being made to look as if he's guilty when in fact he's wholly innocent.'

'It is possible. But that doesn't explain why Warren was so quick to pin the blame on the Swiss and ignore *any* other potential culprit or culprits.'

'So what does?'

'I think he wanted to divert attention from the prince.'

'You mean he wanted to blame someone he knew might be innocent to exonerate the prince?'

'Yes, possibly.'

'Even though the murders might continue?'

'Yes.'

'Why?'

'Well, the obvious answer is that he wanted to avoid a scandal that would damage both the royal family and the state. But it's also possible that he was protecting one of his own.'

'What do you mean by that?'

'I mean he could have been – and could still be – protecting a fellow Freemason. Warren admitted to me that he was a member of that secret fraternity. So too are the prince, the prince's father and the inspector leading the inquiry.'

'You know this for a fact, do you?'

'I do, sir.'

'Well I'm *not* a Mason, though I've long suspected that Bertie was. Even so, I have little patience with tales of Masonic conspiracies, Major Hart. I believe in cold, hard facts. From what you've said, there's clearly *some* evidence that links Eddy to the murders; but none of it is conclusive. Warren seems to have done his best to keep Eddy's name out of the press, probably to protect the royal family as much as a fellow Mason. But I am glad that he has done so, and that he alerted me to your involvement. It is imperative that we bring this whole sorry affair to a close as quickly as possible. The longer it goes on, the greater the possibility that Eddy will be implicated in some way. So I ask you: is there any way to catch the killer – and hopefully exonerate Eddy at the same time – that you can think of?'

George thought again of Mary Kelly's offer. He had been loath to involve her, but Lucy's letter had made him more desperate than ever to solve the case. 'There is *something* that might work,' said he, after a long pause. 'But it would involve putting the life of a young lady in extreme danger.'

'Who is this young lady?'

'She's a prostitute, Irish by birth, and she saved my life.'

'Did she now? Well, I'm very glad to hear that, I truly am,' said the duke in a tone that George now recognized as *almost* paternal. 'What exactly is she offering to do?'

'She's offering to act as bait by luring anyone who matches the description of the killer or killers back to her room where I and a detective sergeant, who, by the way, is as suspicious of Warren's motives as I am, will be waiting to arrest them.'

'That's it?' said the duke, frowning. 'That's your great plan to catch the killers?'

George blushed. 'Yes, sir. I accept it might not work. But it could be worth a try.'

The duke got up and paced the room. At last he turned to George. 'Make no mistake, Major Hart, this is not just a murder inquiry, it's an issue of state importance that could affect the future of the royal family. You might have imagined, if you'd witnessed the Golden Jubilee celebrations last year, that the institution of monarchy was assured for many generations to come. In truth republicanism is on the rise, and has been since the death of the saintly Prince Albert prompted my cousin's long withdrawal from public duties in 1861; the involvement of the heir apparent in a murder inquiry might be the beginning of the end for the monarchy.'

'Sir Charles Warren made a similar point, sir. I have to say I had no idea, when I started on this inquiry, that the stakes were so high.'

'Well they are, take my word for it. Which is why we need to resolve this matter as quickly and as quietly as possible.

So if this prostitute is prepared to help us do that, then maybe we should let her. She will, of course, need to be amply rewarded for the risks she's taking. What about a cash reward? Would that be acceptable to her?'

'Yes, sir, I think it would. She mentioned something about starting a new life.'

'Did she now,' said the duke, stroking his chin. 'Well, that won't come cheap, so what if I guarantee a reward of £5,000 to be split equally between the two of you if you manage to apprehend those responsible?'

'Split between the two of us, sir?'

'Yes, that's right. You'll be running a fearful risk as well.'

It was ironic, thought George, that the duke was unaware of his wife's confession. If he had known, he would surely have used George's own close connection to the royal family to encourage him to take whatever measures were necessary to defend the monarchy. That George was minded to do so, in any case, was probably out of a need to please a man he now knew to be his father. But he also wanted to stop the killings and find the men responsible; and, though he found it hard to admit to himself, the financial incentive of settling his debts, and ensuring a fresh start for Mary, was a far from negligible factor.

'If I ask her to help,' he said at last, 'and it turns out the prince is involved. What then?'

'Well, it depends on how involved he is. If you're asking what you should do if you discover the prince is one of the killers, well you and I both know that isn't going to happen.'

'Yes, sir, I know that. But let's just say, hypothetically, that it did. I have to have all eventualities covered.'

'All right, Major Hart, I'll humour you. *If* you were to discover that the prince is a murderer, you have my authorization – unofficially of course – to do what you need to do. We'd explain the prince's disappearance on a sudden and fatal illness.'

George looked hard at his father. 'Hold on. You're not suggesting that I—'

'Kill him? Yes, that's exactly what I'm suggesting; nay ordering. *If* he's the Ripper, he deserves nothing better than to be shot down like a mad dog. If he's not, then he'll be exonerated and no one will be any the wiser. Do I make myself clear?'

'Perfectly.'

14

George pushed back the battered door, its paint peeling and its glass panels too grimy to see through, and entered the public bar. Apart from a couple of labourers propping up the bar, Jack Fletcher was the only customer. George bought a pint of pale ale and joined him at a corner table.

'The last time we spoke,' began George, 'you suggested using a real prostitute to trap the killers and I said it was too dangerous. Do you remember?'

'I do.'

'Well, I've since been persuaded that if the right girl is prepared to take the risk, we should let her.'

'I agree,' said Fletcher. 'But why the change of heart and who persuaded you?'

'I can't go into details. It's become clear to me, however, that the stakes are much greater than I previously thought. It may sound dramatic, but I think we've already entered very dangerous constitutional waters. If we don't catch the killers soon, the East End might rise up and attempt to overthrow the government. But if we do, and one of them is a member of the royal family, that alone could deal the monarchy a fatal blow.'

'And the solution is?'

'To uncover the killers quickly, so that your colleagues in the CID are not aware, and, if one of them is either the prince, or connected to him in any way, to deal with the problem quietly.'

'You can't be serious, Major Hart? What authority do we have to act outside the law? Who have you been talking to?'

'I can't name names,' said George. 'But our authority comes from the very top.'

'Top of what? Government? The royal family?'

'I can't say. But we won't be left high and dry, I can assure you of that.'

'Well, let's hope it doesn't come to that. So what about this prostitute? Do you have anyone in mind?'

'I do. It's Mary Kelly, the sister of the Fenian who tried to kill me.'

'The one who saved your life?'

'Yes.'

'And what makes you think she'd agree to act as bait?'

'Because she already offered and I turned her down.'

'When was this?'

'After her brother ran off. She was shaking, so I gave her a brandy to calm her nerves. It was then that she offered to help us in return for enough money to start a new life.'

'Why didn't you mention this to me yesterday?'

'Because I hadn't yet been persuaded that it was the right thing to do. Now I have been,' said George, guiltily aware that Lucy's letter had played its part.

'All right, but where are we going to find the money to pay her?'

'Well, there's the £2,000 reward you mentioned. I'm prepared to give her half of that if we catch the killers in the act. And the influential person I've just been speaking to, whose identity I am not at liberty to disclose, has offered her an additional two and a half thousand pounds. The total sum will be more than enough for her to leave Whitechapel and prostitution, and start a new life – maybe in Ireland.'

'It seems, Major Hart, that you've thought of everything. When do I meet her?'

'How about now? Her room is just along Dorset Street, at the back of number Twenty-Six. Let's see if she's home.'

They turned right out of the pub and headed west on Dorset Street. 'Spare a penny?' said a woman sitting against the wall, holding a crying infant.

George paused briefly to hand over a couple of coppers.

'You shouldn't do that,' said Fletcher, as they continued walking. 'It only encourages them to beg. There's always the workhouse.'

Seen by day, the cobbled street was far dirtier and more dilapidated than George could remember. Tall, four-storey tenement buildings loomed up on both sides, many with crumbling brickwork and broken or missing windows. The gutters were flowing with raw sewage and, here and there, rats could be seen snuffling in the piles of litter and rubbish. Between numbers 26 and 27, the latter serving as McCarthy's general store, they came to a brick archway with a sign above it: MILLER'S COURT.

'Wait a moment,' said Fletcher, turning to survey the far side of the street where, almost directly opposite, he could see an alley leading to a separate court or back yard.

'What is it?' asked George.

'I'm just checking for a vantage point.'

'Do you see one?'

'Yes.'

'Good. Shall we continue?'

Fletcher nodded, and the pair entered the narrow covered passage, barely three feet wide. Coming the other way was a dark-haired young woman in her twenties, holding a pile of clothes. 'Hello,' said George. 'We're looking for Mary Kelly.'

'Are you now,' said the women, her eyes flicking from George to Fletcher and back again. 'And what business do you have with her?'

'Never you mind,' said Fletcher. 'This is police work. Just tell us where she lives.'

The woman frowned. 'Next door along. Number Thirteen. She's in bed.'

'How do you know?' asked George.

'Because I'm staying with her.'

'And you are?'

'Maria Harvey.'

'Occupation?'

The woman looked at George as if he was an idiot. 'Well I'm a laundress, aren't I?' she said, shaking her pile of clothes.

'How long have you been living with Mary?' asked Fletcher.

'I don't. I stay occasionally. We're mates. I have my own room.'

'Where?'

'In the next court. Can I go now?'

'Yes.'

They backed out to let her past, then re-entered the passage. The door to Mary's room, number 13, was second on the right. It was chipped and scuffed, its green paint flaking with age. Directly opposite the door was a gas lamp, the only lighting in Miller's Court.

Instead of rousing Mary straightaway, George and Fletcher inspected the rest of the court: a long and narrow paved yard, fifty feet by eight, with doors leading to rooms 1 to 12 and three privies. It smelt of urine and decay. Just beyond Mary's room, however, was a small right-angled extension to the yard – ten feet by ten – that contained a water pump and a large iron dustbin. Mary's only two windows looked out onto this part of the yard; the smaller and lower window, on the right as you looked at the room, was missing one of its four panes, and both were grimy and blacked out by drawn curtains.

They returned to Mary's door and George knocked. When there was no response, he knocked again, this time louder. They heard a groan. 'Who is it?'

'George Hart. You helped me out the other night.'

They could hear movement in the room, and eventually the door opened to reveal a tired-looking Mary, her long blonde hair dishevelled and her eyes red with lack of sleep. She was wearing a thin, threadbare silk dressing gown that did little to conceal her voluptuous figure. Fletcher glanced sideways at George as if to say, *You never told me she was such a looker.*

'Who's he?' Mary asked George, nodding towards Fletcher.

'He's a sergeant in the local CID, hunting Jack the Ripper.'

'I fought you said there was two killers?'

'There probably are. Can we come in?'

'Course. It's a bit of a mess.'

As Mary opened the door wider it banged against something behind it. They entered a small dark room, with the only light coming from embers in a fireplace directly opposite the door. To their left, beneath the intact window, were a simple wooden table and two chairs. Behind the door, to their right, was a smaller bedside table, and beyond that a simple wooden bedstead that had been placed against the wooden partition that separated Mary's room from the rest of number 26. The only other furniture was a small cupboard beside the fire and a washstand next to the bed. Above the fireplace was a popular print of *The Fisherman's Widow* by J. H. Burgers. Clothes were strewn about the room and, even in the half-light, George could see a thick coating of grime on the wooden floorboards and the fading yellow wallpaper. *How could anyone live like this?*

'Take a seat,' said Mary, pointing at the two chairs. She sat on the bed. 'So how can I help?'

'Do you remember,' began George, 'offering to help catch the Ripper and his accomplice by acting as bait. Does the offer still stand?'

Mary nodded.

'Well, we'd like to take you up on that offer. If we're successful, you'll be paid three and a half thousand pounds.'

Mary's jaw dropped. 'You're serious?'

'Deadly serious. The money has been promised as a reward by two interested parties. You'll get your share if we catch the killers, I can promise you that.'

'Gawd! I'll be rich.'

'You will indeed. But first we have to work out how to trap the killers while keeping you safe and sound. There are big risks involved. I'm sure I don't have to tell you that.'

'I'm not afraid.'

'I know you're not, but you probably should be.' George turned to Fletcher. 'Do you have any thoughts on how we should go about this?'

'I do. It's not ideal, I know, but Mary needs to lure the killer back here. That way one of us can keep guard on the room while the other watches out for the accomplice. I noticed before we came in here that there's an alleyway opposite the entrance to Miller's Court. If I hide in there I can keep an eye on anyone trying to enter the court after Mary has taken her client – who has to match or nearly match the descriptions we have of the possible killers – back here. Meanwhile you can hide in the yard outside so you're ready to respond at a moment's notice. We'll both have firearms.'

'How can we be certain,' said George, 'that we'll be able to intervene in time?'

'She'll leave the room unlocked and call out as soon as she senses danger. We can also supply her with a small pistol for her purse. Do you know how to use a gun?' he asked Mary.

She shook her head.

'Well, we can soon remedy that. In any case, we'll be on hand to help. But things could still go wrong, so are you absolutely certain you want to go ahead with this?'

She looked at George, as if seeking reassurance. He kept a neutral expression. 'I—'

'What? Tell me?' demanded Fletcher. 'Are you having second thoughts? Because if you are, we wouldn't blame you.'

'No . . . course not. I'll do it.'

'Good. Well I suggest we start the hunt tomorrow evening at seven p.m. I'll bring Mary a gun and show her how to use it. Everyone happy?'

George and Mary nodded.

'Then I'll be off,' said Fletcher, standing up. 'I have duties at the station.'

Once Fletcher had gone, George's instinct was to stay and tell Mary that everything would turn out fine. He knew she was shouldering most, if not all, of the danger and wanted to reassure her. And despite the squalor of the surroundings, he was enjoying – he could not deny it – the sight of her shapely breasts pressing against the thin material of her dressing gown. But she seemed distracted and keen for him to leave too. 'Do you mind,' she said, rising from the bed, 'I need to get on.'

'No, course not,' said George. 'I'll leave you in peace.'

He paused at the door. 'I – we – appreciate what you're doing, Mary. Not many people would do the same. But remember this: it only takes an accomplished killer like the Ripper a moment to strike; so if you think you're in any danger, any at all, use the pistol immediately. Do you understand?'

'Yes.'

15

13 Miller's Court, Dorset Street

Mary opened the door to her room to find George standing
there. 'Evening, Major Hart.'

'Evening, Mary,' said George, stifling a yawn. 'There's no
hurry tonight. Sergeant Fletcher's been delayed.'

'Just as well. I'm running late. You all right?'

'Yes, I'm fine. Too many late nights trying to snare the
killer. Hopefully we'll get him tonight.'

'You never know,' she said with a smile, holding the door
open.

George followed Mary into her room. Discarded clothes
were lying around, and a half-finished meal was on the side
table. The room smelled of stale beer. 'Take a seat,' said
Mary, returning to a cracked mirror to apply her rouge. 'I
won't be long. So what's Sergeant Fletcher up to?'

George moved a dressing gown off the chair and sat down.
'He's been called to a meeting at Scotland Yard to help brief
the Home Secretary on the latest developments in the case.
He said he'd be finished by nine o'clock at the latest, which
gives him more than enough time to take up his position in
the passage across the street by eleven. If he can't make it by
then, he'll send word by one of his constables who'll stop

outside the arched entrance to Miller's Court and flash his torch three times. If we see the flashes, we delay the plan; if we don't, we go ahead. All clear?'

'I suppose so. Why can't he just come and tell us he's arrived?'

'Because, my dear Mary, we don't want anyone to know he's there, and if he crosses between the two courts he'll bring attention to himself. No, it's better this way.'

Mary looked at George with raised eyebrows.

'No, really it is. We just have to remember to look for the flashes.'

George looked at his pocket watch. It was 10.30 p.m. 'Righto, we've got thirty minutes, which gives me just enough time for a quick nap. Mind if I lie on the bed? I'll give you my watch and you can wake me in twenty minutes. God knows we all need the sleep.'

'Course. You go ahead.'

George lay back, closed his eyes and thought about their collective failure, thus far, to catch the killers. For the previous four nights, from 11 p.m. to 3 a.m., while George and Fletcher waited in their hiding places in and opposite Miller's Court, Mary had trawled the pubs, street corners and alleyways of Whitechapel in search of a man, or men, matching the composite descriptions given by various witnesses: one short and foreign-looking in his late twenties, with broad shoulders, a light brown moustache and wearing a dark overcoat and brown deerstalker; the other taller and a few years older, with handsome features, dark hair and a dark waxed moustache, and wearing a dark coat and a black bowler hat.

She had yet to be accosted by anyone who matched either description, though one or two came close. Was this because, George wondered, the killers – whoever they were – had decided to lie low until the hue and cry had died down a little? The streets, after all, were still well patrolled at night by police and members of the local Vigilance Committee. Or had Mary simply failed to meet up with either of them? He decided that the former was more likely: because if they had been on the prowl they would doubtless have selected and killed somebody else; yet since the double murder, more than five weeks earlier, not a single new victim had been discovered.

The only other alternative was that the Ripper and his accomplice, increasingly fearful of discovery, or their bloodlust sated, had decided to end their killing spree. But Fletcher was having none of this. 'Repeat murderers don't down tools,' he had told George. 'They're either killed, commit suicide or are captured. Mark my words: sooner or later they'll kill again, unless we stop them.'

With that uncomfortable thought playing on his mind, George drifted off to sleep. All too soon he was woken by a hand shaking his shoulder. 'Wakey! Wakey!'

He opened his eyes to see Mary standing over him, watch in hand. 'It's the time you said.'

'Ten to eleven?'

She nodded, handing the watch back.

'Good. I'll go out to check for the torch flashes in a few minutes.'

Mary pulled a chair close to the bed and sat down facing George. 'I've been thinking.'

'What about?'

'What I'll do with the cash.'

'And?'

'I'd like to get a pub in Dublin. I think I could make a go of it. I spend enough time in them. Might as well be earning. What about you?'

'Me? Well, I hadn't thought about it, but now you ask I think I might buy a casino. Until now I've mostly lost money from gambling. This would give me a chance to make some.'

'What say we pool our cash and buy an establishment together, one that has a bar and gaming tables? Maybe even a hotel? We'd make our fortune.'

'It's not a bad idea,' said George, chuckling. 'And I think you're right: we'd do it well. I'd like to be in a position to say yes. But I'm not. I'm married and my wife would definitely *not* approve.'

'So your wife makes all your decisions for you, does she?'

'No, not all. But for big ones like this, we both have a say.'

'Well, that's a shame, Major Hart, because I think we'd work well together. Never mind.'

They heard footsteps passing the front door. 'One of the other residents?' asked George.

'Probably.'

'What sort of people are they?'

'Poor, of course, but good people. Julia Venturney lives over the way in number One. She's a charwoman, but generous. She's often lent me money. I still owe her.'

'How much?'

'A couple of shillings.'

'Do you owe money to anyone else?'

'Yes, to Mr McCarthy, the landlord. He has the shop at number Twenty-Seven. He's a good man. I must owe him at least thirty shillings. I'll pay them both back every penny if I get the reward. Mind you, the money won't buy me happiness, I know that. And I'll miss some things about London, like the Lord Mayor's Show tomorrow. Are you going? I am.'

'I hadn't thought,' said George, looking at his pocket watch. It was five minutes to eleven. 'It's time. I'll check to see that Fletcher has arrived.'

He opened the door and looked down the covered passage to his left. The night was cold, with a very faint drizzle in the air. After a couple of minutes he heard footsteps and saw a caped policeman in the faint yellow glow of a street lamp. The policeman briefly glanced down the passage before continuing on his way. There were no flashes from his torch. Satisfied that Fletcher was in position, George returned to Mary's room. 'He's there. Time to go.'

'Right. Reckon tonight's the night, Major Hart. I got a feeling something's going to happen.'

'Just be careful.'

'I will. With you two looking after me, what could go wrong?'

'What indeed? If you return with someone who matches either description, don't forget to leave the door unlocked. I'll follow you in. If it's who I think it is, I'll put a bullet in him. If it's not but he has a knife, ditto. Jack will deal with his accomplice.'

'You've told me time and time again!' said Mary, 'I'm not an idiot.' She smiled as she put on her bonnet, her face flushed with excitement. 'How do I look?'

'You look beautiful,' said George, *and if I wasn't married . . . who knows?* 'Good luck, Mary. Come back safe.'

'I plan to. Shouldn't be too long!'

As Mary strode purposefully up the covered passage, hips swaying, George was tempted to call her back. Her feeling that tonight was the night had alarmed him because he felt it too. Had they thought of everything? What if the Ripper and his accomplice attacked her before they got back to her room? What if he locked the door and George couldn't get to her in time? They'd have the killer, but Mary would be dead. Was that a price worth paying? He didn't think it was. By now, however, Mary was long gone and, rather than pursue her and have to explain his doubts to her and a sceptical Fletcher, he told himself he had nothing to worry about: Mary was a tough and resourceful girl who could look after herself.

With the die cast, George quietly shut Mary's door behind him and crouched in the shadow of the large coal dustbin that faced her two windows. From there he was hidden from anyone entering and leaving Miller's Court, yet was close enough to the room to see if anyone went inside and to hear what they said. The night was cold and damp, and George was grateful for the extra layer of clothing and dark blue double-breasted navy pea jacket that he had donned before leaving home. He tapped its left inside pocket and felt the reassuring bump of his trusty two-shot Derringer pistol. Tucked into his right boot was a sheathed dagger he had taken from a dead Sudanese warrior.

After an hour, George could feel his leg muscles cramping and shifted position slightly to ease them. He tried to imagine what Mary was doing. Was she in a pub, or walking the streets, or on her way back with someone who resembled the Ripper? Or had she had second thoughts and decided to return home alone? George rather hoped it was the latter, because the more he thought about what they were doing, the more ludicrous it seemed to him. Which begged the questions, why was he doing this? Was it just for the money? Was he trying to impress his father? Solve the murders so that he could be reunited with his family? Or was all this to help the whores of Whitechapel, outsiders like himself, who, through force of circumstance, and no fault of their own, had come to lead such dangerous and degrading lives?

He couldn't decide. He knew that few people were truly selfless, and that most acts of charity expected something in return, even if it was no more than the reputation of a do-gooder. Thus had Alexander Pope written, 'Do good by stealth and blush to find it fame.' George was not a do-gooder by nature, but he liked to think he could do the right thing, and stopping the Ripper was certainly that. But was this ill-thought-out entrapment – with all its attendant risks – the best way to go about it? He was beginning to doubt it.

He was brought back to reality by voices from the passage and a woman's laughter. It was Mary. He could hear a man whispering, and Mary answer, 'All right, my dear. Come along with me. You'll be comfortable.'

He heard more whispering, then Mary again. 'Oh no, I've lost my handkerchief!'

'Never mind,' said a muffled voice. 'Have mine.'

The door to Mary's room creaked open and the pair went inside.

George could feel his heart thumping as he drew his pistol and cocked both hammers. Climbing to his feet, he edged round the corner of the building to Mary's door. He could hear talking and, again, Mary's laugh. *She must think she has the right man or she wouldn't have brought him back, but she doesn't sound worried – not yet.* He put his left hand on the door handle and pressed down slowly until the lock clicked and the door moved a fraction. *Clever girl, she's left it open.* He was about to burst into the room when he heard footsteps to his left. He turned to see a dark figure beside him, the face partially hidden by an upturned collar and hat.

Then something came arcing towards his head. He tried to duck but it was too late. The object slammed into his temple with a thud, scrambling his senses and causing him to sink to his knees. The pain was indescribable; worse than a gunshot wound. He tried to cry out but the sound was just a groan. He could feel blood dripping down his cheek. As he turned his head to glimpse his assailant, he was struck again and blacked out.

*

When George came to, the first thing he felt was an intense, throbbing pain: like a red-hot poker being jabbed into the side of his head. He felt for his left temple. It was bruised and bloodied, but the bone seemed to be intact. He had been teased at school for having a hard skull; now he was grateful. He opened his eyes but could see nothing. It was pitch black. He was lying on his back in some sort of container. He put his hand up and could feel a metal surface above him. He pushed but it wouldn't budge. *Where am I?*

The smell gave the game away: burnt ashes and coal dust, familiar from any open fire. He had to be in a dustbin. Then it all came flooding back: Mary had returned with the suspect and, just as he had been about to enter the room and rescue her, he had been knocked out and put in here. The attack, he remembered, had come from his left. *It can't have been the Ripper's accomplice because Fletcher would have seen him. Unless? Unless?* As the awful truth dawned, George wanted to scream Mary's name. Instead he hammered on the lid above him, desperate to get out and see for himself.

At first nobody responded. But when he persisted a voice cried out, 'Who's in there?'

'Major George Hart. I'm a friend of Mary Kelly. I was attacked last night and put in here. Please get me out.'

'I'll try,' said the voice, 'but there's a piece of bloomin' wood in the lock and it won't budge. I'll get some tools. Won't be long.'

The seconds crawled by as George worried about Mary's fate, only partly encouraged by the man's casual response to his predicament. *Had Mary somehow survived? Was his assault unconnected to the Ripper?* He prayed that might be the case. Footsteps alerted George to the man's return. He could hear grunting and then a loud crack as the lock was forced. The lid opened and light flooded in, causing George to squint his eyes. 'You all right?' asked a fleshy, middle-aged man with a pockmarked face.

'I'll survive. Just help me out.'

The man pulled on George's right arm and got him to his feet.

'Do you know Mary Kelly?' asked George.

'I do,' said the man. 'I'm Tom Bowyer. I work for Mary's landlord, Mr McCarthy. He sent me to collect her back rent, but she's not answering her door.'

Fearing the worst, George staggered the ten paces or so to Mary's door and tried the handle. It was locked.

'I expect she's drunk,' commented Tom.

'Why don't you break it down?

'Because my boss will charge me for the damage. She'll come out eventually.'

George hurried to the nearest window. It was barred, from the inside, by an old coat that was both acting as a curtain and blocking the draught from the hole in the glass. He pushed the coat to one side and peered through the gap into the dark interior. He could just make out Mary lying on the bed, and hope soared inside him that she was asleep. His eyes strayed to a pile of meat on the small table beside her.

What was that doing there? As his eyes adjusted to the gloom, he could see the pile was topped by a white globe with a brown centre. It reminded him of a . . . *My God! It can't be!* He focused on the shape and there was no longer any doubt. It was a woman's breast, hacked from its owner and left atop a pile of human offal.

George looked again at Mary. Wearing the tattered remnants of a linen shift, she was lying in the middle of the bed with her shoulders flat and her head lying on its left cheek, facing in his direction. Her eyes appeared to be shut, but it was hard to tell because the rest of her lovely face had been mutilated beyond recognition by a series of cuts and slashes. Her legs were spread wide apart, and so cut up was the right one that George could see the white of the thigh bone. The abdomen appeared to have been completely disembowelled, with the various organs, flesh and skin spread around the bed, pillow and small table. Mary's blood was everywhere: spattered on the wall behind the bed; soaked in her shift and bedclothes; puddled on the floor. It was now that George noticed the smell in the room: sickly sweet, like an abattoir.

He turned from the horrific scene, fell to his haunches and vomited.

As he wiped the remaining sick from his lips, one thought kept recurring: where was Fletcher and why hadn't he intervened?

'Oh Christ!' said Tom who, following George's lead, was looking through the window. 'Mary's in pieces! 'Oo would do such a fing?'

'Who do you think?' said George. 'Call the bloody police. What are you waiting for?

*

George was sitting with his back to Mary's door, head in his hands, when McCarthy's assistant returned from Commercial Street Police Station, barely 300 yards distant, with a gaggle of detectives and uniformed police. George looked up to see, at their head, Inspector Abberline and Sergeant Jack Fletcher.

'Major Hart?' said Abberline. 'I'm flabbergasted. This is the second time I've found you at the scene of a gruesome murder. The last time you were expressly told by Commissioner Warren to look to your own duties. Yet here you are? So what is the reason, pray tell me, for your presence?'

George glanced at Fletcher, but the sergeant's expression was deadpan, as if they hardly knew each other. He thought about telling the Abberline the truth: that they had tried to trap the Ripper and failed, and that it had cost poor Mary her life. But he decided not to because, on the one hand, he knew that such an admission would cost Fletcher his job; and on the other it wouldn't help to catch the killers. He still didn't trust Warren or Abberline, and suspected they were either protecting the Ripper or involved in some way themselves. So he played for time.

'Why am I here? . . . Well I was . . . I was . . . I'm sorry, Inspector, I'm not making much sense. It must be the crack on the head . . . Give me a moment . . . Ah, yes, now I remember. The poor woman inside did me a good turn by intervening when someone tried to rob me. I came to thank her and offer her some money. But as I waited for her to answer the door, someone knocked me unconscious. When I came to, she was dead.'

Abberline snorted in derision. 'You came here to *thank* her for stopping a robbery? I've heard it all now. Do you think I was born yesterday? You're a big strapping man. How could a mere tart fight off your attacker?'

'She didn't fight him off. She distracted him until a police constable intervened.'

'Who is this police constable? Did you get his name or number?'

'Er, no, but it wasn't far from here, so he must work from the police station on Commercial Street. I'm sure if you make inquiries he—'

'What utter nonsense!' interrupted Abberline. 'But I don't have time for this right now. Where's the body?'

'Inside,' said George, pointing behind him.

'Is the door locked?'

He nodded.

'Well, how do you know she's dead?'

'I looked through a hole in the window round the corner. There's no doubt. See for yourself.'

Abberline and Fletcher rushed to the window. George could hear a groan.

The pair returned white-faced. 'Constable Thomas,' said Abberline to a uniformed officer. 'Stand at the entrance and stop any civilians from entering the court.'

'Sir.'

Abberline turned to Fletcher. 'Sergeant. Take the rest of the men and begin questioning the residents of the court. I want to know if they heard or saw anything.'

Fletcher nodded and went off. That just left Abberline and George outside Mary's room. George rose unsteadily to his feet. 'Shouldn't we break down the door?'

'No,' said Abberline. 'She's obviously dead. There's nothing more we can do for her. My priority now is to keep the scene as it was when the crime took place and gather evidence.'

'Well, surely any evidence worth collecting is in the room? The killer or killers might have dropped something.'

'Yes, and it will still be there when we *do* go in. But we have to wait because the dogs are on their way.'

'What dogs?'

'A couple of bloodhounds were loaned to us after the double murder. I was sceptical at first, but if you give one of these dogs a relatively fresh scent, he will follow it faithfully. We did some trials in Hyde Park, with Commissioner Warren playing the part of the hunted man, and the dogs found him every time.'

'But that's a park. Surely it would be much harder for them to follow a scent in the crowded streets of Whitechapel?'

'Harder, yes, but not impossible, according to the dogs' owner. Which is why I can't allow anyone to enter the room until the dogs arrive. It will confuse them. As things stand, the freshest scent, apart from that of the victim herself, will be from the killer.'

Or me, thought George. He had visions of the dogs going directly from Mary's room to him. He was already the only person to be found at two murder scenes. Now he would be a suspect. 'What about her friends?' asked George, his heart racing. 'Or other clients she might have seen before the killer? Won't the dogs pick up their scent?'

Abberline shook his head. 'As I say, they'll go for the freshest scent. Which brings me back to you, Major Hart. Tell me again why you're here?'

George thought back to his conversation with the Duke of Cambridge. What were his words? *We need to resolve this matter as quickly and as quietly as possible.* Surely, despite everything, that still applied? He decided that there was nothing to gain, and potentially a lot to lose, from telling all. 'As I said, I came here to thank the young woman.'

Abberline looked intently at George, as if trying penetrate to his very soul. George held his gaze, causing Abberline to exclaim in frustration: 'And as I said, I don't believe you! Why would a swell like you come to Whitechapel? It doesn't make sense. I could understand if it was something to do with the case. But you've been warned off, haven't you? So why keep coming back?'

It was a good question, and George responded with the first response that came into his head. 'Because, Inspector, I'm a soldier, and I like to live dangerously. I've fought in many wars, as you know. I enjoy the excitement. Peacetime soldiering can't replicate the thrill of combat, so I seek it when I'm off duty.'

Abberline narrowed his eyes. 'You're telling me that you come to Whitechapel for the excitement? What excitement? Have you had a good look at the place, Major Hart? It's a stinking cesspit, full of the dregs of society: whores, gangsters, conmen and murderers. I know it well. I worked here for ten years before I was moved to Scotland Yard. I'm only here now because of the Ripper case. Why would you come here by choice? You'd have to be insane.'

'Well I'm not, and nor am I alone,' said George, thinking of the prince and his friends. 'I know of a fair few people – some extremely well connected – who make regular trips to the East End. I suspect that, like me, they're attracted to the danger of the place. It's unlike anywhere else in the capital. When your usual haunts are gentlemen's clubs and Mayfair drawing rooms, the pubs and music halls of Whitechapel make a nice change.'

Abberline snorted his contempt. 'I don't get people like you, Major Hart. But then I wasn't born with a silver spoon. Everything I've got, everything I've achieved, I've had to work for. I was a clocksmith before I joined the Met. Did you know that? No reason why you should. First I made sergeant, then inspector, and finally detective inspector with the CID, the best of the best. I've solved most of my cases by slow, dogged, methodical police work. Nothing flashy. So I resent it when someone like you – with your posh voice and your "foreign" looks – tries to interfere with one of my cases. You say you were in the area to thank a whore for saving your cash. Utter nonsense! Oh I know depraved people *like* you come East to despoil the local girls and boys. They don't seem to mind which. But I also know the type, and you're not one of them. You're here because of the case. Why, I don't yet know. You've been warned twice to steer clear. Yet here you are again, at the scene of the crime. A more suspicious man than me might think you were involved in some way. So, to put my mind at rest, why don't you tell me how you know the victim and what really happened last night?'

My God, thought George, *I'm in trouble now! Or is this just another attempt by the Masons to divert suspicion from the prince by pinning the blame on me? Either way, I'd better stick as close to the truth as possible.* 'All right,' said George. 'I haven't been entirely honest, I admit. I met the girl in a pub after the Chapman murder. I was carrying out those unofficial inquiries that I told you about on the night of the double murder.'

'Go on.'

'Well, one thing led to another and we made plans to meet up.'

'Before tonight?'

'Yes.'

'How many times?'

'A couple.'

'So what happened tonight?'

'I said I'd come at a quarter past midnight. I was a few minutes early, but was still surprised to hear voices in the room. I assumed it was a client and was waiting for him to leave when someone clocked me on the side of the head. I woke up in the dustbin.'

'Which side did your assailant approach from?'

'The left.'

'And you were facing the door?'

'Yes.'

'So he was already in the court, while someone else was with Mary. It doesn't make sense.'

'It does if they were acting in concert. One to do the killing; the other to keep watch.'

Abberline stroked his chin. 'Mmm. It's possible, I suppose. The bit that I can't get my head round is your presence at or near the scene of two of the last three murders. You say it's a coincidence. I don't think so. I don't believe in coincidences. There's something you're not telling me, Major Hart, and I intend to find out exactly what that is.'

Rapid footsteps in the passage alerted them to the arrival of a police constable. It was the Polish-born policeman Tom Black. 'Sir, I have a message from the station that the dogs are not coming. The owner took them back two days ago.'

'He took them back? Why?'

'Something about money. The Home Office refuse to pay what he asked.'

'Christ!' said Abberline. 'Those penny-pinching clerks in Whitehall have cost us a perfect opportunity to track this lunatic. Well, it can't be helped. Go and get a sledgehammer, Black, we're going to break down the door. But before you do that, I want you to get a message to Commissioner Warren at Scotland Yard that there's been another killing.'

Abberline took out a notebook and pencil and scribbled the message in capitals for clarity:

THIS MORNING WE RECEIVED INFORMATION
THAT THE MUTILATED BODY OF A DECEASED
WOMAN, BELIEVED TO BE A PROSTITUTE, WAS
FOUND IN THE ROOM OF A HOUSE (NO. 26) IN
DORSET STREET, SPITALFIELD. I AM
CONDUCTING THE INVESTIGATION.
ABBERLINE.

'Have it sent by telegraphic message from the station,' said Abberline. 'Then find Dr Phillips, the police surgeon. He needs to examine the body – or what's left of it.'

'Yes, sir.'

As Black left on his errands, Sergeant Fletcher came out of a nearby doorway. 'Anything useful, Sergeant?' asked Abberline.

'I've just spoken to a woman called Sarah Lewis, sir,' said Fletcher. 'She's a laundress and normally lives in Great Pearl Street. But last night she had an argument with her husband and came to stay with friends at number Two Miller's Court. As she entered the court in the early hours – she doesn't remember the exact time – she saw a tall man in a black bowler hat standing across the street. He was looking up the court, as if he was waiting for someone to come out.'

'Did she see or hear anything else?'

'Yes, sir. She was dozing in a chair in her friend's place when she heard a young woman scream "Murder!" She thinks it was about two or three in the morning.'

'What did she do?'

'Nothing. She didn't even look out of the window. When I asked her why not, she said she thought nothing of it, as similar cries are commonplace in Whitechapel.'

'Christ,' said Abberline. 'What a place this is.'

George felt sick to the stomach that Mary had cried out for help and no one had responded. The poor thing! He and Fletcher had sworn to protect her. They had failed. He looked reproachfully at Fletcher, as if to say, where were you and why didn't you intervene? But the sergeant pretended not to notice. The awkward silence was ended by the reappearance of Black, clutching a six-pound sledgehammer, and accompanied by a man George recognized as the police surgeon from the Stride murder scene in Dutfield's Yard. Seen by day, he looked to be in his fifties and oddly old-fashioned in both appearance and dress, with a grey beard but no moustache, and a black frockcoat that dated from the 1860s.

'Thank you for coming, Dr Phillips,' said Abberline. 'It's another one, I'm afraid.'

'I guessed that, Inspector,' responded Phillips in a soft south London accent. 'Don't thank me. It's my job. Where's the body?'

Abberline pointed to the door beside him and turned to Black. 'Go ahead. Break it in.'

It took the broad-shouldered Black just one well-aimed blow to shatter the lock and open the door. Phillips was the first inside, closely followed by Abberline and Fletcher. George could not bring himself to enter the room properly; but instead peered round the door frame. Though he knew what to expect, the sight of Mary's body at close quarters was sickening. Her throat had been cut with such ferocity that the head was almost severed from the body; and, not content with slashing her face, the killer had removed Mary's nose and much of the flesh on her cheeks and chin. Yet her eyes were still open, and seemed to be staring straight at George with a look of terror. He felt as if he'd been punched in the stomach, and turned away.

Phillips approached the bed, almost losing his balance as he slipped in the puddle of congealed blood beside it. 'Damn!' he muttered.

Mary's left forearm was lying on her torn stomach, as if it had been carefully placed there by the killer. Phillips picked it up and felt the wrist for a pulse, though he knew her to be dead. He then consulted his watch, and declared: 'Confirmation of death, 1.35 p.m.'

'Any idea of the time of death?' asked Abberline, standing with Fletcher a few paces back from the bed.

'It's hard to say until we've done a post-mortem. But from the look of the body, and the fact that rigor mortis has already set in, I would say around two in the morning.'

'What about cause of death?'

'Well, I can see lots of blood on the pillow and sheet behind the head, so I suspect the right carotid artery was severed by a cut. The mutilation would have been after death.'

Thank God for small mercies, thought George. *At least she didn't suffer for long.*

'Thank you, Dr Phillips. That's very useful. In some of the previous cases, as you've pointed out, body parts were removed and taken away. It's too early to be certain, I know, but is there any sign of that in this case?'

Careful to avoid slipping again, Phillips bent over the body and inspected the mostly empty chest cavity. He then sifted through the offal on the table and the body parts on the bed, checking off the severed items he had identified: 'Uterus . . . kidneys . . . one breast . . . liver . . . the other breast . . . intestines . . . spleen . . . but no heart. I can't find the heart.'

'You're certain?' asked Abberline.

'Yes, it's not here.'

Bastards, thought George. *Not content with butchering poor Mary like an animal, they had taken her heart with them. For what purpose, I dread to think. Bastards.*

'Inspector,' said Fletcher, pointing at the fireplace, 'there are ashes and some partially burnt clothes in the grate. Is it possible the killer got a blaze going to burn the evidence of his bloodstained clothes? He must have been covered in gore.'

'Yes, it's certainly possible. But he may also have lit the fire so that he could see better to carry out his devilish work. Most of the candles in the room are burnt to stubs.'

George put his head in his hands, scarcely able to believe that his and Fletcher's actions had caused an innocent young woman to die in such horrific circumstances. *What idiots we've been! To think we could trap the killers with our amateurish scheme! What were we thinking? Would we have taken similar risks with our own loved ones?* He knew the answer. He was desperate to leave the room and its frightfulness far behind; and to speak to Fletcher in private and ask why he hadn't intervened. But the possibility that the room might contain clues left by the killer kept him from fleeing. So he remained in the doorway, scanning the room for anything that hadn't been there earlier. He could see nothing.

As the policemen and the surgeon continued their discussion, he slipped back outside and searched the ground between the doorway and the dustbin. Again nothing caught his eye. He opened the lid of the dustbin and looked inside. Just ash. He sifted the top layer with his hand, almost absent-mindedly, and found only tiny pieces of unburnt coal. He dug a little deeper with the same result. He was about to dust his hands off when he noticed something glinting in the dust. Catching it between thumb and forefinger, he pulled it free and recognized a tiny silver Star of David.

How long has it been there? he wondered. *Could it have been dropped by one of the residents in their ash?* It was possible, but unlikely. A more realistic scenario, he decided, was that his assailant somehow dropped it – or had it pulled from his neck – as he bundled George into the dustbin. That would mean that one of the murderers was either a Jew or pretending to be one. If the former, the most likely suspect was Aaron Kosminski and that fact, in turn, put the prince firmly back under suspicion. *If he is responsible*, thought George, *I won't need my father's authority to kill him. I'll happily do it myself, and hang the consequences.*

'Major Hart?'

George turned and saw Abberline and Fletcher approaching.

'What are you doing over there?' asked the inspector.

'Well,' said George, half turning his body so that he could drop the Star of David into his left pocket without Abberline seeing. 'It occurred to me that my attacker might have inad-vertently dropped something in the dustbin.'

'And did he?'

'Not that I can see. But I've only had a quick look.'

'Well come away, now, and let the experts do their job. This whole area is now the scene of a murder and will be searched with a fine-tooth comb for evidence. In any case, you need to get that cut on your head looked at. You were obviously hit quite hard and it can take a while to recover from such a blow. I suggest you go home and get some rest after you've seen a doctor. But, as I said before, I'm still not entirely happy with your version of events last night. So, to begin with, I'd like you to give a formal statement to Sergeant Fletcher while your memory is still fresh; and then, in a day or two, when you're feeling better, I'd like to ask you a few more questions. Is that all right with you?'

'Well, I've told you everything I know but, yes, of course I'll help in any way I can.'

'Good.' Abberline turned to Fletcher. 'Sergeant, I'd like you to escort Major Hart to the local infirmary and then back to his home. When you consider him fit enough, take his statement.'

'Of course, Inspector,' replied Fletcher, before turning to George. 'After you, Major.'

As they turned to leave, George could see two workmen emerge from the passage, carrying a scratched and dirty wooden coffin. 'In there,' said PC Black, pointing into Mary's room. George slowly shook his head, angry that they were treating Mary's body like that of any common pauper – which of course she was – and made a mental note to buy her a decent gravestone. At least, then, her family could visit her grave.

'Where will they take her?' he asked Fletcher.

'Shoreditch Mortuary's the closest. That's where they'll do the post-mortem.'

'Poor thing,' said George in a lowered voice, not looking at Fletcher. 'You know we're to blame, don't you?'

'Not here, Major.'

Fletcher led the way through the short passage that led to Dorset Street. As George was about to follow, he noticed PC Black staring at him intently. 'Something wrong, Constable?'

Black's face reddened. 'No, sir. I was just looking at the cut on your head. It looks bad . . .'

'It is. But I'm still in one piece. Which is more than can be said for the victim.'

Passing between two burly constables who were guarding the entrance to Miller's Court, George emerged onto Dorset Street, where Fletcher was waiting for him. Directly ahead of them were a horse and tarpaulin-covered cart, waiting to transport the coffin. Beyond the cart, held back by a thin cordon of police, was a large crowd of onlookers, drawn to the murder scene by word of mouth. Almost all were locals, the men holding their cloth caps out of respect for the victim. 'What's happening?' cried one. 'Is it the Ripper?'

Fletcher ignored them. 'The infirmary's this way,' he said, pointing in the direction of Commercial Street. 'If we can get through the sightseers.'

'Forget the infirmary,' said George. 'I need a drink, not a doctor. Take me to the nearest pub.'

16

Britannia public house, Dorset Street

The pub was emptying as they arrived, its shocked customers anxious to witness the removal of the Ripper's latest
victim from a house barely 200 yards away. George marched
up to the deserted bar and ordered two brandies. He handed
one to Fletcher and downed the other in a single gulp, revel-
ling in the fiery liquid's ability to dull his pain. 'Another,' he
told the barman, before turning to Fletcher. 'So what
happened?'

'To *me*?' asked Fletcher, surprise etched on his face. 'I
might ask the same thing of you.'

'I would have thought that was obvious from this,' said
George, pointing to the cut on his left temple. 'I was knocked
out by one of the killers and locked in the dustbin. He must
have been hiding in the shadows before Mary left and I took
up my position. But how would he know where to go *before*
Mary met the Ripper? More importantly, where were *you*? I
saw no signal from the police constable at eleven p.m. and
assumed you were in position.'

'If I *had* been I'd have intervened, you can be sure of that.
But the meeting took longer than I thought. The Home
Secretary kept asking every question under the sun – why

hadn't we thought of this, did it make sense to consider that? – and Warren kept deferring to myself and Inspector Abberline for a response. The hours ticked by and, when I realized I wouldn't get back to Whitechapel in time for our rendezvous, I made my excuses so that I could telephone the station.'

'Who did you speak to?' asked George, before draining his second brandy.

'Police Constable Black.'

'Tom Black? The constable who broke open Mary's door?'

'Yes. I told him to make sure he was outside the entrance to Miller's Court at eleven p.m. sharp, and that he was to flash his light three times. I said it was a stakeout in connection with the Ripper case and a matter of extreme importance. He promised me he would.'

'Well he didn't. I clearly saw a policeman pause at the entrance to the court at eleven p.m. But he made no signal.'

Fletcher looked mystified. 'I don't get it. Black's a diligent policeman. He can't have forgotten, can he? Maybe he got confused and thought I said *not* to signal.'

George shook his head. 'You're clutching at straws, Fletcher. I can understand him confusing three flashes for two, or even one, but not for *no* flashes. If he wasn't supposed to signal, why send him in the first place?'

'Yes. I see that. I'm shocked myself. I can hardly think straight. What if something held him up?'

'What if it did? He could easily have asked a colleague to step in. In any case, none of this explains how the killers knew I'd be there unless . . . unless . . .' George's mouth dropped open. 'My God! That's it! I see it now.'

'See what? Please explain!'

'I will, but first tell me how many policeman work for the Whitechapel division.'

'How many policeman? What's that got to do with anything?'

'You'll see. The number please?'

'I don't know exactly. But more than five hundred.'

'*Five hundred!* And yet the same policeman finds Nichols's corpse, the chalk message and the bloody apron, and was the first copper to attend the Chapman murder scene. This morning he failed to pass on your message, leaving me without support and Mary to her fate. A coincidence? I think not.'

'You think *Black* is involved! First the prince and now Black! You've lost your mind! He's a policeman.'

'I assure you I haven't. I know what you're thinking: Black's a policeman. His job is to save lives, not take them. True enough, but the very fact that Black *is* a policeman makes it all the easier for him to cover his tracks. There are a couple of things about this case that have been bothering me: why, once it was known that a murderer was on the loose, were the victims prepared to go into dark and secluded places with a client they didn't know? And why was it so easy for the killers to leave various crime scenes under the very noses of the police? Both mysteries are explained if either the killer himself, or his accomplice, is a policeman. The women probably knew him and he's the last person they would suspect. As for escaping, he simply has to put on his uniform and pretend he's just come across the scene of the crime, as Black seems to have done on more than one occasion.'

'I can see what you're getting at, but why Black? He seemed so normal.'

'It's impossible to know for sure. But when I spoke to him after Chapman's death, he told me he'd immigrated to Britain from Polish Russia in the early 1880s, and that his original name was Cherniy. I think it's safe to assume that he's Jewish, and that like Kosminski he left his homeland because of the anti-Semitic pogroms. Talking of which,' said George, fishing from his pocket the silver Star of David he had found in Miller's Court, 'have you ever seen Black wearing a symbol like this around his neck?'

'Where did you get it?'

'I found it in the dustbin opposite Mary's room in Miller's Court. If it was part of the fire debris, it would surely have melted. The only logical conclusion is that it was dropped by the killer, or the killer's accomplice, afer he knocked me unconscious and bundled me in there. So I ask again: have you ever seen Black wearing something like this?'

Fletcher rubbed his eyes as he tried to remember. 'It *looks* familiar. Most times you can't see what a constable is wearing round his neck because of his high collar. But I've seen a lot of them change at the station and, yes, I vaguely remember a constable with a star like that. But was it Black? I can't remember.'

'Well, either way he's got a lot of explaining to do. But first I think we should have a word with Aaron Kosminski.'

'Kosminski? Why? If Black's involved, doesn't that put Kosminski in the clear? After all, only one of the suspects matches their general height, colouring, etc.'

'True but, as I said, they share a very similar history: they're both Jewish, of a similar age, and came to Britain to escape anti-Semitic violence in their homeland. Both must have witnessed some terrible things, and I bet you a shilling to a guinea they know each other.'

Fletcher rubbed his forehead. 'What if they do? What will that prove?'

'It might not *prove* anything. But it might help to explain why I was sent that note linking Kosminski with the prince's forays into Whitechapel. If Black is the killer, he might have been using Kosminski to frame the prince. Why, I've no idea. But the more I think about it, the more I'm convinced that there's a connection between Kosminski and Black.'

'Which is why we need to speak to Kosminski?'

'Exactly.'

*

It took George and Fletcher less than fifteen minutes to escape the crowds in and around Dorset Street, and make their way down Commercial Street and along Whitechapel Hight Street to Kosminski's home in Sion Square. The door was opened by Kosminski's sister, Betsy Abrahams, wearing a cook's apron and with her flushed face flecked with flour. She frowned. 'You again! What do you want this time?'

'We'd like another talk with your brother Aaron,' said Fletcher.

Betsy's eyes widened in alarm. 'What about? I told you before. He's done nothing wrong.'

'We believe you. But it's possible he has information about someone who has. Is he here?'

'No.'

'May I remind you, Mrs Abrahams, that obstructing a crime investigation is a criminal offence with grave penalties. So I ask again: is he here?'

'Yes I'm here,' said Aaron Kosminski, emerging from the front parlour where he must have overheard the conversation. 'What do you want to ask me?'

George stepped forward half a pace. 'It's probably better if we talk in private. Can we come in?'

Aaron looked at his sister and she nodded her assent. 'Yes, all right,' he said, before showing them into the front parlour. Mrs Abraham returned to the kitchen.

Once seated round the small table, Sergeant Fletcher began. 'There's been another murder in Whitechapel. It took place in a small court off Dorset Street. The poor victim, barely into her twenties, had her throat slit and her body cut to pieces. The murderer or murderers – and we have reason to suspect that more than one person is involved – even took her heart. For what purpose we do not know. The reason I mention all of this is to stress the wickedness of these acts: almost butchery for its own sake. We have to stop these monsters and we think you might be able to help us.'

Kosminski was blinking rapidly, as if the details reminded him of something unpleasant he'd witnessed. 'It's terrible. Terrible. Tell me what I can do to help?'

'Just answer our questions,' said George, 'as honestly as you can. Do you know a police constable called Tom Black, formerly known as Tomasz Cherniy?'

'Yes, I know him. We lived in same village in Poland. We played together as boys and came to England at same time. I used to see him all time – but not now.'

'Why not? What happened?'

'We . . . I . . .' Kosminski paused, uncertain how to explain. 'He doesn't like me seeing the prince.'

'How did he know that you were?'

'I was good friends with Tomasz, very good friends. Like this,' said Kosminski, hooking one index finger round the other.

'Were you, I wonder,' asked George, 'more than friends?'

Kosminski blushed.

'It's all right,' said Fletcher. 'Just tell us the truth. Please. You won't get into trouble, I promise.'

'Well . . . yes . . . we were more than friends.'

'Thank you,' said George. 'So Black found out about you seeing the prince and was jealous. Is that right?'

Kosminski nodded.

George looked at Fletcher in triumph, before turning back to Kosminski. 'You said before that you'd destroyed all the prince's letters. Was that true?'

Kosminski hesitated. 'No,' he said at last. 'I kept them.'

'Is it possible that Black could have got hold of one, or part of one, of the prince's letters to you?'

'I don't know. It's possible. He was often in my room and could have stolen one, I suppose. Wait here. I'll go and check.'

Once Kosminski had left the room, Fletcher turned to George. 'I have to give it to you, Major Hart. You seem to have an uncanny ability for police work. I must confess I didn't imagine that Black and Kosminski were in a sexual relationship. Did you?'

'No, I didn't. And I'm not sure where it leaves us. It's tempting to conclude that all the circumstantial evidence linking the prince and Kosminski to the murders was manufactured by Black out of sexual jealousy. But, if so, who is Black's accomplice? And might the prince still be involved in some capacity? I just don't know.'

Before Fletcher could respond, Kosminski re-entered the room with a scrap of paper in his hand. 'I found this,' he said, handing it to George.

It was part of a letter from the prince, but missing the letter heading and greeting, which appeared to have been torn off. George read the remaining message:

> . . . I hope you are well and can cut my hair at your home at 3 p.m. this Sunday. Please ensure your sister and her family are out for the day. Yours affectionately, Eddy.

Fletcher was shaking his head in amazement. 'That's definitely it,' he said. 'That's the missing half of the letter fragment that was found by Annie Chapman's body in Hanbury Street. So the writing was genuine after all – it *was* written by the prince – and "My dear A" must refer to Mr Kosminski's chosen name Aaron. Do you think that . . .'

Fletcher was about to ask George if he thought Black had stolen the letter fragment and planted it next to Chapman to implicate the prince and Kosminski. But he paused when he realized that Kosminski did not need to know about this. 'Errm,' he continued, 'sorry, lost my train of thought.'

George turned back to Kosminski. 'Now, listen very carefully. This is important. You are to say nothing of this conversation to anyone – not the prince, not your sister, and certainly not Tom Black. If we find out that you have, you'll be arrested and charged with obstructing the course of justice. You will certainly go to prison, do you understand me?'

'Yes. I won't speak to anyone. I haven't seen Tom for months. Do you think he is killer?'

'We don't know. He might be. Just stay out of his way, do you understand?'

Kosminski nodded.

'One more thing, Mr Kosminski,' said Fletcher. 'We need to take the letter with us. But I promise that no word of it will reach the press and the original will be returned to you as soon as the case is solved. Is that acceptable to you?'

Kosminski did not answer. He was staring into the distance, lost in thought.

'Mr Kosminski!' said Fletcher, a hard edge to his voice. 'Did you hear what I said?'

The young hairdresser turned to look at him. 'Yes, sorry. I heard. I was thinking of Tom. Our friendship. Our love. All gone now.'

'Yes,' said Fletcher. 'All gone.'

*

Walking away from Sion Square, Fletcher turned to George. 'So, let me get this straight, Major Hart. Black steals part of the prince's letter to Kosminski and leaves it next to Chapman's body. Why? To shift the blame from the real killers, Black and his accomplice – if, of course, he has one – and onto his former lover and the prince. And he does this partly because he's angry with Kosminski for preferring the prince to him. Correct so far?'

'Yes, Sergeant, I think that's a fair summary.'

'So does this all mean that Kosminski and the prince are now in the clear?'

'Good question. I *suspect* it does. But until we identify Black's accomplice, we won't know for sure. One outside possibility is that Kosminski and Black are in it together. But as they're similar in build and looks to only one of the possible killers, whereas the other is described by witnesses as taller, with dark hair and light skin, I doubt it very much. The accomplice could, of course, still be the prince. But if he is, why would Black try to implicate him by planting the letter. No. I suspect it's someone else entirely. But who? And, more importantly, how can we *prove* Black is the killer?'

'Well, there might be one way.'

'Go on.'

'We all keep personal items in lockers at the station. It's just possible that Black has left something in his that will incriminate him.'

'Yes it's possible. All right, Sergeant, let's find out.'

17

'Now remember,' said Fletcher, as they approached the porticoed entrance of the large stone and brick three-storey building, 'I've brought you in to take your statement about last night. We'll get you into an interview room and decide what to do next. Sound all right?'

'Fine by me.'

They paused at the steps to the main entrance to allow two constables to leave. The second of the two was Tom Black. 'Hello, Sergeant,' said Black, grinning as he held the door open for Fletcher. 'I see you bring suspect in for question.'

The sight of Black, and the memory of what he and his accomplice had probably done to Mary, prompted a surge of anger in George's breast, and it was as much as he could do to stop himself from grabbing the constable and bashing his head against the wall. But Fletcher calmed the situation by dismissing Black with a wave of his hand. 'I'll trust you to keep your smart Aleck comments to yourself, Constable. Major Hart is not a suspect; he's helping with inquiries.'

Inside the building they were confronted by a portly desk sergeant with magnificent mutton-chop whiskers. 'Ah, Fletcher,' he said, 'just in time. Inspector Abberline wants

233

you in the briefing room. He's received the report from the autopsy. All detectives and uniformed officers in the building are expected to attend. Desk staff excepted, of course.'

'I'll be right there. This man,' said Fletcher, pointing at George, 'is Major Hart. He was in the vicinity of the murder last night and is here to give a statement. Which interview room is free?'

'Number Two.'

'Good. He can wait in there while I speak to the detective inspector. I'll take him up.'

George followed Fletcher up the central staircase to the second-floor landing, where they turned left down a narrow corridor. Number 2 Interview Room was second from the end. Fletcher opened the door and ushered George inside a bare whitewashed room, a small wooden table and two chairs its only furniture. Apart from a small window that provided a tiny bit of natural light, the room was mostly in shadow. Fletcher lit a paraffin lamp, adjusted its flame and turned to George. 'I've just had a thought. The briefing might be our opportunity to see what's in Black's locker. You heard the desk sergeant. Everyone will be there apart from desk and clerical staff, and they're all on the ground floor. The lockers, on the other hand, are in the anteroom to the staff room on this floor. The briefing will last at least half an hour, if not longer. That should give us plenty of time to break into Black's locker and have a look. I say us, but I mean you of course, Major Hart. I'll be in the briefing. Are you happy to take the risk?'

'Of course. How will I know it's Black's locker?'

'They all have name tags. As for getting it open, you'll find some tools that should do the job in a store cupboard in the staff room.'

Fletcher paused at the open door. 'Just follow the corridor back to the main landing and then take the corridor opposite to the end of the building. It's a black door. The lockers, as I said, are in the anteroom. Good luck.'

Once Fletcher had gone, George tiptoed as quietly as he could down the corridor, across the landing and into the second corridor. He paused at the black door and listened, but there was no sound of any occupants. He pushed the door open and stepped into a small room with rows of wooden lockers, eighteen inches wide and two feet high, on both side walls. Below the lockers were wooden benches strewn with odd bits of police equipment: helmets, truncheons, rattles and bull's-eye kerosene lanterns. The lockers themselves were arranged alphabetically, and it didn't take George long to locate Black's. It was secured with a simple mortice lock and George was fairly confident he could break it open with a chisel.

He found one in the store cupboard off the deserted staff room, the latter's tables still strewn with mugs and newspapers. Leaving the storeroom he heard the sound of someone in the anteroom and froze, chisel in hand, heart thumping. He looked around for somewhere to hide and thought the store cupboard might have enough space. But as no one immediately entered the staff room, he realized they must be busy in the anteroom. He crept towards the door and looked through the small, eye-height window. A policeman with his back to George had opened a locker in the vincinity of Black's; he was taking objects from it and putting them in a canvas bag. One was wrapped in a white cloth streaked with red stains. George couldn't think what it might be until the policeman half turned towards him. It was Black. He must have returned to the station and seized the same opportunity to enter the locker room that George had thought to take; which meant the object he was handling, George suddenly realized, was almost certainly Mary's heart. He gagged and gave the door a violent shove, fully intent on driving the chisel he was holding into Black's deranged brain. But the door held fast, though George had turned the handle; Black must have locked it from the inside.

He felt in his pocket for his Derringer, before remembering it had been taken from him. He slammed his palm into the thick glass pane in frustration. It did not break, though the noise alerted Black who looked up and saw George, his handsome features contorted with hate. Ignoring the interruption, Black calmly took a last couple of objects from his locker – one of which, from its dimensions, might have been a knife – and put them in the bag before zipping it up and leaving. He did not look back.

All the while George was hammering on the door and shouting, 'It's the Ripper! It's the Ripper! Stop him!' But nobody heard him, and nobody intervened. They were all on the ground floor, too far away to hear his desperate cries. Realizing that Black was about to escape with the proof that he was a murderer, which he could then hide or destroy at his leisure, George scanned the staff room for another exit. At the far end, near the store cupboard, was a solid door with a key in the lock. He ran to it, turned the key and wrenched the door open. It was a fire exit and led to a metal stairway that dropped two flights to a lane that ran along the rear of the building. George took the steps three at a time, and almost fell as he changed direction at the first-storey landing. But he ran on regardless, prepared to risk all to stop Black escaping.

Reaching terra firma, a dirty lane piled with rubbish, he turned right and then right again, entering Commercial

Street a short way above the police station. It was almost six o'clock in the evening, and the pavement was crowded with the usual hawkers and pedestrians. So George took to the road, dodging a horse and cart, and then sidestepping a swaying drunk as neatly as if he was on the rugby football field again. Reaching the entrance to the police station, he looked right and left. There was no sign of Black and his canvas bag. *Am I too late?*

He ran up the steps and into the station, surprising the desk sergeant who had last seen him heading up the stairs with Fletcher. 'How the heck did you get—'

'I'm sorry, Sergeant,' said George. 'I don't have time to explain. I need to know if PC Tom Black just left the building.'

'Why, yes. Just before you arrived. I'm surprised you didn't—'

'Did he say where he was going?'

'No, why would he? He's probably going home.'

'Where does he live?'

The desk sergeant looked at George as if he'd taken leave of his senses. 'I'm sorry, sir. You know I can't tell you that.'

George clenched his fists in frustration, and realized he was still holding the chisel. He was tempted to use it to threaten the desk sergeant. But he knew that would only lead to his arrest; meanwhile Black was getting away. 'Please,' he said in desperation, 'it's important, a matter of life and death, quite literally.'

'I'm sorry, sir. You'll need to speak to Inspector Abberline.'

Aware he was getting nowhere, and that it would waste too much time to get Fletcher to help, he ran back out of the station. *Which way has he gone?* George wondered. *North up Commercial Street? South? Or down one of the side streets?* Ruling out the side streets, George chose south on a hunch and charged back down Commercial Street, dodging in and out of the traffic on the pavement and road as before. 'Whoa Mister!' shouted one rouged young woman as he barged past. 'What's the 'urry?'

Stopping after a few hundred yards to catch his breath, he noticed he was at the junction with Dorset Street, and just yards from the scene of Mary's murder. His eyes were drawn inexorably up the street, to where the crowd of people was still gathered at the entrance to Miller's Court. 'Bloody vultures are still there,' he muttered. He was about to turn away and continue the pursuit when he noticed the dark outline of a man wearing a police helmet at the near edge of the crowd. *The height's about right; but it can't be Black, can it?* He had read somewhere that multiple murderers often returned to the scene of the crime to watch the police and gloat. *But with a bag stuffed full of incriminating evidence, and so soon after the killing? Only a lunatic would do such a thing. Hold on!* thought George. *Only a lunatic would commit such barbaric murders in the first place. Could it be Black after all? I have to find out.*

As George set off up Dorset Street, walking so as not to draw attention to himself, he tried to keep the police helmet in sight, but it soon disappeared in the crowd. Reaching the edge of the press, he still couldn't see it. *Where had it gone?*

He pushed into the crowd, looking right and left. The only policemen in view were the pair guarding the entrance to the court. Neither of them was Black. He turned full circle and, as he did so, something caught his eye. It was evening now, and almost dark, but he could see something moving in the alley across the street; the same alley that Fletcher had chosen as his hiding place.

He squinted and thought he could see, in the shadows, the outline of someone wearing a police helmet. *Was it Black?* He forced his way out of the crowd and ran the last few yards to the alley entrance, unaware that a woman and small child were approaching from his left. The child, an infant girl, was slightly ahead of its mother and took the full force of George's left knee as it collided with her. The two went down in a heap. As George scrambled to his feet, the girl was lying very still, as if badly hurt. Ignoring the mother's insults, he knelt by the girl to check her wrist pulse. It was faint, but detectable. 'I'm so sorry, but I think she'll be all right,' said George, flipping the mother a coin. 'Please get her checked by a doctor.'

He pulled the chisel from his pocket and entered a narrow alley between two buildings. He could only make out random shapes in the gloom, and had to feel his way with one hand on the wall to his left. When the wall ran out, he stopped and listened. Someone was shouting in the building to his right; but the yard beyond was quiet. He moved forward, chisel extended, one cautious step at a time. Something hard banged against his shin. He put his hands down and felt the hard edge of a wooden crate. He skirted round it and his right shoe slipped on something. The repulsive odour was umistakable: human excrement. He sighed as he wiped his shoe on the ground.

On he crept and, remembering the yard as about twelve feet square, thought he must be near to its far side. He put out both hands and eventually felt the wooden fence that separated the yard from one attached to a building in the next street. George felt for the top of the fence and estimated its height at six feet. It would have been a simple task for Black to scale it, hop down into the yard the other side and exit through the passage into White's Row. George thought he must have done so, and was about to follow, when rapid footsteps sounded behind him. He turned and felt the rush of air as something swung towards him. He raised the chisel just in time and saw sparks as metal clashed against it. *He's got a knife.* Not waiting for a second blow, he lunged forward, his arm fully extended, and felt the blade of the chisel enter flesh.

'Aargh!' screamed his attacker.

He lunged again, but felt as he did so a stinging blow to the top of his hand, causing him to drop the chisel. His right hand was numb and wouldn't grip, leaving him one hand and no weapon to defend himself. All logic told him to flee. But in which direction? His attacker was between him and the exit and he couldn't climb the fence behind him with one hand. It was just as well, because he never would have forgiven himself for running from the man he assumed was Mary's murderer.

His attacker closed in, grunting with exertion and pain as he did so. George dodged to his left, feeling on the ground for a weapon. He felt something solid and tried to lift it. But it was too heavy. He turned back to face his attacker who, wounded and unable to see properly in the dark, was slashing wildly with his knife, hoping for a lucky blow. One near miss thudded into an object beside George's head, jarring the attacker's hand. George thrust his left hand forward and grabbed the knifeman's wrist. *At last I can bring my superior size to bear and overpower him.* But he had underestimated the smaller man's strength. Instead of forcing the knife away, it was as much as he could do to hold it at arm's length. The struggle continued for what seemed like minutes, but was probably just seconds, and all the time George felt his strength ebbing away with the blood from his badly cut hand.

Slowly but surely, George's good hand, and therefore the blade of the knife, was being forced back against his chest. He tried to strike the man's face with his wounded hand, but it was like a slap from a dead fish: unpleasant, but hardly fatal. With just moments to live, he let go of the man's wrist and rolled away to his right, along the front of the fence. As he rose to his knees, half expecting to feel the sharp pain of a blade piercing his flesh, he heard his assailant – Black? – stumbling out of the yard. He wanted to follow; but had neither the will nor the strength. He slumped to the ground, breathing hard.

*

A hard slap brought George round. He opened his eyes and was dazzled by the light from a bull's-eye lantern. 'Don't shine it in his bloody eyes!' barked Fletcher at the policeman holding the lantern.

Once the light had been turned away, George eyes's began to focus. Of the three faces staring at him, the only one he recognized was Fletcher's. 'Thank God!' said the sergeant. 'I thought you were a goner when I first saw you. What happened? No, don't answer that. You can tell me later. That looks like a nasty cut on your hand. Constable Thomas, here, will patch you up and then we'll get you off to hospital.'

A young constable knelt down next to George and examined the wound. 'It looks like a knife wound, sir. He's lost a lot of blood.'

'I can see that. Just bind it up, there's a good fellow.'

Though still groggy, the memory of what had just happened was coming back to George. 'Did anyone see the man who attacked me?' he asked.

'I'm afraid not,' said Fletcher. 'Most of the people in Dorset Street were either looking at Miller's Court or a young girl who was knocked over on the pavement.'

'Is she all right?'

'Yes. She'll be fine. She has a few cuts and bruises, but no bones broken. Why do you ask?'

'Because I'm the one who knocked her over. Accidentally, of course.'

'Well you've no need to worry. She's fine. Now let's get you up and out of this hell hole.'

Fletcher grabbed George's good hand and hauled him to his feet. 'Can you walk?'

'Yes. I think so. But there's one thing your men must do before they leave: search this yard with a fine-tooth comb. I can't be certain, but I think they'll find items that are relevant to the recent Ripper murders.'

'*Here*? Why, did you see something?'

'No, but I think they're here all the same. Trust me on this. Please get your men to search.'

'All right I will. Anything else I should know? Did you get a good look at the man who attacked you?'

'No, but I did manage to wound him with a chisel before he cut my hand.'

'Do you know where?'

'Not exactly. I'd guess the body or the arm. It was too dark to see. But he let out a loud groan so it was more than a scratch. And it's just as well for me it was. He'll try to hide it,' said George, giving Fletcher a pointed look, 'but he was definitely hurt.'

'Thank you, Major Hart. That's very useful.'

18

69 Alnwick Grove, Hammersmith

'How're you feeling?' asked Sergeant Fletcher when George answered the door in his silk dressing gown. To Fletcher, standing on the doorstep, he looked like a battle casualty with his bandaged hand and badly bruised temple.

'I'll live. Come in and we can talk.'

George led Fletcher into the front parlour and gestured to a chair. When they were both sitting, he asked: 'Did you find anything in the yard?'

Fletcher nodded. 'Under an old mattress: a knife with an eight-inch blade and a fleck of blood near its hilt, a brown deerstalker, and a human heart. We think it's Mary Kelly's.'

'So do I. The bastard. He kept it all in his locker. Can you believe it?'

'No, I can't. Now tell me what happened after I left you.'

George did so, ending with the fight in the yard.

'Incredible,' said Fletcher. 'You said yesterday that you wounded the man who attacked you. Did you ever actually identify him as Black? Did he say anything to you?'

'No, but it must have been him. I saw him taking the evidence – the same items your men found under the mattress – from his locker.'

243

'You saw him taking something from his locker, I don't doubt that, and it was almost certainly what you say it was. But think how it would appear in a court of law? The defence would say you were looking through a window at a distance of five or six yards, and that you couldn't possibly have known exactly what Black was handling. You say you saw him take out something wrapped in a bloody cloth. We didn't find any cloth, only the heart. The defence will say we have no proof that the heart we found was the same object that Black removed from his locker.'

George snorted in exasperation. 'What about the other evidence? We know that Black has a possible motive to implicate Kosminski and the prince, and that he almost certainly stole a fragment of the latter's letter and planted it at one of the murder scenes. What about the Star of David that I found in the dustbin? You think you might have seen Black wearing something similar. Then there's the telephone conversation you had with Black before Mary's death. He deliberately didn't do what you asked because he knew it would leave Mary unprotected. Surely all this is enough to arrest him?'

'No, I'm not sure it is. Just listen to the language you're using: "possible", "almost certainly", "might have". Truth is, as you said yourself, we don't have any cast-iron proof. You mentioned the Star of David. Even if I was certain that I'd seen Black wearing it, and I'm not, we still have the problem that you failed to declare it when you found it. I understand the reason: we were suspicious of Abberline and Warren, and thought the prince might still be involved. Now we know he probably isn't, it's too late. As for items found in the yard off Dorset Street, it might be different if you'd seen Black hiding them with your own eyes. But you didn't. You can't even be certain that he was the man who tried to kill you. All our evidence is either circumstantial or unreliable and, as things stand, it wouldn't convince a jury to convict.'

'And if Black has a hole in him that could have been made by a chisel? Is that not an indication that it was he who attacked me?'

'An indication yes, but not proof. He could give any number of reasons for accidentally wounding himself.'

George had heard enough. 'Whose bloody side are you on, Fletcher?' he barked, jabbing his forefinger at the sergeant's chest. 'You were *just as* convinced as I am that Black is either the Ripper or his accomplice. Yet the way you're talking, it sounds as though you're having second thoughts. Are you?'

'No. Not for a minute. I'm certain Black is the killer. But how to prove that? And even if we had more evidence, I'm not entirely convinced that Abberline and Warren would want all this out in the open. Can you imagine the outcry, and the subsequent loss of confidence in the police, if it became known that the Ripper was a copper? Then there's the inevitability that any public trial of Black would be bound to reveal the reason for the prince's forays into Whitechapel. You said yourself that republicanism is on the rise. Well, this scandal, involving the Prince of Wales's eldest son, would shake the monarchy to its core – even if it exonerated the prince of murder. No, we have to think of another way to deal with Black and get him to reveal the name of his accomplice. And the need is doubly pressing because Abberline, on hearing that you were found in the same yard as the knife and the heart, is more convinced than ever that you're involved in some capacity. As he put it, "Why else would he keep turning up at locations where the Ripper has just been?" He has a point, and the obvious way to allay Abberline's suspicion is either to tell him the truth or expose the real killers. The first option would end my career because they'd say, with some justification, that I'd withheld important information about the inquiry. It would also get you into hot water. So I suggest we take the latter option.'

George exhaled slowly. 'All right. I accept we've made mistakes and that a lot of our evidence is not cast-iron. But if we both know Black's the killer, surely there must be a way to *make* him confess? After what he did to Mary, and attempted to do to me, I'd be happy to take matters into our own hands.'

'You mean torture him?'

'Yes, if necessary. If you fight for Queen and Country, like I do, you're bound to pick up some tips from the locals. The Afghans, for example, are not above cutting off a man's toes, one by one, to get him to talk.'

'Uugh!' said Fletcher. 'You're not seriously suggesting we do that to Black? We'd be descending to his level, Major Hart, and that's not something I'm prepared to do. I'm a policeman, for goodness' sake, and sworn to uphold the law. You're an officer and a gentleman. Let's try and solve this problem without becoming criminals ourselves.'

George could see the sense of Fletcher words, but felt himself boiling with frustration. It was not for them to resort to barbarity. *But if they wouldn't, who would?* Suddenly it came to him. 'I think I may have the solution. You may be loath to commit a criminal act, but there are others who are not so squeamish.'

'Who do you mean?'

'The clue's in the name.'

Fletcher looked nonplussed. 'I don't understand.'

'Why criminals, of course. They do this sort of thing all the time; particularly violent criminals.'

'What are you suggesting? That we hire some thugs to do our dirty work?'

'Not quite, because that in itself would be a criminal act. I have a much better idea.'

'Go on.'

'The people I have in mind are both ruthless and violent, and more importantly have a vested interest in punishing Mary's killer.'

'Mary? Why Mary? Why not the other victims?'

'Because none of the other victims, as far as I know, was related to a terrorist.'

'You mean *the Fenians*?'

'That's exactly who I mean. You remember me telling you that Mary stopped her Fenian brother Liam from killing me for foiling an assassination plot?'

'I do.'

'Well, can you imagine what he'll do to Black when he finds out about his sister?'

'And you're going to tell him?'

'I am. I'm going to put a proposition to him that he'll find hard to refuse. What is Black's address?'

'He lives in Mount Street, Whitechapel. Number Twenty-Two. A room on the first floor, I think. Are you sure about this?'

'No. I'm not. But what other options do we have? Wait here a moment. I won't be long,' said George, before leaving the room.

While Fletcher waited, he wracked his brain for a less desperate solution to their problem; one that would deal with the killers *and* preserve their careers. He was still trying to think of one when George reappeared a few minutes later, fully dressed and holding two sheets of writing paper. 'Read this,' said George, handing him the sheets, 'and tell me what you think.'

Fletcher scanned the letter:

Dear Liam,

You will have heard by now of the cruel murder of your sister Mary by the so-called 'Jack the Ripper'. I am the British Army officer, recently attached to the Special Irish Branch, whom she prevented you from killing recently. By all rights I should be straining every sinew to bring you to justice. Instead I have a proposition for you. I know the identity of Mary's killer but, for reasons I won't go into, am unable to bring him to justice. I would therefore like you – her brother – to take care of the problem. I wouldn't presume to suggest how you might do this. But I hope you can get this man to confess his crimes and name his accomplice, for I have it on good authority that he did not act alone. The accomplice is equally responsible for Mary's death. Together they've butchered at least five unfortunates, including Mary. Unless they're stopped, more will die.

If you're prepared to do this – and I cannot imagine it will be a hardship – I will pledge not to pursue you for your attempt to kill me unless, in the future, you commit more crimes against the British state. For the record, I was born in Dublin and sympathize with the cause of Irish self-determination. I agree with your political aims, but not the violent means by which you hope to achieve them.

To prove this is not a trap, I am willing to put myself in your power until you've abducted Mary's murderer and extracted the necessary information. Just let me know where and when you would like me to come. I will then give you the name and address of the murderer.

You can accept this offer by sending a note c/o Detective Sergeant Jack Fletcher, Whitechapel CID, Commercial Street Police Station, Whitechapel. It must reach its destination no later than noon tomorrow.

Yours etc.

George Hart, VC, Major (aka 'Tom Quinn')

Fletcher looked up from the letter. 'Have you taken leave of your senses? Why would you put yourself at the mercy of a Fenian who's already tried to kill you?'

'Because it's the only way to convince him this is not a set-up like last time; and because I'm certain that if he has any shred of humanity, he will put justice for his sister ahead of Fenian revenge.'

'And what if he doesn't? What if he kills both of you?'

'Then I'll be past caring. You have to admit: it's a neat solution.'

'I'll hold my judgement on that, Major Hart. An awful lot could go wrong. And I'm not entirely comfortable about giving confidential information like a policeman's home address to a terrorist.'

'Well, we're not talking about any old policeman, are we? We're talking about a multiple murderer who has terrorized the East End for long enough. If all goes to plan, Liam Kelly and his friends will put a stop to this once and for all.'

'You make it seem so simple. But you do realize, don't you Major Hart, that you're effectively inciting a known terrorist to commit murder?'

'No, I don't agree. Nowhere in that letter is an incitement to murder. I was very careful not to do that. Instead I asked Liam "to take care of the problem". How he does that is his business. Now, are you with me on this or not?'

Fletcher sighed. 'I'm reminded of that great line in *Macbeth*. "I am in blood stepped in so far that, should I wade no more, returning were as tedious as go o'er." I feel the same way.'

'That's impressive,' said George. 'There can't be too many police sergeants who can quote Shakespeare. So we agree on this?'

'I wouldn't go quite that far. But, yes, I'm with you – for good or ill.'

19

The Kingdom public house, Kilburn

A single man was standing at the bar as George entered the pub. He had his back to the door, but George knew it was Liam Kelly from his long dark hair and squat shape. He turned as George approached, a sneer on his face. 'You've got some nerve, I'll give you that,' said Kelly. 'What's to stop me taking you outside and putting a bullet in you?'

'Absolutely nothing. But you should know that Detective Sergeant Jack Fletcher, my colleague in the Whitechapel CID, knows all about you and your links to Irish republicanism. If I don't return safe and sound, he will hunt you down and see you hanged.' George knew that it was a largely idle threat; but he wanted to make Kelly think twice.

'I'm quaking in my boots,' said Liam, shaking his hands in mock fear. 'Don't think 'cos I responded to your letter you're in the clear. You aren't. But I'm prepared to call a truce while I deal with, as you put it, our mutual problem. First things first, what are you drinking?'

'Whiskey and water.'

'Gerry,' said Liam to the man behind the bar. 'Yer man will have a Bushmills and water. Bring it to the table in the corner.'

'Righto,' said the barman.

Liam carried his pint of stout to a round table in the far corner and sat down opposite George. 'I need to know,' said the Fenian, 'how Mary died and why? The papers say she was found in her room. Do you know how she met the killer?'

'Yes I do, and I'm partly responsible. After she saved my life, we went for a drink and Mary told me her life story: how she drifted into prostitution after the death of her husband and eventually settled in Whitechapel; and how she'd refused to help you and the Fenians by seducing a senior policeman so you could murder him.'

Liam's eyes narrowed. 'She told you *that*? A bloody copper? If I'd known I'd have finished her myself.'

Before George could respond, the barman appeared with his whiskey. George took a large gulp. When the barman was out of earshot, he turned to Liam: 'You don't get it, do you? Not everyone shares your fanaticism – not even your family. As I said in my note, I sympathize with your aims; or some of them, at least. But not your methods.'

'My methods, you say? Yet you're asking me to commit murder.'

'Where in my letter does it mention murder? I asked you to take care of a problem that interests us both: namely to get a man to admit to being the Ripper and to name his accomplice. How you do it is your business.'

'A fine distinction, I don't think. You and I both know that if I get my hands on the bastard who killed my sister, he won't emerge with his skin whole. Which suits you because I'll be doing your dirty work. The question is: why? Why can't you arrest him yourself?'

'Because we know it's him, but we don't have that crucial bit of evidence that would convince a jury.'

'But you're certain it's him? No doubts?'

'We're certain. We wouldn't be asking you to do this if we weren't.'

'Fair enough. So you were having this cosy chat with Mary. What then?'

'She offered to help me catch the Ripper.'

'She *what*?'

'She offered to act as bait.'

'Why?'

'For money, so she could start a new life.'

'How much money?'

'Three and a half thousand pounds.'

'You're kidding? Where would you get that sort of money?'

'I can't say. But she'd have got her money if . . .' George's voice tailed away.

'She'd lived? But she didn't, did she? Poor cow,' said Liam. 'She never had much luck. And to think she was trying to start a new life. So tell me what happened?'

George explained, in detail, the plan to catch the Ripper and his accomplice by sending Mary out to pick up someone who matched either of their descriptions; and how he and Detective Sergeant Fletcher would be waiting outside her room to intervene. 'The idea,' said George, 'was to catch them in the act, or just before it. It seems mad after the event; but at the time we couldn't think of another way.'

'No,' snarled Liam, 'and you didn't need to, did you? You had Mary as your bait, and even if she died, you'd still get the people responsible. That's the truth, isn't it?'

'No, it wasn't like that at all. In fact when she first offered to help I turned her down because I knew the risks. But she was prepared to take them and we, in turn, did everything we could to keep her safe.'

253

'So why did you fail?'

'Because, unbeknown to us, one of the killers became aware of our plan, or at least part of it, and took advantage. He made me think that Fletcher was in position when he wasn't. This allowed one of them to take care of me, by knocking me out, while the other killed Mary.'

'All right,' said Liam. 'I've heard enough. Just tell me the killer's name and address and I'll deal with him.'

'His name,' said George, 'is Police Constable Tom Black.'

'A *copper*? How did you find out?'

'I became suspicious when I learnt it was Black who failed to pass on a crucial message from Fletcher on the night of Mary's murder. Then everything fell into place. If Black was the killer, it would explain why he was the first policeman to attend many of the murder scenes; why the victims appeared to have trusted their killer as if they knew him; and why the killer and his accomplice were often able to leave the scene of the crime at the last minute. When he found out I knew, he tried and failed to kill me,' said George, lifting his bandaged hand. 'Unfortunately it was dark and I couldn't identify him.'

'So you've come to me instead.'

'Yes. We both want revenge. It seemed like the obvious solution.'

Liam slowly shook his head. 'You think I'm an idiot, don't you?'

'No, why do you say that?'

'Because what you told me doesn't tally. Oh, I know as well as anyone that the police can make mistakes. They do all the time. But if this was an official police operation, you'd have had a lot more support in case anything went wrong. Instead it sounds like it was just you and this Sergeant Fletcher, and that you were acting alone. Is that right?'

George thought of lying. He had imagined he was dealing with a simple-minded terrorist, but Liam was clearly a lot sharper than that. 'Yes, we were acting alone. I can't go into details, but I will say that senior police officers were not doing all they could to catch the Ripper.'

'Why? Were they trying to protect Black?'

'No, they didn't know about him. Still don't. I think they thought someone else – someone of great influence – was involved and didn't want it to be made public.'

'And might he be the accomplice?'

'No, I don't think so.'

'You're a queer one, Tom Quinn, or whatever your name is.'

'It's Hart. Major Hart.'

'You're a queer one, Major Hart. I can't make you out at all. You look foreign, you claim you were born in Dublin, and you agree with me that Ireland should have its own government; yet you serve the British. Why?'

'It's hard to explain. Suffice to say my background is complicated.'

'That's no excuse. You can't sit on the fence for ever, Major Hart. In the end you have to choose. We all do. Truth is, you've already made your choice, and I've made mine. Which is why, when all this is over, I'll kill you if our paths cross again.'

'They won't.'

'All right: where does this Black live?'

'Twenty-Two Mount Street, just south of the Whitechapel Road. He has a room on the first floor.'

'Any idea why he's been killing the women?'

'Not really. The little I know about him is that he was born Tomasz Cherniy, a Polish Jew. His family immigrated to

Britain to escape the anti-Jewish pogroms of the early 1880s. He might have been unhinged by what he witnessed. Or he might just be a cold-blooded killer who enjoys the infliction of pain. It's impossible to say.'

'Well, if it's the latter,' said Liam, draining his pint, 'he's about to get a taste of his own medicine. As for you, there's a van outside to take you to a safe house. You'll be held there until it's over. Any message you'd like me to give PC Black before it's too late?'

'Yes. Tell him I'm glad I didn't kill him in the yard. Because that would have prevented you from getting your own personal revenge which, I suspect, is going to be much more painful.'

'I'll tell him. Finish that,' said Liam, nodding towards George's whiskey, 'and let's be off.'

George savoured the last gulp, knowing it might be a while before he had another. 'Any idea how long you'll need to hold me?'

'Long as it takes.'

*

George lay staring at the ceiling. It was dark and he'd lost track of time, but he estimated he must have been in the locked room for at least thirty-six hours.

He'd been brought, bound and blindfolded, to the house by two men, and received by another who'd led him down a flight of stairs into what George assumed must be a basement or cellar. There his blindfold was taken off and he got a brief look at both his jailer – a stocky, shaven-headed man in his thirties – and a bare whitewashed room that contained just a simple iron bedstead, a washbasin and a bucket for a toilet, not unlike a normal prison cell. But then the door was closed, plunging the room into darkness, and had remained so for much of the time since, the only exceptions being the all-too-brief moments his jailer had unlocked it to deliver unappetizing food and jugs of water, or to empty his bucket of slops. To relieve the boredom, George had tried to talk his jailer, asking him harmless questions such as 'How's the weather today?' The man did not respond and George gave up asking.

Instead, apart from the odd burst of physical activity, such as calisthenics (which he had learnt in the army) or running on the spot, George had spent most of his time thinking: about Lucy and Jake, and how much he missed them; about the unexpected confirmation from Mrs FitzGeorge that his father was indeed none other than Field Marshal HRH the Duke of Cambridge, Commander-in-Chief of the British Army; and about Liam Kelly's comment that he was a bundle of contradictions who had, nevertheless, chosen to serve the British state. Kelly was right. He had. *But did I ever really have a choice?* George asked himself.

His mind wandered back to his conversation with Fanny Colenso in late 1878, shortly before the British invasion of Zululand in southern Africa. Aware that his mother was half-Zulu, Fanny had asked him how he could fight his own kind. His response had been that they weren't; that he might have had a quarter Zulu blood in his veins, but all his instincts and prejudices were those of a British officer. She was unconvinced, insisting that he had an affinity for Africa because part of him *was* African. He remembered the exact words of his response: 'Maybe you're right. But I'm also a British soldier and my duty now is to fight.'

If that was the moment he had made his choice – by deciding that his British heritage was more important than his African, or indeed his Irish – did he ever really have an option? he wondered. After all, he had been educated in the British public school system from the age of seven; and thereafter at Sandhurst. During those formative years he had been conditioned to think like a member of Britain's ruling elite, and no amount of 'foreign' blood flowing in his veins was likely to change that. Did that mean that nurture was more important than nature, that environment had more impact on your adult self than inherited characteristics? He suspected that it did, though in his case the balance was tipped back the other way by the fact that his father was a both a soldier and a member of the British royal family.

But if his loyalties to Britain were always paramount, that didn't stop him seeing the world from other people's perspectives: he had felt genuine sympathy for the plight of most of Britain's recent enemies – notably the Zulus and Afghans, and even the Boers and the Sudanese – and had supported the cause of Irish self-determination since he was a boy, a political bias he kept well hidden from his brother officers. More recently he had been genuinely moved by the plight of the East End underclass, particularly the women driven by poverty into prostitution, a sympathy that had played its part in his acceptance of Mary's offer to help trap the Ripper in the hope that she could create a better life for herself. Did all this make him a hypocrite? He didn't think so. He had his unbreakable ties: to his family, his friends, his colleagues and his country. But he could also see beyond the narrow viewpoints of a typical man of his class and occupation. That had to be a good thing, he decided.

If he had any slight regrets, one was his unorthodox habit of operating as a loner. This was useful when it came to gathering intelligence in a foreign country; but in recent months, in Britain, his attempt – however justified – to solve the Ripper murders outside official police channels had led to the tragic death of a brave and beautiful young woman who, through no fault of her own, had ended up working as a prostitute. Mary's death was not entirely in vain in that, since the night of her killing (and partly because of it), he and Fletcher had identified at least one of the culprits. But they still needed the name of his accomplice. Then, and only then, could George rest easy that no more women would share Mary's grisly fate.

With his mind a little more at ease, George was contemplating a bit of exercise when he heard steps approaching. A key was turned in the lock and the door swung open, revealing his shaven-headed jailer, pistol in hand. 'Time to go, put this on,' he said, handing George a blindfold.

'Where to?'

'You'll see.'

20

Rural Hertfordshire

The journey in the back of the horse-drawn goods wagon –
the same one that had taken George to the initial meeting
with the Fenian 'Boss' – seemed interminable. For hours it
bumped and rattled its way along roads and tracks. At times
the volume of noise from other vehicles, riders and pedestrians grew in intensity, and George assumed they were passing
through a village or small town. But that hadn't happened
for at least an hour when the wagon finally came to a halt
and the rear door was opened.

'Up!' said a voice, as George was grabbed roughly by the
arm and yanked from a side bench. He stumbled as he was
half-pushed and half-pulled from the wagon, his injured
hand making painful contact with the ground. 'Hell's teeth!'
roared George. 'Take more care, you clumsy idiot! Can't you
see I'm injured?'

He received a stinging blow to the cheek in response.
'Mind yer bloody language, or I'll give yer a proper injury.'

He was then frog-marched across some rough ground and
down a steep slope. George lost his footing numerous times,
and would have fallen if the man had not been supporting
him. As the ground began to level off, George could hear

groans from a man in pain. They got louder as he and his escort approached. Finally George was halted and rough fingers untied his blindfold. It was twilight – late afternoon – but there was still enough light to cause him to blink.

He was in the centre of what appeared to be a deep stone quarry, its jagged sides rising steeply up for more than a hundred feet. It was bitingly cold – even colder than it had been at ground level – and he shivered involuntarily. Directly ahead, at a distance of fifteen yards, stood Liam and another man, both stripped to the waist, their torsos covered in blood. It was not theirs. At their feet was a man on his hands and knees. He was also shirtless, his broad back criss-crossed with livid welts, cuts and burns. On his left side, just below the ribs, was a deep stab wound that might have been made by a chisel.

Spotting George, Liam grabbed a fistful of his victim's dark hair and lifted his head. The face was barely recognizable as human; more like a piece of tenderized steak. The only distinguishing feature was the neatly clipped light brown moustache, caked with blood. 'Just kill me!' croaked Black. 'I can't take any more.'

'You want mercy, do you? Like the mercy you showed my sister, you bloody coward,' said Liam as he thudded a knuck-leduster-clad fist into the side of Black's bowed head. Black toppled sideways with a groan.

Liam beckoned George over. 'I've got good news and bad news for you, Major Hart. The good news is that it was him, all right,' said the Fenian, nodding at the prone body before him. 'He admitted killing all six.'

George slowly exhaled. He had known it was Black, of course, but it was a relief to hear confirmation from the kill-er's own mouth. 'And the bad news?'

'He won't say who his accomplice is. Insists he acted alone. Mumbled he was sorry. Said he was abused. Hated women. That's it, I'm afraid. I spent the last day trying to change his mind. We've whipped, burnt and beaten him to a pulp. We even tied a towel round his face and wet it 'til he almost choked. But he stuck to his story. Which is why I sent for you. Thought you'd like a chance to work on him a little. Don't expect he's got long to go.'

'Can I speak to him alone?'

'Of course.' Liam gestured the other man to follow him.

When both Fenians were ten or fifteen yards distant, George knelt down next to the policeman and said in a whisper, 'Black, it's Major Hart. The man you tried to kill, remember? Well, you failed, and now you're done for. Death will be a blessed release for you, I'm sure. But not just yet, and in the meantime I need to know who helped you kill those women. If you tell me, I'll make sure you're put out of your misery. If not, they can keep this up for days. Do you understand?'

Black nodded.

'Tell me his name.'

Black's battered lips tried to form a word. George leaned closer. Black mumbled something. It sounded to George like 'Prince's friend', but he couldn't be certain.

'Did you say "Prince's friend"?'

Black's head seemed to move forward, but it was such a small incline as to be almost imperceptible.

'Was that a yes?'

Black remained perfectly still. George tried to revive him by shaking his shoulder. There was no response. Eventually Liam strode up with a bucket of cold water. 'Shamming, is he? Well this'll get his attention,' he said, empting the bucket over Black's head.

There was no response. Liam bent down to check the pulse on Black's neck. 'Feck it!' he said, after a short delay. 'He's dead, and good riddance. Well, that's the end of our bargain, Major bloody Hart. We'll deal with the body. You get along, now. If I see you again, you're a dead man.'

*

'I told you it was a bloody stupid idea,' said Fletcher, shaking his head, 'but you wouldn't listen, would you? I'm just surprised the Fenians didn't kill you as well.'

'And a very good morning to you too,' said George, opening the front door wider. 'I see you got my note.'

'Yes, I got it. But it doesn't make a lot of sense. You say in it that Black confessed to being the Ripper, but died before the Fenians could discover the identity of his accomplice. Yet you go on to say you think you know who that person might be. Mind enlightening me?'

'Not at all. Shall we talk inside?'

George led the way into the front parlour and, without consulting Fletcher, poured two whiskies. He handed one to the sergeant and gestured to an easy chair. George sat opposite.

'Bit early for this, isn't it?' said Fletcher, holding up his glass.

'No, I don't think it is,' said George, taking a slug. 'Not after what I've been through.'

'Did you get to speak to Black before he died?'

'Yes, briefly. They'd worked him over something awful. It's amazing he lasted as long as he did.'

'What did he say?'

'Not a lot. I told him that he was going to die a very slow death, and the only way to speed it up was for him to name his partner in crime. Well, he didn't do that, but he did give me a hint.'

'Which was?'

'He said something like "Prince's friend". That's what it sounded like.'

'*Sounded* like?'

'Yes, I'm sure that's what he said. When I asked for confirmation, he seemed to nod, but it was almost imperceptible.'

Fletcher snorted. 'With all due respect, Major Hart, a mumbled reply and an imperceptible nod are hardly definitive, are they? We now know Black was involved; but we'll never be able to prove it. As for his co-murderer, we can only surmise his identity.'

'I think we can do more than that. Black's comment got me thinking about which of the prince's friends would have a reason for implicating him in the murders. Well, if Black was trying to pin the blame on a former lover who had spurned him, could his partner in crime be doing the same thing to the prince?'

'So you think Black's accomplice might be a spurned lover of the prince's?'

'I do, and the prime candidate, in my view, is Jim Stephen. He's the prince's former tutor, and a homosexual who hates women. He even went so far as to say, in my hearing, that the Ripper was doing Whitechapel a favour. I also know that there's a history of mental illness in his family, and that Stephen suffered a serious blow to his head a few years back. It might well have tipped him over the edge. Lastly he matches the description of one of the two people last seen with the deceased.'

'Can you be certain that Stephen and the prince were lovers?'

'No, I can't be certain. But it's highly likely. And if Stephen was replaced in the prince's affections by Kosminski, that might be his motive for revenge.'

'So how does Stephen know Black?'

'Who knows? They were probably introduced by Kosminski and found they had more in common than they'd imagined.'

'What you say is possible. But there's a lot of supposition here, and not much evidence. Even if you heard Black correctly, we can't even be certain he was referring to Stephen, can we?'

George rubbed his forehead with a palm, and exhaled. 'Look, I appreciate we don't have enough to take to Abberline, even if we thought that was the best course of action. But it's the best theory we've got and you can't deny that it makes sense that Black and his accomplice would try to implicate Kosminski and the prince because of sexual jealousy.'

'Yes it makes sense, but it's not the *only* explanation,' said Fletcher. 'But let's say that you're right and Stephen *is* the accomplice. What then? How on earth do we get him to confess?'

'I'm still trying to work that out. I'm tempted to ask Liam Kelly to beat a confession out of him, like we did with Black. But I suspect we've used up all our credit with the Fenians – it certainly seemed that way yesterday – and Liam doesn't have quite the same personal interest in dealing with Black's accomplice, though they undoubtedly both played a part in Mary's death. So on balance I think we need to sort this out ourselves. The question, as you put it, is: how?'

'There is something,' said Fletcher, reaching into his inside pocket. He pulled out a folded sheet of paper and handed it to George. 'Read this. It was authorized by Henry Matthews, the Home Secretary, and has just appeared in the press. Copies are being posted outside all London police stations.'

George unfolded the paper. It read:

MURDER – PARDON – Whereas on November 8 or 9, in Miller Court, Dorset Street, Spitalfields, Mary Jane Kelly was murdered by some person or persons unknown: the Secretary of State will advise the grant of Her Majesty's gracious pardon to any accomplice, not being a person who contrived or actually committed the murder, who shall give such information and evidence as shall lead to the discovery and conviction of the person or persons who committed the murder.

CHARLES WARREN, the Commissioner of Police
of the Metropolis, Metropolitan Police Office,
4 Whitehall Place, S.W.

George looked up from the sheet of paper. 'My God,' he said, shaking his head. 'They're offering to pardon the accomplice if he gives up the murderer. But why?'

'Because,' said Fletcher, 'Abberline, Warren and the Home Office have run out of ideas. They've tried every other way to catch the killer, and failed. This is a last resort. It's also an attempt by the Home Office to appease the public's fury at its failure to catch the killers. Of course they don't know that one of the killers – Black – is already dead, and I suggest we keep it that way. But *we* may be able to use this to our advantage.'

'How so?'

'Why, by offering Stephen a pardon if he gives Black up, of course.'

'Aren't you forgetting something, Fletcher? If Black is dead, how can Stephen give him up?'

'He can't. But he doesn't know that. The most he can know is that Black is missing. He may even have his suspicions. But that won't stop him from trying to save himself.'

'All right. Let's say, for argument's sake, you're right, and Stephen is tempted. But under what authority are we offering him a pardon? It clearly says in the leaflet that a pardon can only be granted if the accomplice neither contrived nor committed the murders. That surely is not the case with Stephen, if indeed Stephen is the accomplice. Is it not possible that we're dealing with two murderers, rather than a murderer and his accomplice?'

'It is. But you're splitting hairs, Major Hart, if you don't mind me saying so. I'm not proposing that we actually obtain a pardon for Stephen. Rather, that we use the offer of one to draw him out. Then, when we know he's responsible, we find a way – a way that is not illegal, I might add – to deal with him once and for all.'

'And how do you propose to do that?'

'By offering him two options: either commit suicide, or face the full severity of the law, with all the disgrace for his venerable family that that would bring.'

George took a moment to ponder the detective's suggestion. 'It's unconventional, I'll give you that,' he said at last. 'But so has been all our work on this case and it's got us this far. All right, let's give it a go. Harry Wilson has invited me to dinner at The Osiers. The prince and Stephen will also be there. It's the perfect opportunity to bring up the issue of the pardon in conversation. Stephen's reaction should be telling. He might even confess there and then. But if he doesn't, I suggest we follow him afterwards and see what he has to say.'

'Good idea, but make sure you're armed. Once Stephen knows he's cornered, he might lash out. I'll wait outside in case he tries to make a run for it.'

George raised his glass. 'A toast. To you, Sergeant Fletcher, one of the Met's finest, and to solving the crime of the century. It's been quite an adventure, but I feel the end is in sight.'

Fletcher clinked glasses. 'Me too. Let's just hope we're on to the right man, for a change.'

21

Chiswick Mall, west London

George paused outside the front door of The Osiers to adjust his bow-tie. Much had happened since that first dinner in August when Stephen, in particular, had made no bones about his hatred for woman. The prince's former tutor had also expressed his unwelcome opinion, George remembered, that soldiering brought out the worst in men. *What a load of nonsense! And what a hypocrite! Well, it was time to expose him.*

George turned his head to make sure Fletcher was in position across the road. After the last debacle, he wasn't taking any chances; he was relieved, therefore, to see the back of the detective sergeant's head, topped by a bowler hat. He was sitting on a bench, well wrapped up in coat and scarf, staring out across the River Thames as if contemplating life. But George knew that he would be watching the front door of The Osiers like a hawk.

He rang the bell and was let in by the butler who took his top hat, coat and scarf. 'Mr Wilson and the other guests are in the drawing room, sir.'

As he mounted the stairs, George patted his inside jacket pocket and felt the reassuring firmness of his Derringer twin-barrelled pistol. The door to the drawing room was

269

directly opposite the first-floor landing. He paused with his uninjured hand on the door handle and took a deep breath, then entered the room. Wilson and the prince were seated on one sofa; Stephen directly opposite. Standing between them, facing the fire, was Druitt.

'Ah George, it's good to see you,' said Wilson, rising to his feet. Noticing George's bandaged hand, he asked, 'What happened to you?'

'Oh, it's nothing. A stupid accident. How are you all getting on?'

'I'm afraid we're not in the best of spirits.'

George looked from Wilson to the others: all were grim-faced, particularly Stephen, or so he seemed to George. *He couldn't have told them, could he?*

'Whatever's the matter?' asked George.

'It's Monty,' said the prince, also rising to greet George. 'He has very bad news.'

George looked at Druitt who, by this time, had turned from the fire. His handsome face was pale and drained of blood. He seemed stunned. 'Monty,' said George, 'tell me what's happened?'

Druitt stared past him, as if in a trance.

'Anyone?'

'He just lost his job at the boarding school in Blackheath,' said the prince. 'Nasty business.'

'But I thought Monty was a barrister,' said George, 'like Harry and Jim.'

'He is,' said the prince, 'but he supplements his income as an assistant schoolmaster.'

'What happened?' asked George.

It was Druitt, back in the present, who responded. 'The housemaster found us together.'

'Found who together?'

'Me and one of the senior boys: Charlie Philips. I went to his study to bid him goodnight, but he persuaded me to get into bed with him. I knew it was a mistake but I did it anyway. I must have fallen asleep. The housemaster discovered us in the morning. Charlie's been sent home and I've lost my position. If this gets out, I'm finished. I might even be prosecuted, though I doubt Charlie would testify. Either way, I'll be disbarred and effectively disgraced.'

'What possessed you to have a relationship with one of your pupils?' asked George.

'I don't know. I've been such an idiot.'

'Look on the bright side, Monty,' said Stephen, trying rather awkwardly to lighten the atmosphere, 'at least your father, the good doctor, is not alive to witness your disgrace.'

'Jim, please,' said Wilson. 'That sort of comment is not helpful.'

'Excuse me a moment,' said Druitt, 'I need some air. I'll take a turn in the garden.'

Once Druitt had left the room, George said quietly to the prince: 'I didn't know Monty's father was a doctor.'

'Yes indeed, and a very good one, by all accounts. He practised as a surgeon in Dorchester, and had high hopes for Monty's career.'

'Hopes that had every chance of being fulfilled,' interjected Wilson. 'Monty was a brilliant debater at Oxford and seemed destined for politics. But his father's sudden death in eighty-five seemed to knock all the stuffing out of him, and he's just drifted in his career since then. His work as a barrister has dried up, which is why the loss of his teaching job at Blackheath has hit him so hard.'

'Yes,' said the prince, 'and he's also had to contend with his mother's condition. He hasn't been himself lately.'

Druitt returned, and the men moved to the oak-panelled dining room to eat. The polished mahogany table looked beautiful with its silver cutlery, crystal glasses and starched white napkins, all lit by two candelabra. Wilson sat at the head, flanked by the prince in the place of honour on his right, and Druitt on his left. George was next to Druitt and opposite Stephen who, much to George's surprise, was looking remarkably relaxed and unconcerned. It was he who broached the subject of the Ripper. 'So tell us, George, the latest on the Whitechapel murders?'

George saw his opportunity. 'Well, the police still haven't caught the killer, as I'm sure you're all well aware, which is why they're desperate enough to issue this.' He took the copy of Matthews' offer of a pardon from his pocket and waved it in front of him.

'What's that?' asked Stephen, his eyes narrowing.

'It's an offer from the Home Secretary to grant a pardon to any helper of the Ripper who's prepared to turn Queen's evidence and give up the murderer.'

George looked for a reaction from Stephen but there wasn't any. Instead, Druitt asked: 'May I see that?'

'Yes of course,' said George, handing him the piece of paper.

Druitt scanned it. 'It relates,' he said, 'to the most recent murder. It says the Secretary of State will advise the Queen to grant a pardon to any accomplice, and here's the crucial bit, "not being a person who contrived or actually committed the murder, who shall give such information and evidence as shall lead to the discovery and conviction of the person or persons who committed the murder". So not quite what you were suggesting, George. That's a shame.'

George turned to face Druitt. 'What do you mean by that? And why is it a shame?'

'Oh, nothing. It's just that you were implying that the pardon might apply to someone who'd helped the Ripper carry out his murders. That *might* have done the trick – which is why I said it was a shame. But what the offer actually states is that a pardon will only be granted if the person had no part in either the planning or the committal of the murder. You'd know that, George, if you had legal training,' said Druitt, contemptuously. 'Truth is, it's directed chiefly at family members and friends who might be suspicious, rather than someone who is actually helping the Ripper, and for that reason it's unlikely to do any good.'

'So are you saying,' responded George, 'that a different wording might have produced a different result?'

'Yes, that's exactly what I'm saying. It's quite obvious from the press reports that someone is helping the Ripper. He's the one they should be concentrating on. An offer of a pardon to him might be the only way to crack the case.'

George turned to Stephen. 'You asked the original question, Jim. Do you agree with Monty?'

'About what? He's certainly right about the point of law. The offer won't encourage a genuine accomplice to hand himself in, because it doesn't apply to him. Nor could it. There'd be a public outcry if someone involved in the murders cheated the gallows. So on that point, Monty and I will have to disagree. It's not a shame the offer wasn't targeted at the Ripper's actual accomplice – if indeed he has one – because that was never a viable option. The Home Secretary would have been crucified.'

George listened to Stephen's reasoned argument with mounting concern. His whole manner since the start of the evening – cool and dispassionate – could not have been further removed from the flustered and nervous reaction that George was expecting. Even the news of a possible pardon had had little effect on him. Instead, Stephen had dismissed it as an irrelevance. Was this the behaviour of a brutal killer whose co-murderer had recently disappeared? George didn't think so. If anyone was behaving strangely, it was Druitt, but he certainly had good reason.

'One thing I forgot to ask,' said Stephen, a mischievous look in his eye. 'Is Eddy still a suspect?'

'No, not at all,' said George. 'The police do believe, however, that someone was trying to implicate the prince.'

'How so?' asked Stephen.

'By planting a section of one of the prince's letters at the murder scene.'

'I think,' interjected the prince, 'you mean planting a forgery of one of my letters, don't you George?'

'No, Your Royal Highness, I mean what I say.'

Stephen rose from his seat. 'How dare you accuse—'

'Hear me out,' said George. 'His Royal Highness had a very good reason for denying authorship of the letter, and it has nothing to do with the murders. That's right, isn't it, sir?'

'I don't know what you're talking about.'

'I think you do,' said George. 'I've spoken to Aaron Kosminski. I know about the letter.'

The prince reddened. 'How do you know about Aaron?'

'Does it matter?'

'No,' said the prince with a sigh, 'I don't suppose it does. All right. I confess I did write the letter. It was addressed to Aaron Kosminski, a young Jew who used to cut my hair. I told George it wasn't my handwriting because I was terrified that Aaron was involved in some way. But I met with him recently and he put my mind at rest. I only lied to protect him.'

'So if Eddy wrote the letter, but didn't leave it at the murder scene, who did?' asked Wilson.

George looked directly at Stephen. 'Why don't you ask Jim?'

'Jim,' said the prince. 'What's this got to do with him?'

Stephen stared at George open-mouthed. 'You think I . . .? You've clearly gone insane.'

Before George could respond, Druitt interjected: 'It was me.'

All eyes turned to Druitt. 'You planted the letter, Monty?' asked the prince.

'Yes.'

'Why?'

'Because,' said Druitt, tears in his eyes, 'you don't love me any more.'

As Druitt rose from his seat, George realized in a flash his error: he'd suspected the more voluble Stephen of being Black's co-murderer; instead it was the quieter, more intense but no less misogynistic Druitt. *He* was the spurned lover of the prince who must have met Black through Kosminski, and together they'd carried out the murders. Like Stephen, Druitt matched the description of the man seen with some of the victims shortly before their death. The son of a surgeon, he must have known the basics of human anatomy. And though not heavily built, he had particularly strong forearms and wrists from playing cricket, which would have made it easier for him to strangle his victims before cutting them up.

'Stay right where you are, Monty!' shouted George, drawing his pistol.

Druitt ignored him and fled the room. George followed, though he had further to go to reach the door. Bounding down the stairs he found the front door open. It was dark outside. 'Fletcher!' shouted George.

'I'm here, Major Hart,' said Fletcher from across the street.

George ran over to join him. 'Did you see which way he went?'

'Do you mean the man who just left? That wasn't Stephen.'

'I know. It was Druitt. He's the man we're looking for, not Stephen. Where did he go?'

'Down there,' said Fletcher, pointing to the entrance of a small footpath that led to the river.

'Follow me.' George led the pursuit down the winding footpath. After a couple of hundred yards the path took a sharp turn to the right and there, just a short distance ahead, they could see Druitt standing on a low wall, facing the fast-flowing river.

George and Fletcher stopped about six paces from Druitt. 'It's over Monty,' said George. 'Tom Black told us everything.'

Druitt half turned. 'I don't believe you. Tom would never squeal. You thought it was Jim, didn't you? It was obvious from the way you were speaking at dinner. So much for your talent as a detective. I should have finished you when I had the chance in Miller's Court.'

'Why didn't you?'

'Because you saved the prince's life, and because he holds you in such high regard. I still love him, despite everything.'

'And yet you and Black tried to frame him for murders he didn't commit by dressing up as soldiers, and leaving the letter and button by the bodies?'

'I was angry. Upset. One minute I was blissfully in love. The next I was discarded like old shoe, for that uneducated hairdresser, for God's sake. What could he have seen in him? I wanted to punish both of them, but particularly Kosminksi. How dare he think he could replace me? What does he know of high culture, or even love? What could he give the prince that I couldn't?'

George could think of one thing – happiness – but thought better of mentioning it. Instead he asked: 'Why risk the prince's life and reputation if you still love him?'

Druitt's eyes narrowed. 'That's a ridiculous question. I knew he would never be hanged for the murders. He wasn't even in Whitechapel for the last one – I made sure of that. I would never do anything to harm him properly.'

'But the same doesn't apply to defenceless women, does it?'

'You mean those prostitutes? They deserved to die.'

'Why?'

'Because they're temptresses, sent by Satan to spread pestilence and lead men from the Righteous Path.'

'And killing them is Righteous?'

'It must be,' said Druitt, his eyes shining with an almost mystical fervour, 'because I received the order to do so from God himself.'

'Then why not do the killing yourself? Why let Black do some of your dirty work? Was he also instructed by the Almighty?'

'No, he just hates women. And he'd do anything to please me. We've spent a lot of time together since . . . since . . .' Druitt frowned, unable to finish the sentence.

'What caused such hate?'

'The *cause*? Many things. His sisters for a start. Such

277

monsters! They caught him masturbating as a boy and told his mother, who beat him. Then they forced him to perform oral sex on them. Can you imagine anything worse? I'd have struck them down there and then. Later, during the pogroms, he saw some terrible things: children being torn limb from limb, rapes, murders. It must have been awful, awful. It unhinged his mind! But he's not a bad person.'

For a brief moment, while Druitt spoke of the sexual abuse his friend had suffered, George felt sympathy for the young Tom Black. Then he remembered what the adult had done and the sympathy dissolved. 'What did you do with the body parts you took?'

'You mean the heart, uterus and kidney? We ate the first two.'

'So you *did* send the kidney with the letter "From hell" to Lusk?'

'Tom did. I wrote the other letter.'

'Who came up with the name "Jack the Ripper"?'

'I did. My second name is John. It was a tiny clue that I knew you would never get.'

'What about the cuts on Eddowes' face, hinting at a Freemasonry connection?'

'That was my idea as well. I thought it would make Warren and Abberline more wary of unmasking the killer.'

George shook his head with grudging admiration. 'My God, you thought of everything, didn't you? There's one more thing I need to know. Were they always dead before you cut them up?'

'Most of them were. But the last one took her time to die and squealed a bit when Tom cut her breasts.'

'You bastard!' shouted George, his finger tightening on the trigger. 'I should shoot you down like the dog you are.

But I won't because that would make me a murderer. Instead I'll give you two choices. You can surrender, face trial and certain execution by hanging. But that would drag our friend the prince into the story. So it's far better if you just jump into the water. It's fast flowing and cold, and you won't survive long. Then we can say it was suicide – which it will be – and put the blame on your sacking and impending disgrace. No one needs to know the truth.'

Druitt turned back to face the river, weighing up his options. 'All right,' he said at last, 'I know what I have to do. Pass me a couple of those, will you.' He was pointing at a pile of stones beside the path. 'I need to do this properly.'

George picked up a couple of the heavier stones and handed them to Druitt, who put them in his outside pockets.

'My only reget,' said Druitt quietly, 'is leaving Tom to face the music alone.'

'You've no worries on that score.'

'Why not?'

'Because he beat you to it. He's already dead.'

'You killed him?'

'No, I left that to your last victim's brother who, it just so happens, is a Fenian terrorist and a ruthless bastard. He was quite prepared to use any method – however savage – to extract a confession from Black. It seemed to do the trick. Just be thankful he didn't get his hands on you. It was, I'm pleased to report, a very slow and painful death. I was there at the end and Black was begging us to put him out of his misery.'

'Oh God! Poor Tom.'

'Poor Tom! Save your sympathy for the families of the poor women you butchered.'

'Those whores deserved to die. My only regret is not killing more.'

'Enough!' shouted George. He closed his eyes and remembered Mary as she was when he'd last seen her alive: wearing her best bonnet, her pretty face flushed with excitement. But this happy thought was soon interrupted by horrific images of her torn body lying on the bed, its throat cut and its stomach opened from breastbone to pubis. The lovely face so badly slashed and mutilated it was unrecognizable; her severed breasts, once pressed so provocatively against George's chest, heaped on the table beside her. *Who would do such a thing?*

George opened his eyes and the answer was before him. He strode forward, fully intending to speed up Druitt's demise by pushing him into the water.

Aware of his intention, Fletcher ran forward to stop him, shouting, 'No, Major Hart!'

But before George could make contact, Druitt jumped. There was a loud splash and a groan. George and Fletcher peered out over the wall into the gloom. There was no sign of Druitt: just icy blackness and the swirl of a fast-moving current.

22

6 *Queen Street, Mayfair*

'That's quite a story, Major Hart,' said the Duke of Cambridge, twiddling his white moustache between thumb and forefinger. He was sitting opposite George in the drawing room of his Mayfair townhouse, glass of brandy in hand. George was drinking whisky. 'I'm not sure I'd have believed it,' continued the duke, 'if I'd read it in a novel.'

'No, sir,' said George, still trying to adjust to the fact that the man before him, the country's leading soldier, was his father. 'Though truth is often stranger than fiction.'

'Yes indeed. For who could have imagined that the killers would turn out to be a policeman and an Oxford graduate, eh? Thank God Eddy wasn't involved. It wasn't looking good at one stage. But that's all in the past now, thanks to you and Sergeant . . . whatisname?'

'Fletcher, sir.'

'Yes, Fletcher. Well, I must see if I can't persuade the new commissioner to give him a promotion.'

'Did you say new commissioner, sir? Has Sir Charles Warren stepped down?'

'Yes. He resigned a few days ago and was replaced by Sir James Munro, the former head of the CID. The official version of events is that he rowed with Matthews over an article he wrote in the press on the running of the police. The real reason, of course, is the Met's failure to catch the Ripper. And, that, sadly, is how it must remain: an unsolved case in which the murders simply stopped. Of course, there'll always be people who'll say that other, later killings in the East End are by the same hand. That's inevitable. But we know the truth: they started with Turner and ended with Kelly. Six in all, and it would have been more but for you and Fletcher.'

The duke gave George a look that might have resembled paternal affection, before continuing: 'It pains me, Major Hart, that we can't give you any official credit. But there it is: it wouldn't do to expose the failings of the Met, or to have it known that a policeman and a close friend of the heir apparent were behind the murders. Nor can it ever get out that the same heir apparent frequents homosexual clubs and forms close friendships with working men. The consequences for law and order, and the popularity of the monarchy, would be incalculable. You do understand, don't you?'

'Yes, of course, sir, and anything you can do for Sergeant Fletcher would be much appreciated. I couldn't have cracked the case without him.'

'No, I can see that. It's a shame there aren't more like him in the Met. Do you think Warren and Abberline ever suspected a policeman was involved? That might explain their extraordinary myopia when it came to actually solving the case.'

'I don't know, sir. I don't think so. I think it's far more likely that they were worried about a possible royal connection – and those fears were not without justification. There was a royal link, just not the one they were expecting.'

'No.' The duke rose to his feet. 'Another drink?'

'Thank you, sir.'

The duke took both glasses to the drinks tray and refilled them. Having handed one back to George, he stood by the fireplace, lost in contemplation. After a minute or so, he turned back to George. 'I originally asked you to shadow Prince Eddy for a year. That was just over three months ago. But in that time you've foiled a Fenian assassination attempt and kept Eddy's links both to homosexuals and to the Whitechapel murders out of the newspapers. You've more than kept your side of the bargain and we – that is the royal family – owe you a huge debt. I intend to pay it. Wait here.'

The duke left the room. A few minutes later he returned with a bank cheque and handed it to George. 'You deserve every penny.'

George looked at the cheque. It was made out to him for the sum of six thousand pounds. 'Sir, I don't know what to say. It's far too much.'

'Nonsense. I agreed to pay you a thousand for keeping Eddy safe and an extra five thousand for catching the Whitechapel murderer, to be split between you and that young Irish prostitute. Sadly she's no longer with us, so you get the lot.'

Was this just another example, George wondered, of his father using money to salve his guilty conscience? He suspected that it was, and that a prouder man than he would have refused to accept it. He did not have that luxury, though he'd have been happy with half the amount. 'Thank you, sir,' he said after a pause, 'I'm very grateful for my share. But it doesn't feel right getting Mary's as well.'

'Nonsense, my boy. You were very nearly a victim yourself. You've earned it. But if it makes you feel uncomfortable, feel free to donate some of it to Fletcher or any other good cause you can think of.'

George thought at once of poor Mary. Her body had just been released by the coroner and was due to be buried the following day in a pauper's grave in St Patrick's Roman Catholic Cemetery at Leytonstone. He would pay for the funeral and arrange for a proper coffin and gravestone. He would also send some money Fletcher's way and pay Mary's debts. It was the least he could do. 'Good idea, sir. I'll do just that.'

'You are henceforth relieved of your duty to protect Eddy. We have, in any case, a clever ruse to keep him out of any more trouble.'

'Which is, sir?'

'Why marriage, of course. His mother has found the perfect match: a young German princess called Mary of Teck. She's handsome, clever and strong-willed. Just what Eddy needs.'

'Will he agree to the match, do you think, sir?'

'Of course he'll bloody agree. He has no choice. In any case, he understands his duty. He'll be king one day. He must have a queen. But enough of Eddy. There is still one matter to be settled for you. In return for protecting Eddy, I also promised you a step in rank and a posting of your choice. From tomorrow you will be gazetted a substantive lieutenant colonel. Where would you like to serve?'

George looked at his father's benign expression and thought, *Mrs FitzGeorge was right. Despite his abandonment of me and my mother, he is at heart a good man who wants only the best for me. It's better to know that late, than never.* 'I really don't know, sir,' said George. 'I'd like to spend some time with my family and then I'll decide. It's too late to join the expeditions to Sikkim or Equatoria. Maybe South Africa, where I certainly feel I have business left to complete. Tell the truth, sir, I don't really care as long as it's overseas. If the last few months have taught me anything, it's that I'm not cut out for Home Service.'

EPILOGUE

The bells were tolling as George approached the intersection of Shoreditch High Street and Hackney Road. It was a cold, crisp day and a huge crowd, well wrapped up and many thousands strong, had gathered outside the gates of St Leonard's Church. George looked up at the church's magnificent soaring steeple, at least 200 feet in height, atop a giant but delicate four-columned portico. It was, he decided, a fittingly majestic departure point for Mary Kelly's funeral procession.

At 12.30 p.m., four men emerged from the mortuary beside the church, carrying on their shoulders the handsome polished oak and elm coffin, with metal fittings, that George had chosen for Mary. The sight of the coffin caused the men in the crowd to doff their caps and hats, while some of the women, their faces wet with tears, cried out, 'God have mercy on her!' and 'Forgive her her sins!' Many were unsteady on their feet, having drowned their sorrows in nearby public houses as they waited for the coffin to appear.

A horse-drawn open hearse was waiting on the thoroughfare. As the gates opened to let the pallbearers through, the crowd surged forward in an effort to touch the coffin. It was held back with difficulty by a thin cordon of constables, some of whom drew their truncheons to keep order. George watched all this from a raised pavement on Hackney Road. He had made all the funeral arrangements through a Mr Wilson, the sexton of St Leonard's Church, explaining that he was a wealthy admirer of the deceased who wished to remain anonymous. As such he had declined Wilson's offer to accompany the chief mourners in two carriages behind the hearse. He had assumed that Mary's brother Liam would be in attendance. In the event, Liam stayed away and the carriages were occupied by Mary's recent paramour Joseph Barnett and a number of her closest female friends, most of whom were prostitutes.

George was both astonished and moved by the huge crowd's very public demonstration of grief as it surged around the hearse and the two mourning carriages, making it almost impossible for the procession to make any headway on its journey to Mary's final resting place at St Patrick's Roman Catholic Cemetery in Leytonstone. It took more than half an hour for the police constables on duty to clear a path through the crowd to Shoreditch High Street so that the procession could head south towards Whitechapel. It was not the most direct route to Leytonstone, but it afforded the people of the East End the chance to say goodbye to one of their own.

He followed the procession in a hansom cab, and it was only when the hearse got beyond the huge crowds lining the Whitechapel Road that the traffic thinned and the horses were able to break into a trot. The procession finally reached the little chapel of St Patrick's at two o'clock. Having passed through a sizeable crowd at the gates, the coffin and mourners were met by Father Columban of the Order of St Francis, two of Columban's acolytes and a cross-bearer. George's hansom cab pulled up outside the gates as Mary's coffin was being lifted down from the hearse. He watched from the road as Father Columban and his assistants led the coffin and the mourners to an open grave in the northeast corner of the graveyard. It was a fair distance away, but George could see Barnett and the other mourners fall to their knees as the coffin was lowered into the ground. The sound of their weeping easily carried across the cold still air to where he was standing.

Only when the funeral service was over, and the mourners had repaired to the nearby Birkbeck public house, did George enter the cemetery and approach Mary's grave. The grave-diggers were about to fill in the hole, but George stayed them for a moment. Looking down at the coffin, with its simple brass plate that read 'Mary Jane Kelly, died 9 November 1888, aged 25 years', he thought of the beautiful, brave and vibrant young woman he had known for those few short weeks.

'Goodbye Mary,' he whispered, dropping a handful of soil on the polished oak. 'You deserved better.'

AUTHOR'S NOTE

With the exception of George and his immediate family, Sergeant Fletcher, PC Tom Black and the Fenians, almost all the characters that appear in this novel are based on real people. They include HRH Prince Albert Victor Christian Edward ('Eddy') and his friends Harry Wilson, Jim Stephen and Montague Druitt; HRH the 2nd Duke of Cambridge and his 'wife' Mrs FitzGeorge; the policemen Sir Charles Warren, John Littlechild, Frederick Abberline and James McWilliam; the Ripper's alleged victims Martha Turner, Polly Nichols, Annie Chapman, Elizabeth Stride, Catherine Eddowes and Mary Kelly; the witnesses Pearly Poll, Mrs Long, Mrs Fiddimont, Louis Diemschutz, PC William Smith, Joseph Lawende and Israel Schwarz; and the suspects John Pizer, ('Leather Apron'), Joseph Isenschmid and Aaron Kosminski.

The Special Irish Branch of the Metropolitan Police (later just the Special Branch) was formed in 1883 to deal with the terrorist threat from Irish Republicans that reached its height in the mainland bombing campaign of 1884-85, though Fenian terrorism remained a danger to internal security for many years thereafter. The main act of terrorism depicted in this book – the bombing and assassination attempt in Mayfair – did not take place, though it might have.

There was a male brothel run by Charles Hammond at 19 Cleveland Street in Fitzrovia. It was at the centre of a major scandal in 1889 when a fifteen-year-old telegraph boy admitted to police that he had been working as a male prostitute at the club. The patrons included Lord Arthur Somerset, a major in the Royal Horse Guards and the Prince of Wales' Master of Horse, the Earl of Euston and a Colonel Jervois of the 2nd Life Guards. Somerset's solicitor claimed that Prince Eddy was also a client.

The details in the book about the Whitechapel Murders are mostly based on the historical record, from the killing of the victim generally acknowledged as the Ripper's first (Martha Turner) on 7 August 1888, to the last (Mary Kelly) just over three months later. They include the two 'Jack the Ripper' letters sent to the Boss of the Central News Office, the chalk message and torn apron found in Goulston Street, and the package (containing a letter and half a female kidney) sent to the head of the Whitechapel Vigilance Committee. The descriptions of Whitechapel are partly gleaned from author Jack London's *The People of the Abyss*, an eyewitness account of life in the East End at the turn of the 20th Century.

Despite countless books on the subject, the identity of 'Jack the Ripper' (and his accomplice, if he had one) has never been established beyond doubt. Among those identified as chief suspects by recent books are Prince Eddy, his friend and former tutor Jim Stephen, the artist Walter Sickert, the author Lewis Carroll and the American singer and composer Michael Maybrick, the protagonist in Bruce Robinson's *They All Love Jack* (2015).

Prince Eddy first entered the frame in 'Jack the Ripper – A Solution?', an article by eminent physician Dr T. E. A. Stowell that appeared in the *Criminologist* in 1970. Though Stowell did not name the Prince, his description of 'S' could not have been anyone else. 'After the education traditional for an English aristocrat,' wrote Stowell, 'at the age of a little over 16 years, "S" went for a cruise around the world with a number of high-spirited boys of approximately his age group.' Later Stowell later refers to his subject's nickname as 'Collars and Cuffs'. Stowell's theory is that 'S' contracted syphilis on one of his 'many shore parties' and it was during the periodic fits of madness brought on by this illness that he killed his victims.

The theory has been repeated and embellished by various writers, and is not without some foundation. Eddy was almost certainly bisexual, a frequent visitor to the East End and, as newly discovered letters reveal (*Daily Mail*, 26 February 2016), was receiving treatment in 1885 and 1886 (and possibly later) for a venereal disease like gonorrhea that he probably caught from a prostitute. Yet contemporary documents – in the form of the *Court Register* – prove that Eddy could not have been in London at the time of the murders.

So who might have been responsible? The policemen involved in the case narrow the possibilities down to just two or three people. In a famous memorandum of 1894, CID Chief Constable Melville Macnaghten wrote: 'A much more rational and *workable* theory . . . is that the Ripper's brain gave way altogether after his awful glut in Miller's Court and that he then committed suicide, or, as a *less* likely alternative, was found to be so helplessly insane by his relatives, that they, suspecting the worst, had him confined in some Lunatic Asylum . . . I enumerate the cases of 3 men against whom Police had very reasonable suspicion: Mr M. [Montague] J.

Druitt, [Aaron] Kosminski and Michael Ostrog. Of Druitt and Kosminski he wrote:

> No. 1 Mr M. J. Druitt, a doctor of about 41 years of age & of fairly good family, who disappeared at the time of the Miller's Court murder, and whose body was found floating in the Thames on 31s Dec. i.e. 7 weeks after the said murder . . . From private information I have little doubt but that his own family suspected this man of being the Whitechapel murderer . . .
>
> No. 2 Kosminski, a Polish Jew, who lived in the very heart of the district where the murders were committed. He had become insane owing to many years indulgence in solitary vices [masturbation]. He had a great hatred of women with homicidal tendencies. He was (and I believe still is) detained in lunatic asylum about March 1889. The man in appearance strongly resembled the individual seen by the City P.C. near Mitre Square.

Macnaghten added: 'I have always held strong opinions regarding No. 1, and the more I think the matter over, the stronger do these opinions become.' In his memoirs he wrote: 'The Whitechapel murderer, in all probability, put an end to himself soon after the Dorset Street affair in November 1888.'

Sir Robert Anderson, head of the CID from early September 1888, was convinced Kosminski was responsible. He wrote: 'One did not need to be a Sherlock Holmes to discover that the criminal was a sex maniac of a virulent type; that he was living in the immediate vicinity of the scenes of the murders; and that, if he was not living absolutely alone, his people knew of his guilt, and refused to give him up to justice . . . The Police had made a house to house search for him, investigating the case of every man in the district . . . And the conclusion we came to was that he and his people were low-class Jews, for it is a remarkable fact that people of that class in the East End will not give up one of their number to Gentile justice.'

He added: 'The only person who had ever a good view of the murderer [Israel Schwarz] unhesitatingly identified the suspect the instant he was confronted with him; but he refused to give evidence against him. In saying that he was a Polish Jew I am merely stating a definitely ascertained fact.'

Donald Swanson confirmed that Anderson was referring to Kosminski when he wrote in the margin of Anderson's book: 'He knew he was identified. On suspect's return to his brother's house in Whitechapel he was watched by police (city CID) by day & night. In a very short time the suspect with his hands tied behind his back, was sent to Stepney Workhouse and then to Colney Hatch [Asylum] and died shortly afterwards – Kosminski was the suspect.'

A recent book by Russell Edwards (*Naming Jack the Ripper*, 2014) claims to have DNA evidence (taken from Catherine Eddowes' torn shawl) that Kosminski was the killer.

Yet, despite the fact that various key witnesses have identified a possible accomplice, no one has made the case that Druitt and Kosminski either acted together or with someone else. I chose the latter scenario, with Druitt assisted by a deranged (and fictional) police constable, Tom Black.

As portrayed in the book, Druitt committed suicide by jumping into the Thames at Chiswick. His badly decomposed body was found on New Year's Eve, 1888, and was assumed to have been in the water for at least a month. His father had died of a heart attack in 1885 and his mother was committed to a mental asylum in July 1888.

Kosminski was treated at the Mile End Workhouse and diagnosed as having been insane for the previous two years on 12 July 1890. Released three days later into the custody of his brother, he was returned to the workhouse infirmary on 4 February 1891. Shortly after he was transferred to the Colney Hatch lunatic asylum and later to Leavesden Asylum for Imbeciles where he died in 1919.

Since the publication of *Hart of Empire* – the second in the Zulu Hart series – in 2010, I've received many emails and letters asking about the next in the series. I could never have imagined, even with my teaching and non-fiction commitments, that it would take eight years! Or that it would be set in London rather than Africa. I apologize to all fans of the series, and hope it's been worth the wait.

My thanks, as ever, to my excellent and super patient publisher Nick Sayers and his team at Hodder: Cicely Aspinall, Juliet Brightmore, Aaron Munday (who designed the wonderful cover) and the copy editor Penny Isaac. I'm grateful, also, to my agent Peter Robinson who suggested I try my hand at crime fiction; to my wife Lou who read (and improved) the manuscript with her sage if blunt advice; and to my youngest daughter Tashie who suggested the title (and would have been the book's dedicatee if I hadn't taken so long to write it).